A Dash
of
Death

A Dash

of

Death

A COCKTAILS AND CATERING MYSTERY

Michelle Hillen Klump

CROOKED
LANE

NEW YORK

Published in the United States by Crooked Lane Books, an imprint of The Quick Brown Fox & Company LLC.

Crooked Lane Books and its logo are trademarks of The Quick Brown Fox & Company LLC.

Library of Congress Catalog-in-Publication data available upon request.

ISBN (hardcover): 978-1-64385-937-8
ISBN (ebook): 978-1-64385-938-5

Cover design by Brandon Dorman

Printed in the United States.

www.crookedlanebooks.com

Crooked Lane Books
34 West 27th St., 10th Floor
New York, NY 10001

First Edition: February 2022

10 9 8 7 6 5 4 3 2 1

To my mom, who never doubted
this was possible.

Chapter One

Samantha Warren zipped up her second-best dress, its silk skirt swishing against her bare legs as she walked into the kitchen to box up the last of three hundred bottles of home-made bitters. The petite blue bottles with their creamy white labels should have been tucked into gift bags to be enjoyed by her wedding guests. But since her fiancé, Gregory Price, had dumped her three weeks earlier, there'd been a slight change in plans. She wouldn't walk down the aisle tonight. Instead, she would show up for the Highlands Historic Home Tour to serve cocktails and sell the cherry-vanilla bitters she'd made as wedding favors.

Samantha had hemmed and hawed when her friends Marisa and Beth encouraged her to take part in the Historic Commission's benefit, filling in last minute for a local brewery that had canceled. Marisa had practically forced her to sign the contract, convincing her it would do her good to participate. Now she could admit she was grateful to have a reason to dress up and a place to go on what should have been her happiest night. She leaned down to give a quick pat to Ruby, the orange-and-gray tortie cat who circled her ankles. Box in hand, she turned out the light and slipped out of her garage apartment, descending the stairs into the humid Houston night.

Within moments, her friends pulled up in a silver Cadillac, well-appointed with leather seats, a sunroof, and illuminated door handles. Heated seats, unnecessary on a May night in Texas, were a luxurious treat for Samantha, who shivered at the first hint of a cool breeze.

Marisa Lopez stepped out of the car, as striking as a runway model in a purple sheath dress, which complemented her auburn bob. "I know it's silly, but we decided the occasion warranted some style." Marisa gestured toward the car and popped the trunk. "You look beautiful, by the way."

Often self-conscious, Samantha indeed felt beautiful in a vintage, off-the-shoulder black cocktail dress, second in finery only to the lace brocade wedding dress, still hanging, unworn, in her closet. Her blonde hair, which normally curled around her face in messy waves, had been tamed and pulled up into an elegant chignon designed to show off her honeyed highlights.

"It's not exactly the outfit I had in mind for tonight, but I can still clean up pretty well." Samantha placed the box of bitters in the trunk and climbed into the back seat. She smiled at Marisa's girlfriend, Beth Myerson, in the front seat. Beth, a landscape architect who wore a T-shirt and cargo pants nearly every day, had traded in her khakis for something sparkly. Samantha admired her sequined top. "You two are ravishing!"

Beth bit her lower lip, her voice timid. "I cut the phlox you asked for this morning. It's in the back. Are you sure you're okay with this?" Though she and Samantha had grown closer in the two years Beth had been dating Marisa, Beth often faded to the background when the three of them were together. As the one who had arranged the home tour gig, she sounded worried about her role in dragging Samantha out.

Samantha nodded. "I'm good." She needed a night free of second- and third-guessing her life choices, and the home tour, the premier social event for the tony Highlands community, would offer plenty of distraction.

Hundreds of people attended every year for the chance to glimpse some of the community's most historically significant homes. Each home showcased a different local product, from pastries to coffee to soap. Attendees sampled the products during the tour and, if they liked, used prepurchased tickets to buy extras to take home. Vendors competed fiercely for the opportunity to participate, so Samantha had been shocked to be invited to fill in at the last minute, even with Beth's connections to the commission. After all, she didn't even own a local business. A freelance writer, she dabbled with bitters and cocktails on the side.

At the Reilley house, the fourth stop on the home tour and Samantha's station for the evening, the trio pulled around to the back entrance. The four-story Victorian mansion, one of only two original homes built by the developers of the Highlands neighborhood, sat perched at the top of a hill. There the white house towered, like a benevolent king, over the surrounding bungalows. Walking into the kitchen through the open back door, Samantha admired its gingerbread trim, which gave it a fanciful quality and softened its features.

Samantha unloaded Beth's flowers and her bottles of homemade bitters and placed them on the counter next to the alcohol provided by the commission and trays of warming appetizers dropped off by a catering van still parked outside. She planned to make several batches of cocktails, with the bitters she'd intended to use as wedding favors serving as the star ingredient. Since each drink used only a dash or two of bitters, she would still have plenty of bottles to sell to the hundreds of guests attending the home tour.

Her ingredients at hand, Samantha began mixing and muddling large pitchers of Attorney's Privilege—a rye-orgeat combination brightened by her special bitters. The rose-colored concoction, poured into a chilled coupe glass, hit the right notes—not too sweet, not too bitter, but smooth and tasty. For guests who didn't enjoy the brown stuff, Samantha mixed pitchers of Cherry Gin Fizz, which would show off her bitters' versatility. The bright-pink drink with its crown of foamy froth tasted as festive as it appeared.

After prepping the cocktails, Samantha prepared garnishes with the tiny white-and-pink phlox blossoms, picked that morning from Beth's garden. The flowers would add a slight spiciness to cut the sweetness of the drinks and promote the elegant garden-party theme.

"Everything looks beautiful, Sam." Marisa laid out the last of the glassware and took a sip of a gin fizz. "And tastes delicious . . ."

Their preparations finished, Beth, who occasionally worked with the Historic Commission, insisted on giving Marisa and Samantha a tour of the home. The owners, who lived most of their time in a palatial loft downtown, rented the home out for weddings and other special events but always allowed it to be included in the commission's annual home tour.

The three women began at the front entrance, where the library tower at the top of the house reminded Samantha of widow's walks seen in Victorian homes in the Northeast. She imagined a lonely ship captain's bride pacing the length of the tower, on the lookout for her seafaring husband. *At least she has some hope. I know Greg won't be coming back.*

She shook her head, as if to shake the bad thoughts from her mind, and followed Beth and Marisa into a lovely garden abounding with distinct colors and textures. Beth pointed out sunflowers, foxglove, and ranunculus blossoms and explained that the garden bloomed at all times throughout the year.

The three women walked around the wraparound porch, already twinkling with fairy lights, and headed toward the front entrance. The home opened into a grand foyer with rich green velvet drapes and delicate floral wallpaper. The adjacent parlor was smaller and cozier. A short hallway led to the dining room, which featured a hand-carved oak table, and a music room to the left, outfitted with a grand piano and a golden harp.

Finished with the tour, the three friends walked back into the kitchen to make their last preparations. As Samantha stirred her final-batch cocktail, a tall man with wavy salt-and-pepper hair and a two-hundred-watt smile sauntered into the kitchen. It was Bob Randall, president of the Historic Commission.

"Oh, Beth—there you are. And these must be your friends." Bob offered Samantha a firm handshake. "Everything looks great. We appreciate you filling in on such short notice."

Samantha pegged Randall as a rye drinker and offered him the Attorney's Privilege. "Care for a cocktail?"

"Delicious." He downed it in one gulp. "Now, pardon me . . ." He left the kitchen to open the doors for the first patrons.

Guests wandered into the kitchen to grab cocktails and snacks as they made their way through the rest of the house and out into the garden. The drinks were a hit, and the bitters were going fast. By seven, Samantha had already amassed enough tickets to fill a julep cup. As each ticket was worth eight dollars, she had already recouped her costs and hoped to turn a small profit.

By seven thirty, Samantha couldn't keep up with the demand. The waitstaff, who carried trays of drinks and appetizers through other parts of the house, continued to return with empty trays, so Samantha enlisted Marisa and Beth to make more trays to circulate at peak periods.

Long stretches of nonstop activity kept Samantha's mind occupied, but every hour the crowd turned over so the earlier wave could move on to the next stop of the tour, creating a lull in the action. During one of these lulls, Samantha strolled through the elegant rooms, hoping the effervescent party atmosphere would raise her spirits, like the bubbles that fizzed and popped to the top of a champagne flute. Sadly, it seemed, her champagne was mostly flat. A lump formed in her throat as she looked at her watch and marked time in an alternate universe, where her own party went on as planned—*This is when I would have cut the cake. This is when we would have danced our first dance.*

She curled her fingers into a fist, and her fingernails dug half-moons into her palm. She counted to five as her heart slowed to its normal pace, until, calm again, she wandered out into the garden to take solace in the sunset. As she stopped to smell a rose, she spotted Marisa and Beth, hands entwined, at the other end of the garden. Beth, petite but strong like a gymnast, with a messy brown braid perpetually swinging against her back, lacked Marisa's sophistication. Yet they fit comfortably together. The sight made Samantha's heart lurch.

Isn't there anywhere I can go to escape?

Ashamed to begrudge her friends their loving moment, Samantha pivoted and walked away before they could spot her. In the process, she nearly ran headfirst into one of the waitresses—a slight young woman with a headful of corkscrew curls. She was wiping away tears, her mascara smudged, as she sobbed into a napkin.

"Oh, excuse me . . ." Samantha touched the woman lightly on the shoulder. "Are you okay?"

The girl flushed and nodded her head, causing her curls to bounce slightly. "I'm fine. It's just my boyfriend being jealous, as usual." She pushed past Samantha and rushed back toward the house.

Samantha gave her a few minutes' head start before she headed back into the kitchen to continue pouring drinks.

By ten, the crowd had thinned. Samantha was mixing a few last drinks in the kitchen when she jumped at the sound of an ear-piercing shriek. Rushing into the dining room, she discovered a crowd clustered around a bronzed, brawny man sprawled backward in a roped-off parlor chair, meant to be off-limits to guests. A blonde woman in a pink cocktail dress fanned the man with her program as others in the crowd asked if he needed assistance.

"Stop it, Darcy. I'm fine." The man, red-faced and sweating, his suit disheveled, appeared embarrassed by the attention.

"Mark, you're not fine. Everyone in here saw you fall."

"I'm a little nauseous. It's nothing." The man stood unsteadily and grabbed the woman's shoulder for support. "We should probably leave, though. I'm really not feeling my best."

As the couple walked toward the exit, Bob Randall rushed in from the garden. "Mark! I just heard . . . are you all right?"

The woman swiveled toward Bob, still supporting Mark with her arm around his waist. "He's not well. I'll take him home."

The incident dampened the festive atmosphere as people exchanged worried glances. Bob, in an effort to enliven the crowd, offered to show the remaining guests some of the off-limits rooms. As the crowd followed him upstairs, Samantha retreated to the kitchen with Marisa and Beth.

"I hope that guy's okay." Marisa filled a sink with water and dishwashing liquid.

"Me too." Samantha let out a pent-up breath as she gathered dirty glasses and handed them to Marisa.

Beth laid out a dish towel for Marisa to place the clean glasses on to dry. "Mark's the commission's newest member. He looked terrible."

"Hopefully a night of rest will do him good." Despite her cocktail gown, Marisa shoved her hands deep into the soapy water. "I've gotten into a rhythm here. Why don't you two gather the glasses left in the other rooms, and I'll keep at it."

The remaining crowd slowly filtered out as closing time neared. Samantha and Beth wandered around the house to collect glasses—most of them empty.

"Looks like your drinks were a hit. I told you people would love them." Beth grabbed another couple of glasses from a side table.

"Thank you for convincing me to do this. I stayed so busy I didn't have time to think." Even as Samantha said the words, she realized they weren't exactly true. Thoughts of Greg had pushed through periodically during the evening, causing a faint tightness in her chest, but she figured Beth didn't need to hear about her lapses.

Samantha dropped off another tray in the kitchen and stopped to count the pile of tickets in the overflowing julep glass. After a few calculations, she determined she'd made more than $2,000. Even considering the supplies for making the bitters and the taxes she would have to pay on her income, that wasn't a bad haul for a night's work.

Just as she headed to the living room for more glasses, Samantha heard Beth cry out from the powder room on the first floor. She and Marisa ran to find her.

"What is it? What's wrong?" Marisa rushed to Beth's side.

"This glass—I found it in the bathroom."

Marisa glanced at it. "Yeah, so . . ."

"The flower . . . look at the flower."

Samantha grabbed the glass and inspected its contents. "That's not the same flower we used for the garnish. What is that?"

Beth's hands shook without the glass. "It's oleander. It's poisonous."

"How did it get in the glass? We didn't have any oleander in the kitchen." Samantha set the glass on the counter and pushed it away, as if trying to escape the flower's toxins. "Remember the sick guy? What if he drank from this glass?"

Beth ran out of the room and toward the stairs. "I'll go find Bob."

Moments later, Bob came down the stairs with Beth behind him. "Let's not worry too much. We don't even know if that was Mark's glass. I'm sure it's nothing, but I'll give him a call just to be safe."

The three women waited as he pulled out his cell phone and made the call. In a moment, he hung up. "Went straight to voice mail. I'll try Darcy."

He punched some new numbers into his phone. "Darcy? It's Bob Randall with the Historic Commission. I wanted to check in on Mark. How's he doing?" His eyebrows lifted in surprise. "He's in the hospital? Oh my God!"

Though Samantha couldn't make out the words coming from the other end, she heard the pitch of the woman's voice. She sounded frantic.

"Darcy, listen. I need you to stay calm so I can explain something. We found what looks like oleander flowers in a glass. Do you think it could have been Mark's? It might be the reason he got sick." Bob paced as he listened to Darcy's response. "I'm not sure how it got in there. What's important is that the doctor knows about it so he can check whether Mark has any symptoms of oleander poisoning. Call me back when you know something else. Tell Mark we're all thinking about him."

Bob hung up and slowly turned toward Samantha. "He apparently fainted once he got home, and they couldn't revive him. He's in the hospital. It doesn't sound good."

Samantha winced. "Oh no—I hope he'll be all right. How could this have happened?"

Bob shrugged. "Who knows? There are oleander bushes all along the back fence. Maybe a flower fell in his drink as he walked outside. Anyway, you girls should head out. I can handle anything else."

The three friends boxed up Samantha's remaining bitters and the other bar supplies and drove home in shocked silence.

Samantha paused as she climbed out of the car. "Let me know if you guys hear anything." Anxiety about Mark, mixed with the high emotions of the day, had created a pit in the bottom of her stomach.

Back in her apartment, Samantha's stomach soured further as she remembered that her original plans for the evening had included a night in the honeymoon suite of downtown's St. Regis hotel. She cursed Greg, alternately wondering how he had spent his day and wishing she had never met him.

Ruby followed Samantha into her bedroom and hopped up on the bed as she began to change. Samantha stroked her velvety ears. Unable to help herself, she began, for perhaps the hundredth time since Greg had left town, to puzzle over the beginnings of their relationship and wonder what clues she'd missed that should have foretold her eventual heartbreak.

They'd met five years earlier when Samantha joined the staff of the local newspaper, the *Gazette*. It hadn't exactly been love at first sight. Though conventionally handsome, with blue eyes and dark, wavy hair trimmed short, Greg initially struck Samantha as stuck up and conceited. The navy-and-white Yale scarf he always left in plain sight on his desk irked her, almost as much as his lobbying for front-page placement for nearly every one of his stories. It took months for Samantha to realize he never meant to slight anyone. He was genetically wired to believe in himself.

Eventually, once they'd been thrust together for a few late nights on a breaking news story, she could begrudgingly admit that he worked hard. It took several more months for them to become friends. Finally, nearly nine months after they'd first met, Greg took their relationship a step further, comforting Samantha after she'd received some bad news. An old editor at her former newspaper had emailed to offer a tragic update to a story she'd written years earlier. An elderly woman had died, murdered by someone Samantha had helped to set free from prison. Samantha couldn't forgive herself.

Even now, the memory brought a pang to her chest. The news of the woman's death had crushed her, causing her to question her judgment about everything. Greg had listened and assured her she wasn't to blame. When she wasn't convinced, he kissed her to redirect her focus away from her inner turmoil.

Now Samantha wished the kiss had never happened, even as her heart pounded with the memory. She took off her dress and threw it across the room. As she pulled the bobby pins out of her hair and freed her curly waves from the tight bun, she experienced another pang from wishing away the years of happy memories and wondered if she would ever feel the same closeness with anyone else again.

Chapter Two

S amantha woke to a frantic phone call from Marisa.

"Samantha, he's dead. And the police want to talk to us."

Still groggy, she didn't immediately understand. "Dead? Who? What are you talking about?"

"It's Mark, Sam. He died last night. Bob called Beth. The police want to talk to all of us."

The gravity of the situation hit her as she remembered the scene from the previous evening. "Oh my God! Dead? That's crazy. But why do they want to talk to us?"

"They said it was oleander poisoning. The police want to talk to everyone involved with making the drinks. I'm sorry we got you involved in this."

"They can't believe we had anything to do with it, can they?"

"Bob said they're calling it a suspicious death for now, but he's sure they'll realize it had to have been an accident."

"That poor man, and his poor wife . . ." Samantha fell silent for a moment as she recalled the couple she'd seen the night before. "When do we have to meet with the police? What should we say to them?"

"They want everyone to meet back at the Reilley house at ten this morning. I think they want to go over what happened last night."

"This is crazy."

"I know. Beth and I will pick you up around nine forty-five, and we can go over together. I don't imagine any of us want to face this alone."

After hanging up, Samantha jumped in the shower and riffled through her closet for the outfit most likely to identify her as a respectful, law-abiding citizen. She opted for a pair of jeans and a navy-blue-and-white-striped top. She pulled her blonde waves into a low ponytail and put the barest amount of makeup on—just enough to cover her blotchy skin from her night of restless sleep. *Okay, I look presentable, like an upstanding member of society.* She went downstairs to find her friends already parked out front.

Samantha jumped into the back seat of Beth's Prius, biting her lip. "They can't blame my drinks, can they? Nobody else got sick, as far as we know."

Marisa turned from the front seat to glance at her friend. "Don't panic. I'm sure it's a formality. They want to ask everyone in attendance last night some questions."

The friends were silent for the rest of the brief drive to the Reilley house. When they arrived, police were already on-site and ushered them into the sitting room, where they joined a crowd of people, including Bob and the waitstaff from last night.

"Have a seat right here, please." A tall, lanky policeman with a pompadour reminiscent of James Dean pointed toward a sofa in the corner. "We need to take everyone's statements. Which one of you made the drinks last night?"

Samantha stared hard at his glossy brown hair and black-rimmed glasses, trying to decide if he looked more like Elvis or Buddy Holly. Amid her musings, it took her a minute to register what he had said. Finally, she raised her hand. "I made the drinks."

"All right, we'll start with you." He waved her toward the kitchen and introduced himself as Detective Jason Sanders. "Walk me through last night. When did you get here? What did you do?"

They stood at the large kitchen island where Samantha's drinks had been displayed the night before.

"I came with my friends, Marisa and Beth. We arrived at around five thirty and immediately set up my display of bitters and prepared the drinks. Then we took a tour of the house." She walked around the island and showed Sanders how she had arranged the room. As she pointed, she tried to steady her trembling hands. "Around six, when the tour began, we poured the drinks into glasses and prepared trays for the waiters to pass around."

Sanders scribbled her responses onto a small notepad. "Did you make these drinks to order?"

"No. There were too many people. I made two large batches, and they were served as guests arrived. A small sprig of phlox floated in each glass as a nod to the garden-party theme."

He looked up from his notepad with a quizzical expression. "Flowers in your drinks? Doesn't sound real appetizing."

Samantha laughed nervously. "I know it sounds strange, but phlox gives a nice spicy flavor. It's an essence more than anything else, but it adds to the flavor profile of the drink."

"These flowers . . . where did you get them?"

"My friend Beth cut them from her garden."

Sanders leaned against the counter and struck a relaxed pose. "Any chance some oleander got mixed in with the other flowers?"

The forced casualness of the question sounded to Samantha like a trap. "Of course not! Beth is a landscape architect. She tells us all the time about ripping oleander out from gardens where people have small children or pets. She would never grow it in her own garden."

Sanders stood straighter, allowing his height to tower over Samantha. "Until we get the autopsy results, we're working under the assumption that Mr. Brantwell ingested the oleander in his drink. Now, my problem is, if you didn't put it in there, how did it get there? You and your friends made the drinks, right?"

Samantha instinctively took a step back. "Yeah, we made the drinks, but there were three or four waiters and waitresses who served them. Beyond that, some people came back and grabbed drinks on their own or for other people. Plus, there was the food brought by that catering company. There were hundreds of people here last night."

Sanders pulled out a stool and motioned for Samantha to sit. He pulled out a second one for himself. "What do you remember about when Mr. Brantwell fell ill?"

Samantha took a deep breath and tried to focus. "I'm not sure. I was in the kitchen when someone screamed. We all rushed out, and he had fallen into a chair . . . a woman tried to help him up. He didn't look good."

Sanders nodded. "Did he have a drink then?"

"No. Beth didn't find the glass with the oleander until after we began to clean the house after everyone had left. Since oleander is poisonous, we worried it might have been Mark's glass.

Bob called Mark's wife to explain what we had discovered so she could tell the doctors who were treating him."

He nodded again and stood. "Do you remember anything else important from last night?"

Samantha shook her head as she stood as well. "No. I wish I could."

"Okay. That's all for now." Sanders led her back to the sitting room.

While Sanders conducted the other interviews, Samantha wandered into the dining room. She wanted to take another peek at the scene of Mark's collapse, curious if it would jog any memories.

Though the room had looked empty when she entered, she soon noticed the crying waitress from the night before, partially hidden behind a Victorian silk screen in the corner. The woman whispered to someone completely hidden on the other side. The pair hadn't yet noticed Samantha, who'd been about to leave when she overheard the girl. "Please tell me you didn't . . ."

A young man's voice sank into a whisper. "Are you crazy, Mila? Keep your voice down."

Suddenly, the couple went quiet, as if aware of another presence in the room. Samantha made a quick about-face, trying to pretend she'd made a wrong turn. As she raced back into the parlor, she ran into Bob, which gave her an excuse to talk to someone else. "It's all so horrible, isn't it? How is Mark's wife?"

An expression of momentary confusion clouded Bob's face. "Oh, Darcy? She's not his wife—she's his girlfriend. He's been separated from his wife for the last eight months."

"Oh . . ."

Bob, still the gracious host from the night before, stood to offer Samantha his seat. She took it. "What about the wife? Do you know her?"

He shook his head. "All I know about her is what I heard from Mark. But from his descriptions, she's a piece of work."

"How about Darcy? How's she doing?"

"She was in terrible shape last night. I couldn't calm her enough to get a word in edgewise. It's a shame. Mark had just been telling me she'd seemed a little off lately—in a fragile state, I think he said. I'm not sure how she's going to handle all of this."

Samantha nodded, unsure of what else to say or do.

Before long, Beth and Marisa returned from giving their statements. The police had given them all permission to leave, with the caveat that they might need to answer more questions later.

It was now afternoon, and the three women were hungry. They headed to their favorite taco stand on the edge of the Highlands and began to compare notes on their interviews with Detective Sanders.

"He didn't act like he believed Mark's death was an accident." Marisa parked Beth's car in front of the weathered bungalow turned taco shack. A line snaked out the door, but the welcoming scents wafting from the building promised to compensate for the wait.

"His questions made me think he blamed me." Samantha placed her order for two chorizo, egg, and cheese tacos and a fresh-squeezed lemonade. The woman behind the counter handed her an order of chips and queso for the table, and Samantha and her friends grabbed seats at a booth in the corner. As they ate, Samantha filled them in on her talk with Sanders and on her conversation with Bob afterward.

"Please stop me the next time I mention I've got a great idea." Beth picked at her food. "None of this would've happened if I hadn't gotten you involved. This is such a mess."

"It's not your fault." Samantha grew silent as they cleared the table to leave.

Marisa tried to cajole her into a good mood. "Wait. We can't end the afternoon like this. Let's do something to take our minds off everything."

Samantha scrunched her nose. "Ugh . . . don't worry about it. There isn't much else I want to do now."

"Doesn't matter." Marisa grabbed the car keys from Beth again. "Come on—I've got an idea." As the women climbed into the car, Marisa tuned the radio to a classic rock station. "We're going to Hermann Park."

The words made Samantha smile. Hermann Park was Houston's answer to Central Park. With 445 acres in the middle of the Museum District, the park drew thousands of Houstonians from all walks of life every day. In the park, city dwellers could breathe and get away from the traffic and the twelve-lane interstates. Samantha loved how it reflected the true diversity of the city, with singles and families mingling on the playgrounds, exploring the zoo, or maneuvering paddle boats through the small lake while couples took photos in the Japanese Tea Garden or strolled in the Centennial Gardens. Samantha often visited the herb garden there in search of inspiration for her unique bitters combinations.

Beth parked in a side lot, and the three women walked under a tunnel of live oaks, past the amphitheater, and across a small bridge to the boat launch on the other side of McGovern Lake.

Marisa led Samantha to the pedal boats. "You've always wanted to do this at least once. Now's your chance."

Within a few moments, the three were balancing together in the boat and listening to the steady rhythm of the boat's

19

paddles thumping water against the hull. They pedaled around the fountain and trailed a family of ducks from one end of the lake to another, but nobody really enjoyed themselves.

Samantha, who controlled one of the boat's two sets of pedals, stopped pedaling. The peaceful setting couldn't still her thoughts. "I can't stop thinking about that detective and his questions. You don't think there's any chance he'll blame me for Mark's death, do you?"

Marisa shook her head. "No way. What's your motive? You didn't even know the guy."

"My drink killed him . . ."

Marisa turned to face her friend. "Sam, if a drink killed him, and that's a big if, then someone else doctored it. It's not your fault. This is no time for your martyr complex."

Samantha flinched as if someone had slapped her. "Martyr complex? What're you talking about?"

Beth laid a hand on Marisa's shoulder and shot her a warning look.

"I know I'm supposed to treat you with kid gloves right now, but I want to say something. You've blamed yourself for years for that woman's death just because of one story you wrote. Her death wasn't your fault, and this isn't your fault either."

Samantha leaned away from her friend. "That's not fair. I didn't say this was my fault."

Marisa stared straight ahead at the water. "No, but I know how your mind works. Within four hours, you'll have twisted this into a scenario where you blame yourself for this man's death."

Samantha raised her gaze as she looked at her best friend of five years. She couldn't believe Marisa could say such things. She hunched over.

Marisa turned and put her hand on Samantha's knee. "I'm sorry if that came out wrong. It's just . . . ever since that woman died, you've carried around this guilt like an anchor and don't trust yourself or your instincts anymore. Greg let you get away with it. He was a crutch. You let him make all of your decisions for you, but you need to learn to stand on your own two feet now."

Samantha yanked her knee away and turned to face the water, stung by her friend's words. "Let's go home."

On their way back to the dock, the only noise came from the *kathunk, kathunk* of the paddle as it hit the water. During the awkward ride home, nobody talked amid the tension of words left unsaid.

When they pulled up to Samantha's apartment, Marisa turned to the back seat and looked at her friend. "Sam, you're my best friend. I want you to find the happiness you deserve. Call me if you need anything."

Still stung from the previous exchange, Samantha nodded as she opened the car door. She climbed out without saying anything and trudged up the steps to her apartment as the weight of Marisa's words caused her shoulders to slump.

Ruby mewed at the door, and Samantha scooped her into her arms. "At least I have one friend who doesn't judge me."

As she stroked the cat's fur, Samantha considered what Marisa had said. Was there any truth to it? She wasn't responsible for Mark's death. She hadn't poisoned his drink. But the other woman? If Samantha hadn't written those stories for the newspaper, the woman never would have died.

A cold shame spread through her body, but Samantha pushed the thoughts aside as she performed a litany of mindless tasks. She cleaned her apartment, attempted to read a book, and tried to write in her journal before setting it aside to eat a sandwich for dinner. Usually journaling helped her to work through her feelings, but not today. The memories kept coming, forcing her to relive the terrible time when she'd learned a woman she had helped to free from prison had murdered again.

The story stemmed from her first job out of college at a small newspaper in central Texas. She'd been itching to write an article big and important enough to catapult her to another, larger newspaper. Rumors had swirled for years about an overzealous prosecutor who cut corners to secure maximum sentences in nearly every criminal case in his district. Samantha dug into court records and interviewed defense attorneys, defendants, and their families until she pieced together a pattern of malicious actions on the part of the prosecutor, who had either ignored or failed to pass along exculpatory evidence to defendants. There were rumors of even more egregious cases where the prosecutor, desperate to get a conviction, had planted evidence.

Samantha wrote a series of stories outlining her case against the prosecutor, but she needed a particularly grievous case to bring the story alive to readers. She stumbled upon the perfect subject in Laurie Cavendish, tried as an adult at fifteen and sentenced to life in prison for murder.

Interviews with Laurie's foster parents, and later with the girl herself, convinced Samantha of Laurie's innocence. Laurie, young and desperate for acceptance, had fallen in with a dangerous crowd. She insisted she had waited in the car and hadn't known about the robbery and certainly hadn't been in the house at the time of the murder.

During her trial, the prosecutor had entered strands of Laurie's hair into evidence, claiming they'd been collected in the dead woman's room. The evidence had been key to the guilty verdict. A source had slipped Samantha a copy of the initial evidence catalog, which didn't include any strands of hair.

For two days, Samantha owned the front page with stories about the prosecutor's record, including a centerpiece story about Laurie and her case. The series won several awards and led to calls for state intervention, including in Laurie's case, in part because of Samantha's stories.

The clips proved Samantha's investigative abilities and earned her a spot at the *Houston Gazette*. All was well until two years later when her old editor forwarded Samantha a new story about Laurie, who'd been free since her overturned sentence. According to that story, Laurie had killed another innocent woman.

The news devastated Samantha, and it had been Greg who'd listened for hours to her self-recriminations.

Was he really a crutch?

Samantha liked to believe she approached decisions the same way she would approach a problematic bitters recipe—she went slow and investigated each ingredient in isolation, taking her time to identify any overpowering flavors so as to decide on a counterbalance. Had she sought too much input from Greg and not relied enough on her own palate, so to speak?

Samantha shook her head, not wanting to further analyze herself. She carried Ruby into the bedroom with her. As she climbed into her cold bed, thoughts of Mark and of Laurie twisted together in her head as she tossed and turned. Ruby nestled in at the foot of the bed, out of reach of Samantha's scissoring legs, her soft snores soon the only sound in the room. Samantha begrudged the cat her ability to fall asleep instantly. Samantha's mom used to call it "the sleep of the innocent." In the dark hours of the evening, Samantha feared she would never experience it again.

Chapter Three

After a night of restless sleep, Samantha woke early Monday on what should have been the first day of her honeymoon in Spain. She'd canceled the trip but still hadn't taken on any new assignments or scheduled any interviews for the period when she'd planned to be away, deciding she owed herself a vacation after all she'd been through.

Samantha had worked as a freelance writer and editor for the past nine months, after she and twenty of her colleagues were laid off in the latest purge at the *Gazette*. It was a tough time to be a journalist, with newspapers everywhere scaling back due to lost advertising revenue. Now she supported herself by writing articles for the local business journal and a lifestyle magazine as well as a handful of other niche publications, coasting along while she tried to figure out what she wanted to do with her life. Greg's connections had helped her land her most steady and lucrative assignment—helping to edit the quarterly magazine for City University, where Greg had attended law school. It meant two or three weeks of steady, well-paid work every three months. She had been set to help put together the summer issue once she returned from her honeymoon.

Today, with nothing much planned, Samantha went outside to find the newspaper, planning to read it leisurely with a cup of hot chai tea. She'd read newspapers cover to cover every day since high school, and she'd remained a loyal reader, despite losing her job. She slipped off the thin bag, unrolled it, and stripped out the classified ads and the auto and real estate sections until only the best parts were left. Buried deep in the B section, she found a little blurb about a "suspicious death" during the Highlands home tour.

Mark Brantwell, 48, of Houston, died Saturday night after attending the annual Highlands Historic Home Tour. Details of the death weren't immediately available, though police have declared it suspicious.

Witnesses say Brantwell grew ill during the event and left for home around 9:30 p.m. Hours later, he was pronounced dead at Memorial Hospital. Police declined to comment on the manner of death.

Brantwell, a local contractor, recently joined the Highlands Historic Commission. A native Houstonian, Brantwell moved back to Houston eight months ago after working in the Galveston area for ten years.

After finishing the story, Samantha sighed in relief when she found no mention of herself. Her relief dissipated as dread clouded her thoughts.

Eventually more details will leak out. If they connect me to this man's death, my reputation will be ruined.

Samantha couldn't handle any more thoughts about Mark and decided to burn off her restless energy with a bike ride along the bayou.

People who didn't know Houston loved to complain about the endless freeways and concrete, a sprawl that spread like fungus from every corner of the city into endless suburbs. The city was dense and in some places gritty, but government leaders had spent millions building bike trails to give residents an opportunity to commune with nature. Samantha had explored most of the trails, having spent many sunny afternoons using them as a launchpad for exploring far-flung neighborhoods.

Today she wanted routine, and so she fell into a simple rhythm on one of her regular rides, following the bayou through woods and neighborhoods to a clearing with a beautiful view of the city's skyline.

After meandering for a few miles, almost without realizing it, Samantha turned her bike toward a familiar street with a quaint yellow bungalow for sale, barely on the wrong side of I-10 but still technically in the Highlands. She hadn't fallen in love with the house immediately. Greg had convinced her it would be the perfect place to start their new life together—close enough to his future job as an assistant prosecutor that he wouldn't suffer the usual Houston commute and still the kind of place where they could raise a family. After repeated viewings, she'd finally seen past the cracks in the walls and the uneven floors to its potential, including a nice backyard, where she could imagine kicking a soccer ball around with some future child.

They'd been set to close on the house when Greg announced he couldn't go through with any of it. His words still echoed in her brain. He didn't want to buy a house, he didn't want to stay in Houston, and he didn't want to get married. He fled the city for a life of fifteen-hour days and billable hours in New York City and left Samantha to pick up the pieces.

She'd grown to love the house and wrestled with whether to try to keep it, but her mom had convinced her she couldn't handle all of that now. She'd lost her earnest money but saved her down payment when she pulled out of the deal after Greg flew the coop.

What a waste. She pedaled past the house, trying to put it and all it represented behind her. As she rode, her mind turned to the future and what she might want now that her plan A had gone out the window. She supposed she could hunt for a different job, but she wasn't sure what she wanted to do. Her mother had encouraged her to consider a fresh start in her hometown of Corpus Christi, but going home would feel like a step backward.

With her head full of other possibilities, Mark's death had briefly escaped her mind when she biked past her landlord's bungalow and down his driveway to her apartment, located above the garage in the back. To her surprise, she discovered the crying waitress from the party perched on her bottom steps. Samantha instinctively rolled backward on her bike as the girl stood and rushed toward her.

"Samantha, right?" The girl continued to move closer as Samantha stumbled, dismounting from her bike. "It's Mila. From the party the other night?"

On the short end of petite, the girl couldn't weigh more than 115 pounds. Still, Samantha took a step back.

"Please. I just want to talk to you."

Samantha eyed the girl, careful to keep her bike between her and Mila. "What do you want? How did you find me?"

"Oh, I bought a bottle of your bitters at the party. Using your name, I looked up your address. Anyway, I want to talk to you about what you overheard yesterday."

Samantha recalled the scene in the dining room the day before. Though Mila was hardly intimidating, Samantha hadn't seen the man who had been behind the screen. He could be six foot five and built like a linebacker, for all she knew. She would need to consider her words carefully.

"I didn't really hear anything." Samantha rolled her bike toward the storage space underneath her apartment but kept her gaze on Mila.

The girl frowned and looked at the ground. "Listen, I know you overheard me ask my boyfriend about . . . you know. I also know you saw me that night in the garden, crying. I didn't want to leave you with the impression . . . well, that Eric had anything to do with it. Because he definitely didn't."

Samantha locked her storage space and turned back to face the girl. "How do you know for sure?"

Mila's voice rose. "Because I know him, okay? He would never hurt someone, much less kill them."

A twinge of worry needled Samantha. She'd encountered domestic violence cases as a reporter and knew jealousy sometimes masked more sinister tendencies. What if Eric had somehow caused Mark's death? In that case, not only would Mila be in danger, but so would Samantha.

Samantha looked the girl up and down, searching for any telltale bruises, but found nothing obvious. "You were pretty upset on Saturday night. Does Eric get jealous a lot?"

Mila took a step back. "No, no. It's not like that. Anyway, I obviously shouldn't have come here."

The girl hurried down to a car parked at the end of the driveway. She flung herself into the driver's seat and drove off.

Samantha stood still, stunned by the encounter and unsure what to make of the girl or her story.

That was weird. She walked up the stairs and into her apartment.

Inside, Samantha considered calling Marisa to describe her encounter with Mila, but she resisted the impulse. Her friend's comments on Sunday still rattled in her mind. Unsure what to do with her afternoon, she began to research some new bitters recipes and dove into the large to-be-read pile of books by the side of her bed. After dinner, she decided to veg out with some HRN—the Home Renovation Network—and flipped on the television. It wasn't long before she had curled up on her couch with Ruby and was bingeing on a house-flipping show.

* * *

After her HRN marathon the night before, Samantha woke Tuesday morning resolved to give her own space a makeover. She would break out of her funk with a thorough cleanout of her apartment.

When I'm done, there won't be a trace of Greg left here.

She began in her closet and was filling a bag with old clothes to give away when her breath caught at the sight of her wedding dress hidden in the back. She backed away and closed the door, ready to move on to something a little less fraught.

At her desk, Samantha pulled out her drawers and made a promising start by filling two grocery sacks with old bills and receipts. Ruby sat on the floor, pawing at a stray bit of paper that had missed its mark and landed outside the sack. Samantha laughed at the cat's antics and continued to yank out papers until a dancing-hamster birthday card, given to her by Greg as a joke, stopped her cold. She threw the card back into her desk and slammed the drawer shut.

Who am I kidding? I'm not ready for this.

She grabbed the sacks of bills and was descending the stairs outside to throw them in her trash bin when a male voice behind her called out, "Samantha Warren?"

She dropped the trash, grabbed the aerator next to her compost bin, and spun around, afraid Mila's boyfriend had come for a follow-up visit. Instead, a shaggy-haired kid with a patchy hipster beard stepped forward and handed her an envelope. "You've been served."

"Served? What's this?" She ran after him, but the kid ignored her and sprinted down the driveway.

She ripped open the envelope to find documents naming her as a defendant in a lawsuit. Shocked, she dropped the papers as if they had scalded her. After a moment, she picked them back up and carried them into her apartment. She sank down onto her green sofa and skimmed through the legalese to get to the important details. She, individually, and the Highlands Historic Commission collectively were being sued for the wrongful death of one Mark Brantwell.

"You've got to be kidding me!" Samantha paced. She read more of the details as she walked laps around the circumference of her living room rug.

Gabby Brantwell of Galveston, Mark's wife, sought the princely sum of eight million dollars for the loss of her husband's earnings potential. She and her lawyers had apparently decided that Samantha and the entire Highlands Historic Commission were to blame.

Why me?

The lawsuit alleged that the Historic Commission was legally responsible for hosting the event and hiring a bartender who, through either negligence or malfeasance, had poisoned Mark by putting oleander in his drink.

"I did not!" Samantha shouted to nobody. "I told those police I would never put oleander in a drink."

She hated to say it, but she needed a lawyer, and quick. A story like this would find its way into the papers, and her name would be dragged through the mud.

Forgetting her earlier fight with her best friend, Samantha called Marisa, who agreed to come right over.

* * *

"Marisa, what am I going to do? I can't afford this . . ."

Marisa leafed through the lawsuit while Samantha resumed her loop around her living room rug.

"Sam, I'm only a first-year law student, but even I understand this lawsuit doesn't have any merit. As far as we know, the case is still an open investigation with the police. Until they complete their investigation, nobody will pay attention to this."

Samantha stopped pacing. "I'd feel better if you had a second and third point. What should I do now? The only lawyer I know dumped me and moved to New York."

"You mean Greg? Please. He hasn't even passed the bar yet. How about the law firm he interned with last summer? David Dwyer has a great reputation."

Not a bad idea.

Greg had once described David as one of the best legal minds in the business, even though he hadn't yet hit his forties. Samantha most remembered his kind and unassuming nature. Last summer he'd invited Samantha and Greg to a gallery opening in Montrose to view his latest collection of paintings. Samantha had worried that the gallery opening would be pretentious, but David had made it fun. Calling him might be awkward now that she and Greg had split, but she needed someone she could trust.

"Maybe I'll call him."

"Do it, and in the meantime, don't panic. Call me as soon as you've talked to David."

After Marisa left, Samantha Googled Dwyer's law firm to find his phone number. His head shot showed off the warm smile she remembered.

Should I really call him? Won't it be too weird?

She spent some time searching Yelp for other law firms, but there were too many, and she couldn't imagine what criteria one should use to decide who was good and trustworthy. With too many options, she settled on the safest one and called David.

It was only two in the afternoon, so she hoped he'd be in the office. However, the call went straight to voice mail. She left her name and number and asked him to call her back.

Within an hour, her phone rang.

"Samantha? How are you? It's David Dwyer." His voice sounded friendly.

"Oh, I didn't expect you to call back so quickly."

"It's great to hear from you. But you sounded concerned in your message. Is it about Greg? I was sorry it didn't work out between the two of you."

Samantha groaned at the reference to Greg. It still hurt when she thought about him. Consequently, she avoided the topic as much as possible.

"No, it's not about Greg. It's a legal situation, and I hope you can help. I mean that I could hire you . . . or that you could recommend someone or something." She winced. *Ugh. This is so awkward!*

"What kind of legal situation?" David's voice sounded concerned. "Do you want to come down to my studio to discuss it?

I've been trying to paint, but I've got a bit of a creative block at the moment. I could use a distraction."

"Your studio?"

"I had a light day today and took off a little early. Must answer the muse when she calls and all that. The muse must have gone for the afternoon, though, so I'm free now. I've got a full schedule tomorrow."

Samantha took a deep breath. She needed time to slow down. She couldn't think when everything moved too quickly. Logically, she knew she needed to talk to a lawyer, but she didn't like to make decisions without weighing all the pros and cons. She didn't have that luxury now.

"Okay." She exhaled. "I'll be right over."

She followed his directions to a studio in an old rice silo, now transformed into a space for artists of all kinds. Samantha had visited the studios once during an open house, when the silos bustled with artists selling their wares and crowds eager to buy them. This afternoon, however, footsteps echoed in the silent hallways. Only a few lights shone from open studios, the rest being tightly locked and closed off.

When she found David, she almost didn't recognize him. He'd exchanged the three-piece suit of the courtroom brawler for a paint-splattered T-shirt and ratty jeans, which hugged his muscular frame. He ran his fingers through wavy black hair that flopped over his brow, revealing intense green eyes that warmed with his smile when he turned to her in the doorway.

"Samantha, I'm so glad to see you again." He wiped his hands on his jeans and shrugged an apology. "I'd shake your hand, but . . ."

"No, please, don't worry. Thanks again for seeing me so quickly. I'm sorry to disturb your work."

He pointed to a nearly blank canvas in front of him. "Well, as you can discern, there's not a lot of work to interrupt at the moment. It will do me some good to focus on something else. What's this legal matter you mentioned?"

"It's a lawsuit. I'm being sued for wrongful death." Samantha trembled. It seemed impossible that the words she spoke could apply to her.

"What? Whose death?"

She pulled the summons out of her purse and handed it to him.

He scanned through it and glanced at her with a quizzical expression. "A bartender? I didn't know you do bartending."

"I don't. It's a long story, but . . ." Samantha blushed. "You might remember I originally had other plans for Saturday night?"

"Your wedding."

"My friends were trying to keep me busy and, well, also help me get rid of the three hundred bottles of homemade bitters I'd made as wedding favors. Anyway, long story short, I filled in as a guest bartender at the Highlands Historic Commission's home tour on Saturday."

David nodded, as if this made total sense, though as she said it out loud, the entire story sounded ludicrous to her. *What was I thinking?*

"While we were there, this man, Mark Brantwell, got sick and later died. We found an oleander flower in a drink and later learned he died of oleander poisoning."

"His wife is the one suing you?"

"I guess so. Though he attended the home tour with another woman. Apparently, Mark and his wife were in the middle of a messy divorce."

David read back through the documents carefully, scratching paint from his fingernails as he flipped through the pages.

"The first thing I'll say is if the police are still investigating, they haven't filed a criminal case against anyone. Any decent attorney would advise against filing a civil case before police have ruled out criminal charges."

The knot in her stomach loosened a bit.

"However, you've still got to answer this. Since this was a spur-of-the-moment job, I don't suppose you have liability insurance?"

The knot tightened again. "What? No. Do I need it?"

"Well, unfortunately, in cases like this, liability insurance could help pay a claim, but without it, it's all on you. Now, that might work in your favor. If they realize you don't have any assets, they might drop you from the case."

"What if they don't?"

"Well, then it could be bad . . ."

Samantha rubbed her temples as a tension headache began to form.

"I still believe the best-case scenario is the most likely. The police finish their investigation, find the guilty party, and a judge throws this suit out of court."

"What's the worst case?"

"If a judge or jury rules against you, there could be a hefty judgment and wage garnishment for years to come."

Samantha became light-headed and looked around for a place to sit. She slumped onto a stool and rested her head in her hands as she tried to absorb the ramifications of the lawsuit.

"Again, that's a long shot. However, to recoup some of your losses, you might want to file a countersuit."

"Why would I do that?"

"Say, for instance, a newspaper or a television station picked up this lawsuit and mentioned your name in connection with this murder. That could hurt your reputation for years to come. A countersuit would be your only opportunity to get compensation."

Samantha's tension mounted, spreading to her shoulders as she considered David's words. "This is such a mess. My life is such a mess. It's no wonder Greg left."

David shook his head and stepped closer to Samantha. "Greg has tunnel vision when he focuses on something. It's a good skill for a lawyer, but it will hurt him in other parts of his life."

Samantha turned away as she wiped away tears. Why had she mentioned Greg? She couldn't handle thinking about him on top of everything else.

David closed the distance between them and briefly touched her shoulder. "I'm sorry. Listen, would you like a drink?"

Samantha looked into his kind face. "You know what? I should say no, but I would."

David walked to a small bar in the corner of his studio and pulled out a bottle of Knob Creek. "All I can offer you is a little bourbon and water."

"Perfect."

As he poured the drinks, Samantha walked to the wall to admire some of David's finished paintings. Although no two were alike, each conveyed a specific mood as colors bled into one another in astonishing ways.

"How do you do this? It's like you've captured emotions and let them pour out onto the canvas."

"In a way, I do. I paint what I feel, which is why this creative block is driving me nuts right now."

David handed her a frosty glass with the bourbon poured neatly over a globe of ice.

Samantha swirled, sniffed, and took a sip. "This is nice."

"I'd say cheers, but . . ."

She clinked her glass against his. "To renewing our acquaintance. Thank you for listening to me."

"Anytime. I want to help. I'm swamped with a few other cases, but I can make room for you. If it gets too complicated, I might recommend someone else, but it should be fine. Often in cases like these, the initial filing includes everyone even tangentially related to a case before narrowing in on the actual party at fault."

Samantha let out the breath she had been holding in. She wanted to believe David could solve this for her with a few well-written filings. However, the tightness in her chest filled her with dread rather than hope about the future. She took another sip of her drink, hoping the warmth of the bourbon would relax her, before she realized she might fall asleep in David's studio if she didn't stand. The past few days and weeks were catching up to her. "Thank you. I don't want to take up more of your time. I should head home."

"Wait—" David grabbed her arm and turned her toward him. "I promise this will be okay, Samantha."

He let go of her arm and patted her again on the back. "I've got some contacts in the police department. First thing tomorrow, I'll try to find out the status of the investigation. I don't want you to worry about this. We'll handle it."

"I can't thank you enough." Samantha offered her hand for him to shake.

He set down his drink and clasped her hand in both of his. "Try not to worry, Samantha. Hopefully the police will solve this case soon and all of this will be a formality. I'll be in touch."

"Thanks. It was nice to see you again. Have a great afternoon." Samantha turned and walked out of the studio. She hurried as she left, chasing her own shadow down the halls of the nearly empty silos. As much as David had tried to reassure her, she couldn't help but sense danger lurking ahead.

Chapter Four

After leaving David's studio, Samantha was still a little on edge. The prospect of a trial or of the last few weeks of her life being blasted across the pages of the *Gazette* or, worse yet, blared on television during the news report caused the tension to settle even more firmly in the back of her neck. She massaged her shoulders, trying to release the knot in her upper back.

Now back home, Samantha wanted another drink—something to help prevent a full-fledged panic attack. She settled on a Battle of New Orleans, a bourbon drink with hints of absinthe and bitters, which frosted her glass as she spun ice cubes with a bar spoon. The drink had a bite but mellowed as it warmed her throat on the way down.

Cocktail in hand, she walked laps around her living room rug as she cataloged the series of unfortunate events that had upturned her life: she'd been laid off from the only job she'd ever loved; her fiancé had left her; she'd given up her dream house, canceled her wedding, stumbled on the scene of a potential murder, and wound up being sued by someone connected with the case. She was spiraling and could find nothing to stop her from veering completely off any sensible course.

While Marisa and David had tried to convince her of the lawsuit's flaws, Samantha couldn't help but consider the outcome if it proceeded. What if the newspapers found out about it and sullied her reputation? She might lose her clients and have no way to pay rent.

She finished the drink and decided she needed more. This time, she poured in more bourbon and splashed in a few dashes of the orange bitters. It wasn't as smooth, but it would get the job done.

She sipped her drink as she resumed her path around the rug. *Not only could I lose my clients but also any money I have saved.* She couldn't imagine making eight million dollars over several lifetimes, much less this one. They'd garnish her wages from now until the end of time. *Then what can I do but move back home with Mom and Dad?*

With that last musing, she finished her drink and collapsed onto the sofa, waking Ruby, who'd nestled into the corner.

I'll spend my entire down payment on attorney's fees.

The booze counteracted her racing thoughts, and the room spun as she closed her eyes. Ruby climbed onto her lap and curled up. It was only five in the afternoon, but the alcohol and the stress caught up with Samantha, and she fell into a light sleep.

A ringing cell phone startled her awake an hour later. Too groggy to notice the name on her caller ID, she pressed the button to answer and waited.

"Is this Samantha Warren?" The voice on the other end of the phone sounded young and uncertain.

"Yes. Who's this?" At least she didn't slur her words!

"This is Lori Huffing at the *Gazette*?" The statement came out like a question and confused a half-asleep Samantha.

"Yes?"

"Well, I'm calling to ask if you want to comment."

"To comment? On what?" Samantha's heart raced.

"The wrongful-death lawsuit."

"No comment." Samantha jabbed the key to end the call and slammed her phone down on the cushion beside her.

Wow. So that's what it feels like. She'd been on the receiving end of many "no comments" in her career, but she'd never considered what it would feel like to have to say the words herself. Even after she spoke them, the ramifications of the reporter's questions loomed large. There would be a story.

Samantha's hands trembled, and she clasped them together to stop the shaking as the prospect of a newspaper article hit her. She experienced a brief flash of empathy for all the sources she'd left tossing and turning from her questions at night before brushing the recollection away to focus on her own dread. Now she was wide awake.

At times like these, she missed Greg the most. For four years she'd been used to having someone around, and she hadn't yet figured out how to fill the lonely hours without him. She drifted from the newspaper crossword to the pile of books by her bedside to her journal, where she jotted a few random thoughts before returning to the television, which had become her most reliable source of mindless comfort. After a Meg Ryan marathon with *Sleepless in Seattle* and *When Harry Met Sally*, Samantha finally stumbled toward her bedroom, where she struggled to will herself back to sleep. She finally succeeded around two in the morning.

At five thirty AM, the phone rang. Groggy, Samantha assumed it was the newspaper again, and she spoke without giving the caller a chance to say anything. "What part of 'no comment' don't you understand?"

The voice on the other end of the line sobered her quickly. "Baby? Are you okay?"

"Greg? What? Wait . . . why are you calling?"

Samantha's breath caught in her throat as she replayed his words in her head. *He called me baby.* She sat up in her bed.

"I read the *Gazette* this morning. What the hell have you gotten yourself into since I left?"

As suddenly as it had come, any lingering tenderness the endearment had evoked dissipated into ear-pounding rage. She jumped out of bed, needing to move to release her anger. "Don't . . . you . . . dare . . ." She didn't know how to finish her threat, but the tone of her voice seemed to startle Greg.

"I'm sorry. I'm sorry. I was just worried about you."

"Greg, I don't need or want your sympathy."

"I wanted to make sure you're okay. If you want, I can make some calls. Help you straighten this whole mess out—"

"No thanks. You don't want to be in my life, so why are you butting back in?"

"Samantha, please. Don't be like this."

Samantha hung up on him, steaming. *The nerve of him. I can't believe he would call me. What makes him think he has the right to try to solve my problems anymore?*

She stomped into the kitchen and downed a glass of ice water to cool herself off. The two calls had unnerved her. A part of her wanted to give in, call Greg back, and ask if he could offer a solution. Another part of her wanted to prove she didn't need his help. The newspaper story presented the most immediate concern. By now, it should have landed on doorsteps and desktops across the city.

Samantha shooed Ruby into the next room so she wouldn't make a break for it before running down the stairs in her pajamas and grabbing the paper from the front lawn. The story hadn't landed on the front page, but she spotted it in the B section. "Historic Commission Sued for Wrongful Death." Samantha blew out a sigh of relief to find the headline below the fold. It could have been much worse.

She read through the story:

The Houston Highlands Historic Commission and former Gazette *reporter Samantha Warren are named in a wrongful death suit stemming from the death of Mark Brantwell, 48, of Houston, who died Saturday night after attending the annual Highlands Historic Home Tour.*

Ugh. Her name had made the lede. She continued to read the article as she sat on the bottom step of her outdoor staircase.

Houston police are still investigating Brantwell's death, which they have labeled suspicious. Police declined to comment on the ongoing investigation.

The lawsuit, filed by Brantwell's wife, Gabby Brantwell, states Mark Brantwell died from oleander poisoning caused by a beverage consumed while attending the home tour. Warren, described in the suit as a bartender, was said to have made the drinks that caused Brantwell to fall ill.

When she flipped to the jump on the second page, she stifled a scream. Her photo stared her in the face. The newspaper had used an old head shot taken by a staff photographer to go along with a series of stories she had written about a backlog of DNA tests at the crime lab.

"Are you kidding me?" She finished reading the story.

The lawsuit seeks $8 million in damages for wrongful death from Warren individually and the Highlands Historic Commission collectively.

Warren declined to comment when reached at her home Tuesday night.

Bob Randall, chairman of the Historic Commission, said the commission was cooperating with the police investigation but declined to comment further.

Samantha's stomach roiled as she imagined her current clients and potential clients, not to mention half the city, reading about the lowest point in her life. She walked back up the stairs and into the kitchen, where she picked up Ruby and hugged her until the cat grew impatient and jumped to the ground.

Samantha set her teakettle to boil in hopes that some caffeine would spur her to action. Lost in her own head, she didn't notice the shriek of the kettle's whistle until a few moments had passed. She shook her head and poured the boiling water over one of her chai bags. As she warmed her frigid hands on the teacup, her phone rang.

Linda, her contact at the university, spoke, informing her that the head of university relations had seen the story in the paper and worried about any blowback to the university. "I told him you're not set to come in until next week, so there's a little time . . ."

The pause alerted Samantha to another shoe about to drop.

"I'm sure this will all blow over by then, but if it hasn't . . . well, we have to protect the university's image."

Counting silently to five to avoid saying anything she might regret, Samantha calmed her voice. "Um, what exactly does that mean?"

"I don't want you to worry about anything right now. Like I said, I'm sure it will all blow over." Linda hung up the phone before Samantha could respond.

The phone call had been another punch to the gut; she felt like she'd been dumped again, this time by someone she didn't even especially like.

Unsure what to do, she decided not to do anything. She turned the ringer of her phone off and crawled back into bed, hoping sleep would help her drown out the rest of the world.

* * *

When Samantha awoke a few hours later, she checked her phone messages. Three from Marisa, two from her mother, and one from David. Unable to face her mother, she called Marisa back first.

"Sam! Are you all right? I've been worried. You haven't been answering your phone."

"Yeah, I've been a little busy trying to pretend nothing bad is happening."

"I can't believe they ran such a story. They essentially accused you of murder. At least it wasn't on the front page. Maybe most people will miss it."

"Nice try, Marisa. If even half of the subscribers read the story, we're talking about over one hundred thousand people. Not to mention, you know it will lead every local television news report. I'll never be able to show my face again."

"It's not as bad as you're imagining."

"My contact at the university called. She hinted that I might not be welcome to come in next week for my editing assignment. I'm a little freaked out about it, to be honest."

"That's nuts! They can't really believe there's anything to this."

"I don't know what they think, but they seem concerned about me tarnishing the university's stellar reputation."

"That's awful, Sam. Listen, I have to get to my torts class. Call me back this afternoon. Beth demanded I invite you for dinner. You shouldn't be alone after all of this."

"I'll be fine, Marisa. Thanks."

"I'm serious about dinner. Be there."

"Okay, okay." Samantha ended the call.

Though she should call her mom back, she called David instead. She'd been postponing the call, afraid of his reaction to the situation, but she needed to hear what he had to say.

"Um, David? This is Samantha. How bad is it?"

"Samantha. Hi. I read the paper this morning. This has escalated quicker than I expected. It looks like we may need to go into crisis-control mode."

"Oh God." Samantha's stomach swayed as though she might be sick. If the situation made calm and collected David concerned, she was positively petrified.

"It's bad, but not as bad as it could be. Glad you declined to comment. That's the right thing to do at this point. Can we meet today? A client's hearing was rescheduled, so I have some free time."

Samantha groaned. "I can be there in about an hour."

"Perfect. I'm in the office. See you then."

Samantha usually enjoyed the drive down Kirby through River Oaks, the wealthiest part of the city, where the old-money mansions fought for attention with new-money mansions, each competing with the others for the most ostentatious display of wealth. Today she couldn't even enjoy the azaleas lining the road, blooming in every shade of pink and white.

She arrived at David's office tower and parked in the adjoining lot. A yawning security guard buzzed her into the building and called David to collect his visitor. She clutched her purse to her chest, waiting for the elevator to ding. David, dressed in a suit and tie, his hair parted to the side, smiled reassuringly. She stared, disbelieving, at his transformation. The handsome lawyer before her offered an alternate-reality version of the bohemian artist from the day before.

"Samantha, I hope you haven't been too worried."

"It's a nightmare, David."

He escorted Samantha to his office on the seventh floor and offered her a seat across from him.

Bouncing her leg up and down, she couldn't help but notice a group of girls practicing field hockey at a local high school across the street. "Interesting view." Samantha motioned toward the girls.

He laughed, a warm baritone. "That's Lamar High School. I went to school there, so it's fun to peer out the windows and remember when."

Samantha bit her lip. "What do we do? Where do we begin?"

David's expression turned serious. "I'm glad you didn't comment for the *Gazette* story. You don't want to give the media any ammunition to twist the story one way or another. But you can expect continued media attention. Consequently, you need to consider mounting a serious defense."

Normally such generalizations about "the media" as some monolith out to destroy people annoyed Samantha, but in her panic, she brushed it aside as she took several quick, shallow breaths. David's words were no longer reassuring. "You're frightening me a little."

"I'm sorry. I don't mean to. I still believe all of this is premature, at least until the police complete their investigation. However, this has become a trial by media, which is a whole different situation. You should consider a countersuit against Gabby Brantwell for defamation. Sometimes, in these situations, it's best to go on the offensive."

"I don't know if I can stomach another lawsuit." Samantha rubbed her throbbing temples.

"At least consider it, okay? If nothing else, it could be a bargaining chip to get this woman to drop the case against you."

That idea appealed to Samantha. Anything to end this whole situation would be a godsend.

"All right. I'll consider it. Also, before we go any further, I want to be up front about it. What are your fees?"

David looked at his desk, where he tapped a pencil's eraser on a notepad. "Oh, we're old friends. We can work it out later."

Samantha shook her head. "No, I insist. I want you to charge me what you would charge anyone."

She held on to the edge of her chair, her fingers white at the knuckles, a little frightened of his answer.

"I understand." He smiled at her. "I'll charge a fifteen-hundred-dollar retainer to handle my fees, plus any court filing fees. Anything above the retainer gets charged at my hourly rate of one hundred fifty dollars an hour."

Samantha added the numbers in her head. The fee would consume half her checking account, a scary prospect, since David likely had given her a massive discount. If the case dragged on, she could always dig into her down-payment money in her savings account, but she hoped it wouldn't come to it. She hoped to save that money for some sort of fresh start.

"Okay, I'll do it." She signed some paperwork and wrote out a check. Her hand shook a bit at the princely sum. "Thanks again, David. I don't know what I would do without you."

"Try not to worry too much, Samantha."

They shook hands, and he walked her to the elevator.

By the time she got back home, Samantha could barely stand from exhaustion, but she felt encouraged by David's taking control of the situation. Still, the thought of 2.3 million people gawking at her face on the five PM news made her want to crawl into her bed and hide.

Chapter Five

Samantha brewed some ginger tea, hoping the ginger would help to settle her stomach a bit. Hiring David had been a good decision. He could handle any legal situation, but all of his talk about going on the offensive didn't reassure her that there would be a quick conclusion to this mess.

What happened to all of this disappearing after filing a few motions?

Samantha looked at her phone and saw eight increasingly frantic text and voice mail messages from her mom. Now she wanted to talk to her more than anything. While her mom might not be able to help with specifics, she was always good for a pep talk.

"Samantha! Finally, you call me back. I was about to jump in the car and head up there. Are you okay?"

"Hi, Mom." She tried to put a little extra pep in her voice to deflect her mother's ability to identify all manner of emotions from a few spoken words.

"I read the story. It popped up when I did a search for your latest bylines. What in heaven's name have you gotten yourself into? Who is this woman suing you? Why is she accusing you of murder?"

"It's been quite a week, Mom."

"Honey, you sound tired. Are you all right?"

Samantha tried to hold it together, but the warmth in her mom's voice made her want to confess how far from fine she truly felt. She filled her mother in on the party, the murder, the lawsuit, and the lawyer.

"Now the university is acting like they may cancel my contract if this doesn't blow over. I'm worried this will tank my reputation."

"Is this lawyer a good one? Can he help you?"

"He suggested a countersuit, but I'm not sure I can handle another lawsuit right now, emotionally or financially. The newspaper is bad enough. I don't even want to contemplate how the television stations will report this."

"Honey, this is awful. Do you need me to visit? Or better yet, why don't you come down here and get away from everything."

"Mom, I can't. There's too much going on."

They talked for a few more minutes about David's strategy and debated whether Samantha should proceed with a countersuit. Her mother tried to assure her that the lawsuit wouldn't go very far because nobody who met Samantha could possibly imagine her a murderer.

"Thanks for the vote of confidence, Mom."

"I'm serious. If you want to get away for a while, you can always come home."

"I know, Mom. Thanks."

While she welcomed the support, Samantha had hoped for more actionable advice. Feeling adrift, Samantha wished there were some road map she could follow.

Her cell phone rang.

When she answered it, a breathless Marisa spoke. "Did you hear the news? The police say Mark was definitely murdered!"

"What? No! How do they know?"

"Bob told Beth that Mark died from oleander poisoning, but the small bunch of flowers we found in the glass wouldn't have been enough to kill him. According to the toxicologist, the drink contained a significant amount of dried oleander powder, which is why Mark died so quickly."

"What's oleander powder?"

"I don't really know. I looked it up, and apparently it can be made by drying the leaves and flowers of the plant and grinding them. Someone must have slipped it into Mark's drink."

"Wow!" Samantha shivered. She'd been in the same room as a murderer. "Do they have any suspects? Besides me, I mean?"

"Bob didn't say, though I would assume the wife should be suspect number one—especially since they were going through an ugly divorce. Anyway, remember, you promised to come by for dinner tonight. We can talk about it more then."

* * *

Marisa and Beth lived in a small Victorian-style cottage in Montrose—one of the few original homes on a street overtaken by townhomes and Garage Mahals, as Samantha liked to call the narrow houses with garages as their central feature. Dwarfed by the surrounding homes, the house contained only two bedrooms. But Beth had filled a decent-sized backyard with multiple gardens of both herbs and flowers. When Samantha arrived at their back gate, the couple were outside, Marisa grilling carne asada and Beth pouring sangria into plastic goblets on their outdoor table.

"Sam!" Marisa put down her tongs and moved to give her friend a hug. She pulled away and looked her up and down.

"I'm fine, Marisa. You don't need to keep evaluating my emotional state every time you see me."

"Sorry. I'm just worried about you." She turned back to the sizzling meat.

Samantha detected the scent of citrus and cilantro wafting from the grill. "It smells delicious."

She settled into one of the patio chairs and grabbed a goblet of sangria.

Marisa slid meat onto a tray and threw tortillas onto the grill. "Tell me, what's the latest with this lawsuit?"

Samantha took a long sip of her sangria before filling her friends in on her meeting with David. "I like David, but I've got to be honest, I left more nervous than when I went in there."

"Good. He's not sugarcoating things." Marisa sliced the meat and set it in the middle of the table, gesturing for the others to make their tacos. "This is a serious situation. I hope you made things official with him."

"I signed the paperwork this morning." Samantha loaded her tortillas with the smoky meat and mentioned David's suggestion that she file a countersuit against Gabby.

"It's not a bad idea. I like David more and more." Marisa gave a satisfied smirk as she bit into her taco.

"What's your next step, Sam?" Beth passed Samantha a bowl of homemade guacamole.

"I don't know. David will handle the legal stuff for now. I feel sort of helpless. What else can I do?" Samantha spooned the dip onto her taco, now filled almost to bursting.

Marisa raised one eyebrow incredulously. "Are you serious? Girl, you're a reporter, last time I checked. David says you need to go on the offensive. Why don't you use your skills and find out what you can unearth?"

The words took Samantha by surprise. "Do you really think I should? The police are already investigating—"

Marisa flicked her hand dismissively. "Have you forgotten everything you learned as a reporter? You can't count on the police to have your interests at heart. Approach it like you would any story."

Marisa's words made it sound simple. Samantha found herself intrigued by the idea. *Am I really equipped to investigate a murder?* She took a bite of her taco, enjoying the citrusy tang of the meat. "How would I start?"

Marisa refilled her glass with more sangria. "I don't know, Nellie Bly. I'm a lowly photographer turned law student. You're the reporter. You tell me. How do you start?"

Samantha laughed at the nickname but began to ponder how she would approach the case if it were a story. She realized there was at least one very loose thread to follow in the form of Mila, the waitress who had visited her apartment on Monday.

Samantha told Marisa about Mila's visit and on the conversation between Mila and her boyfriend in the dining room on Sunday.

Marisa's eyes grew wide. "Sam, you need to inform the police!"

Samantha winced. "I hate to get the girl any more involved in this if she didn't have anything to do with it."

"This is a murder investigation."

Samantha nodded. "I know, I know. You're right." She agreed to fill Detective Sanders in on her encounter with the waitress.

She took another sip of her sangria as she considered the matter further. "However, if oleander powder rather than the flower itself killed Mark, it had to have been premeditated.

Unless Mila's boyfriend somehow knew Mark and had a reason to want him dead, he doesn't seem like the likeliest suspect."

Marisa carried her plate into the kitchen. "Sam, you don't know anything about the guy. Maybe he and Mark had a history."

Samantha followed with her own plate. "It seems unlikely, but I guess it's possible."

"What's possible?" Beth passed the two women as she stepped through the patio doorway with a plate of cookies.

After they deposited the dishes in the kitchen and walked back to the patio, Marisa caught Beth up on Samantha's encounter with the waitress. "Can you figure out who the commission hired to handle the servers? It wouldn't hurt to learn a little more about who they were."

"I can ask around." Beth bit into a homemade gingersnap.

"I also want to find out everything I can about the Brant-wells." Samantha grabbed her own cookie. "What do you know about them, Beth?"

Beth shared what she knew about Mark, which wasn't much. He had moved to Houston about eight months ago from Galveston, after the split from his wife. He'd been active in restoration of historic properties there and was pretty well-known regionally for that kind of work. When he became involved in similar projects in Houston, some members of the Highlands Historic Commission took notice. They'd asked him to join the board about seven months ago to fill a vacancy.

"How did he get along with the others on the board? Any problems?" Samantha grabbed her glass for another sip of sangria.

"I can't recall anything in particular. But I'm not on the board and haven't seen all the interactions." Beth stood to clear away the cookie plates.

"Can you remember anyone who might have had a problem with him?" Samantha palmed her sangria glass back and forth between her hands.

Beth sat, silent for a moment. "Now that you mention it, I do remember something. I don't know if it's relevant or not, but one Highlands resident threw a fit at a board meeting because they wouldn't approve his variance request to double the size of his garage. The man raised a huge stink with the entire board, but Mark expressed the most vocal opposition."

Samantha remembered when the board had been created and the complaints certain residents had raised about infringement of their property rights. Tensions had been high at the time, but Samantha couldn't believe someone would kill another person over a garage. "I guess it's worth looking into."

"I'm sorry I can't tell you more. I didn't know him very well."

"What about Bob? Would he talk to me? He's bound to know something. Plus, we're both being sued by Mark's wife."

"It's worth a shot. I'll call him in the morning to try to arrange it." Beth carried the plates into the kitchen.

"Thanks."

"What about the wife? Could she have done it?" Marisa leaned back and reached her arms in the air to stretch out her long neck.

It was an obvious question, but Samantha didn't have the answer to it . . . yet. She made excuses to leave, eager to get home and map out a strategy.

Beth raced back outside. "Oh, before you go, I have some herbs for you." She took a set of clippers to the garden and snipped stalks of green with dark-purple buds. Once she had a handful, she tied it with twine and handed it to Samantha. "It's lavender. It's grown like crazy in my garden. You can use it in one of your bitters recipes."

Samantha inhaled the sweet fragrance. "It smells amazing."

"Wait, one more thing." Beth snipped a handful of peppers from bushes in her garden and threw them in a bag for Samantha. "I thought you could make some use out of these too."

Samantha hugged Beth and then Marisa. "Thanks for everything, guys. I don't know what I'd do without you."

They waved as Samantha walked to her car.

* * *

At home, Samantha tied the lavender in several bunches to hang upside down in her closet. As it dried, it would make her clothes smell fresh. In a few weeks, she planned to infuse it with orange peel and ginger to make spicy, flowery bitters. As she worked, Samantha considered the irony that her bitters-making hobby, which she'd begun as a shared interest with Greg following a couple's cocktail-making class, was now her escape, not only from him but from anything bothering her.

Ruby batted at the lavender bunches as Samantha tied them to the closet rod. Samantha shooed the cat out of the closet and closed the door, changing into some pajamas and pulling out her laptop. She'd inform Detective Sanders about Mila tomorrow, but for now, Samantha intended to learn more about Mark Brantwell and his estranged wife, Gabby.

The first stories she came across confirmed what she'd already learned—Mark had recently been appointed to the Highlands Historic Commission after moving from Galveston. The stories offered only the bare minimum about his background. He'd won a few architectural preservation awards for a

Victorian home he renovated in Galveston. Even though the story about his death described him as a native Houstonian, Samantha couldn't find a scrap of information about his life prior to his move to the island.

After an hour on the computer, Samantha had uncovered little beyond a nasty comment on a website from an unhappy customer.

She changed gears and dug for information about the woman who had filed the suit—Gabby Brantwell. She came across a few stories about her business, Brantwell Interiors, which had won some local awards for interior design. Photos showed a fashionable fortyish woman with a brunette bob and a dimpled smile as she flipped through fabric samples. Then . . . *this is interesting.*

Samantha found a small blurb, more of a police blotter, from last year.

Local woman Gabby Brantwell, 42, was charged with harassment Tuesday for defacing property and waging a social media assault on a local realtor. Brantwell is alleged to have painted graffiti on local real estate agent Darcy Meadows's signs and written malicious comments on Meadows's social media pages. Brantwell was released on bond with the promise that she would refrain from contact with Meadows.

Hmmm. Gabby's no stranger to legal problems. And the name Darcy can't be a coincidence. Samantha could hardly believe her luck. The blurb proved Gabby had a history of unhinged behavior, which might help in a countersuit. She copied the item and emailed it to David.

Could she have been so angry at her husband about the affair that she wanted to kill him?

In some ways the explanation seemed too simple, but in at least half the murders Samantha had covered as a reporter, the spouse or partner of the victim had committed the crime. The more she considered it, the more it made sense. The question was, how could she prove it?

Samantha reflected on how she would have approached a complicated story in her newspaper days. Unfortunately, the first step would likely have been a lengthy conversation with Greg, who'd been her desk mate for a time at the *Gazette*. When she started, he'd covered courts and she'd covered crime. Often they worked together on stories, but even when he wasn't involved, he listened to her talk through the details and served as a sounding board for ideas on who to interview or how to get an unwilling source to talk.

He'd left the paper three years earlier to go to law school, but Samantha had still talked through most big stories with him. He'd offered suggestions to guide her when she wasn't sure which direction to take. Any sort of investigation into Mark's death would be a serious undertaking. *Can I even do this without Greg or someone else to help me?*

She brushed the worry aside as she pulled up Gabby's design website and took time to explore all its pages. She clicked through photos of the Victorian beach houses Gabby had helped to design and discovered a photo of Gabby with Mark and their daughter posed outside a colorful Victorian in Galveston's historic district. Titled "My Passion Project," the caption contained details about the home's restoration to its original grandeur.

Gabby looked down-to-earth. She smiled for the camera, and her dimples lit up her face.

Samantha struggled to imagine the person in the photo as a murderer, but past experience as a reporter had taught her that anyone could be driven to kill with a strong-enough motive.

She shut down her computer and decided that Thursday would be the perfect day for a trip to the beach.

Chapter Six

The next morning, Samantha called Detective Sanders and filled him in on Mila's visit to her apartment and on what she'd overheard at the Reilley house on Sunday.

Sanders seemed annoyed. "Why are you only telling me this now?"

"I didn't want to cause the girl any trouble if it wasn't necessary. Do you think it's important?"

"We're focusing on a lot of different angles right now. Please, in the future, if something else *occurs* to you, let me know right away."

Chagrined, Samantha hit end.

Despite Sanders's annoyance with her for not calling sooner, he hadn't seemed particularly interested in her story about Mila and her boyfriend. His lack of interest confirmed to Samantha that she should focus on Gabby.

She riffled through her closet, past her sensible work clothes and casual jeans, hunting for the perfect outfit for the role she needed to play.

This will do the trick.

She pulled out a red-ruffled sundress, often mistaken for designer, and a pair of white wedge-heeled sandals. With a

61

brown pixie-cut wig she'd once bought for an Audrey Hepburn Halloween costume and a pair of cat-eye sunglasses she'd bought as a joke last summer, Samantha decided she might be mistaken for a socialite with money to burn. She fed Ruby and gave her a pat on the head before she grabbed an oversized handbag and walked outside. A bejeweled toy poodle to stuff inside the purse would have completed the ensemble, but Samantha would have to go without.

She hopped onto I-45 and headed south toward Galveston, the quaint but faded beach town Houstonians loved to disparage—before filling its beaches every weekend.

Samantha had grown up in Corpus Christi, which sat a couple rungs above Galveston on the Gulf Coast's beautiful beach index. While Galveston's beach wasn't as pretty as her hometown's, Samantha could always breathe a little easier on the water. The first sign of the saltwater marshes from the causeway or a flock of brown pelicans flying in a V formation, like storm troopers on their way to battle, made her want to fill her lungs with salt air. Today was no different. Even if Samantha didn't find a scrap of fresh information for her investigation, the trip to the beach would do wonders for her psyche.

When she exited the freeway, she headed to the East End Historical District, home to a collection of Victorian mansions, which offered viewers the best glimpse of what turn-of-the-century Galveston would have looked like in its heyday.

Samantha drove slowly and kept an eye out for the home in the picture from Gabby's website. The photo caption hadn't included an exact address but had mentioned Post Office Street. Uncertain how she would recognize it, Samantha spotted the home at the corner near Fifteenth Street. A beautiful home painted in Wedgwood blue and white with gingerbread accents, it hearkened back to the days of Galveston's zenith as one of the most important cities in Texas. Lovingly restored, it had a simple flower garden and a wrought-iron fence.

A small Toyota parked out front suggested someone was home. Samantha's heart beat a little faster. She wasn't ready to visit yet. A journalism professor had once told her never to ask a question if she didn't already know the answer. The advice, boiled down to its essence, meant always do your research. Before Samantha had enough answers to ask any questions, she needed more information. She prepared the first stage of her plan. With a list of addresses compiled from Gabby's website, she headed out to determine what she could learn about Gabby from her own customers.

At the first house on her list, a small shotgun-style beach cottage a few blocks from the water, Samantha knocked on the door and waited. After receiving no answer, she moved on to the next house on her list and still the next two after that. Her knocks finally summoned a woman to the door of the fourth house—a modern mansion on stilts.

The woman, a middle-aged blonde, replete with oversized diamonds on her rings and necklace, surveyed Samantha as if appraising her net worth. "Can I help you?"

"Oh, thank you for answering. I'm Allison." Samantha stuck her hand out to shake.

The woman, flustered, barely grasped it, letting her fingers slip away as if afraid of contracting a disease.

"I'm from Houston, but my husband and I plan to buy a beach house out here in Galveston, and I wanted to ask you about Gabby Brantwell. I understand she worked as your interior decorator?"

The woman rolled her eyes. "Is this about the television show? Because it's not happening anymore."

"Television show? What are you talking about?" Samantha's surprise must have shown, because the woman suddenly opened up, as if Samantha were her long-lost friend stopping to hear some gossip.

"You mean you don't know?" She gestured to one of the Adirondack chairs on the wide front porch and motioned for Samantha to sit down.

Although she hadn't made it inside the house yet, Samantha decided she'd passed some initial test. "No. This is the first I've heard of any television show. That concerns me. The last thing my husband wants or needs is publicity. A friend of mine who lived down here ages ago recommended Gabby. I saw a picture of your house on her website and thought it looked beautiful."

The woman smiled. "Yes, well, she did a suitable job here. What do you want to know?"

"Oh, you know—how she was to work with, whether she was responsive, did she stay in budget. Basic stuff."

"She did our house about two years ago. I liked her suggestions. She did an impressive job of listening and figuring out our style—well, my style, really. Ted doesn't care much." Her laugh was high and tinkling. "My, it's hot out here. Would you like to see the house? I'm Amy, by the way."

Samantha nodded. "I'd love to, Amy. Thanks. The pictures were beautiful, but I find you get a better sense of a room when you can stand in the middle of it."

Amy stood and ushered Samantha into the house. Inside, it appeared much as the pictures had shown—pale pastel colors and creamy whites, with sea shells and sea glass in quaint jars on shelves.

"It's very serene." Samantha looked around the room admiringly. "You must love it here."

"I do. It's my little escape from the world. Would you like some iced tea?"

In her days as a reporter, Samantha had learned never to reject the offer of any beverage. It meant the conversation would last a little longer. "I'd love some. I'm a little parched after my trip down here."

They walked through the sitting room/living room area through a dining room, with Samantha making the appropriate cooing sounds here and there. They finally made it into the kitchen, where the woman poured two glasses of sweet tea.

Amy pointed to sleek white cabinets filled with turquoise china. She handed Samantha a glass and gestured at her to take a seat on a stool next to the kitchen's island.

"What's the deal with the television show?" Samantha took a sip.

"Oh, it was one of those Home Renovation Network shows—*Island Time* or something silly like that. Gabby's husband is a contractor, and the network wanted the two of them to star together in some show about renovating beach houses. Except Gabby and her husband were constantly at each other's throats. The husband dumped Gabby and they canceled the show before it even started."

"What happened?"

"She and her husband broke up, and then she went and made matters worse for herself."

"What do you mean?"

The woman tilted her head toward Samantha's and lowered her voice. "Now, I don't like to gossip . . ."

"Of course not. But I appreciate anything you can tell me."

"You can find out about this anyway from Google, so I guess there's no harm in sharing. It might give you an indication of how erratic Gabby can be."

"Oh, thank you. My husband would be furious if I got him involved in any scandal."

The woman nodded, as if confirming that Samantha's non-existent husband was right to be concerned.

"I told you the television show never happened, right? Well, that's because Gabby discovered her husband had been having an affair with her best friend."

Samantha gasped. "How horrible for her."

"I know. It's awful. Now, I can't say I might not feel the same if I ever caught my Teddy cheating on me. We southern women can sometimes be emotional, but we know to keep it out of the papers."

The woman strung Samantha along, stretching out the story without telling her anything. Samantha wanted to throttle her, but she opted instead to wait with a smile on her face. "Oh dear. What happened?" She took another sip of the overly sweet iced tea.

"The story is she caught her best friend in the act with her husband in one of the friend's real estate client's houses."

Samantha's jaw dropped open, which seemed to be enough of a reaction for the woman to continue her story.

"Obviously, she was furious, as we all would be. She posted these nasty messages about her friend all over her social media accounts and left critical Yelp reviews and low ratings anywhere possible. And then . . ." The woman took another sip of her iced tea, as if to build more suspense. "A few weeks later, in the middle of the night, someone went around the island and painted 'home wrecker' on every one of the for-sale signs with Gabby's friend's name on it."

"Wow. I mean, it's hard to blame her, but one would hope she would know better than to make such a public display." Samantha stood, assuming she'd gotten all she could from Amy.

"Exactly. Anyway, what kind of house are you and your husband considering?" The woman led Samantha back toward the front door.

"Oh, it's nothing nearly this large. It's just a little shotgun cottage. We'd only come down on the weekends sometimes."

The woman seemed to lose interest in the conversation upon hearing the news that Samantha's own home would be less impressive than her own. "Well, good luck to you. Like I said before, I got along with Gabby all right, but she comes with some baggage."

"I appreciate you filling me in, Amy. Thank you for your time." Samantha followed the woman outside, glad to have gotten more information to add to her portrait of Gabby.

While she'd already seen a story about the graffitied signs and other harassment, the mention of the canceled television show intrigued Samantha. She wondered if there might be more to learn and decided she should visit a few more houses to locate a few more women who liked to gossip.

The next home was even larger than the last, with three floors and wraparound porches around each of the stories. It looked more like an inn than a house. Samantha walked up a grand staircase and knocked on the immense oak door.

After a few minutes, a woman with dark-brown hair cut in a smooth, stylish bob opened the door. "Can I help you?" The woman's southern accent practically dripped sweet tea.

"I'm Allison. I'm thinking of hiring Gabby Brantwell as an interior decorator for our beach house. Amy suggested I ask you about your experience with her." Samantha guessed that the two women might be acquainted. Both seemed to be in the same age range, and both were likely members of Galveston's social register.

"Oh, for heaven's sake. Okay. Come in. I'm Tina." She shook Samantha's hand with a firm but cool grip and led her into the grandest foyer Samantha had ever seen. "Go on, have a seat." She pointed to an L-shaped sea-green leather-fabric sectional covered with seashell- and star-shaped pillows.

Samantha sank back against the plump sofa cushions. "This is lovely. Did Gabby design this for you?"

"She started it, but I had to hire someone else to finish it."

"Oh no! What happened?"

"Listen, she's a lovely woman, and all things considered, she did excellent work. It just didn't work out between us." The woman looked anywhere but at Samantha.

"I don't mean to pry. I like Gabby's style, but my husband would never forgive me if I didn't do my due diligence. Please, can't you share your concerns?"

Tina stared at Samantha for a few minutes and nodded. "Okay. I don't like to spread gossip, but I don't want others to experience what I went through." She spoke a little more softly. "Now like I said, she's a pleasant woman, and she really does exemplary work, despite some incidents from last fall. However, I caught her stealing from me."

Samantha gasped. She hadn't expected such immediate confirmation of criminal behavior.

"She claimed she only borrowed the money, and no doubt she needed it. Her husband dumped her for another woman and moved to Houston, leaving her without a way to pay for her house. And she has a daughter in middle school. I can appreciate she needed the money, but I can't have someone I don't trust working for me."

"Of course not. What happened?"

"I found around five thousand dollars missing from the decorator account, and I confronted her with it. At first she told me it paid for some drapes, but eventually she came clean and claimed to have borrowed it. I told her that where I come from, it's called stealing."

"Exactly right! Did you call the police?"

"No. She begged me not to. She said she'd only taken the money because she needed it to make the house payment so she and her daughter didn't end up on the street. She told me the entire sob story about how her husband left her—of course, that particular story had already made the rounds once or twice. I sympathized with her. She paid me back, and we called it even."

"How kind of you. I'm grateful you told me. My husband would murder me if I hired someone with those kinds of problems." Samantha choked on her choice of words.

"I'm only telling you because I didn't want you to experience what I went through. I do sympathize with her. I heard her husband recently died."

Samantha took the reference to Mark's death as her cue to leave. "Oh dear, how awful. I hope something turns around for her, but I don't think I'll take a chance on hiring her for our beach house."

"I know some other designers, if you want a recommendation. Come on, I'll show you around."

Samantha didn't want the woman to recognize her if she ever read a story about the lawsuit. "Oh, thank you, but I didn't notice the time. I need to head out, but I appreciate your help."

She walked toward the door and shook Tina's hand before leaving her slightly puzzled in the doorway.

As she got into her car, Samantha decided she shouldn't let her trip to Galveston go to waste. She drove to the seawall for a walk on the beach. She had plenty to contemplate.

She parked on the boulevard between the sporting goods store and the souvenir shop. Galveston didn't do itself many favors in the tourism department, but if you turned away from the strip malls, you could gaze out at the Gulf of Mexico. The churning waves constantly kicked up sand, leaving the water muddier and murkier than Florida's picture-postcard beaches, but Samantha never minded. To her, the ocean was the ocean.

She yanked off her wig and walked toward the Pleasure Pier—a tourist-trap collection of small roller coasters and carnival games intended to hearken back to the piers of old. She took off her sandals and walked on the beach, enjoying the sensation of the warm sand against her toes, as she considered what she had learned.

Gabby has a temper and is a little desperate for money these days. Very interesting.

Part of her wanted to go back to Gabby's house and confront her, just to learn what she would say about the theft or Darcy's tryst with her husband. It would be satisfying to observe Gabby's face when she realized how much Samantha knew about the skeletons in her closet.

She deserves it after filing a lawsuit against me.

Samantha imagined Gabby's countenance when Samantha appeared on her doorstep. The vengeful part of her brain wanted to knock on the door now, but the rational part realized she would have only one opportunity to catch Gabby off guard.

I need more information. If Gabby killed Mark, how did she do it? Did she know he'd be at the house tour? Did she show up there or hire someone else to kill him?

Samantha realized she needed to know who had attended the tour—information more likely available in Houston than in Galveston.

On the way back to the city, Samantha checked her voice mail and heard a message from Beth saying Bob could meet that afternoon. Thankful to have left Galveston before rush hour, she raced home, eager to find out what he could share. Gabby had become a serious suspect with plenty of motive. The question remained: how could Samantha prove Gabby's guilt?

Samantha arrived back in Houston at three thirty and drove straight to Bob's office in one of the little bungalows on Highlands Boulevard. Besides being president of the Highlands Historic Commission, Bob Randall was a well-known contractor in the area. His signs sprouted from lawns all over the Highlands, advertising his role in many significant historic renovations.

Samantha walked inside, straight into what in a traditional home would have been a living room but in Bob's office served as a comfortable lounge area of sorts. A receptionist took Samantha's name and asked her to take a seat.

She didn't have long to wait.

"Samantha, right?" Bob smiled as he walked into the room. "Nice to see you again, though I'm sorry about the circumstances."

Samantha followed him back to a comfortable office, where he sat behind a mammoth desk. She took a seat in a wingback chair on the other side of the desk, presumably where his wealthy customers would outline their visions for their dream homes. A photo of a much younger Bob and a brunette girl sat on a credenza behind his desk.

Samantha often tried to disarm potential interviewees by asking about a photo on their desk. "Lovely picture. Is that your daughter?"

He swiveled around to glance at the photo. "Yes, that's my Jennifer. She's off in South Carolina now, a doctor. Anyway, Beth told me you wanted to discuss something?"

"Well, it's about this lawsuit. Since we're both party to it, I hoped we could work together. Obviously, I had nothing to do with Mr. Brantwell's death. The faster we can clear it up, the faster I can get out from under this suit."

"I'm sorry you got sucked into all of this. It's all such a crazy situation. The commission also would like it resolved. We don't need the adverse publicity. How do you think I can help?"

"My lawyer thinks it would be good to gather a little information on Mrs. Brantwell. I'm wondering . . . you mentioned Mark was in the middle of a difficult divorce with his wife. Could she have done this? Is there any chance Gabby attended the event on Saturday?"

"I only know Mark's side of that story, and only a limited version. He described it as an acrimonious divorce. I believe there is a daughter involved, which creates more difficulty. As to whether she attended the event, I don't know. There might be a way to check."

"Really?" Samantha's spirits lightened.

"Yes. In fact, I sent a copy of the footage from the security cameras to the police this afternoon. The cameras were on the front door and should have captured everyone who walked in the house, all eight hundred of them. It's four and a half hours of footage, so it's a bit of a slog."

"I'd love a peek. Any chance you could share that with me?" Samantha's fingers tingled as her excitement bubbled up. She wasn't afraid of research, particularly with the possibility of a big break.

"I'd love to help, Ms. Warren, but we have to be considerate of privacy concerns."

"I understand. Of course, the police will have to turn it over to my lawyer eventually. I'm only asking for a little sneak peek."

Bob smiled. "I guess that's true. It's not like you'll publish it, will you?"

"No, of course not. I only want to examine it myself."

He nodded. "Okay, then. Stop by the receptionist on the way out. She'll save the videos on a flash drive for you. If you find something, please let me know."

"Of course." Samantha stood to leave. "Oh, before I go, Beth mentioned a resident who fought with Mark at a board meeting?"

Bob looked thoughtful and nodded. "If I recall, the argument stemmed from a garage project a few months ago. He created quite a scene at two meetings. Mark dealt with him. It seemed like the entire situation died down pretty quickly after the meeting."

"Okay. Thanks again for the videos." She restrained herself from running outside, given her eagerness to dig into this new information.

Chapter Seven

She arrived home a few minutes before five. In a past life, she might have called Greg to convince him to go out for Tex-Mex, her version of comfort food after an interminable day. They had rotated through a handful of restaurants, sampling enchiladas, chile rellenos, and margaritas across the city. Samantha could use a margarita and a sounding board right now. She could always call on Marisa and Beth, but she didn't want to get in the way of their own relationship. She decided security videos and DoorDash were her answer to Thursday night.

First, she would make her own margarita as she waited for her enchilada delivery. While many people swore by the frozen version of the margarita, Samantha couldn't handle the sticky sweetness, not to mention her susceptibility to experiencing brain freezes. In her view, a good margarita must be shaken hard and served in a coupe with tiny frozen slivers of ice on top.

When her food arrived, she pulled her coffee table toward her, set it with her dinner and drink, and cued up the first security video. Though it would take forever to watch all the videos, she wanted to start, believing the videos might offer the first solid lead in the case.

The videos began around five PM, a few moments before she and her friends had arrived. The video quality was nearly perfect—the camera must have been mounted right above the door. It offered a clear view of everyone who walked inside. Samantha caught a glimpse of herself, Marisa, and Beth arriving after their tour of the grounds. A few minutes later, a few more workers walked into the house. The crowds arrived around five thirty. The video played in excruciating slow motion as Samantha checked the face of every person who walked through the doors. Though she recognized some faces from the tour, many of them were complete strangers. She counted on Gabby resembling her photos enough that she would be able to identify her.

After she spent about an hour and a half watching, rewinding, and rewatching, Samantha's concentration broke when her phone rang.

This time, she looked at the caller ID before she answered—Greg. Ugh. She didn't relish another fight right now.

"Greg, what is it now?"

"I wanted to check on you. I'm sorry about yesterday, but you've been through a lot. I wanted to make sure you're okay."

Some of her resolve to maintain a stiff upper lip loosened. It would be nice to unburden herself for a bit.

"It's been a rough few days. Is there anything else?"

He paused. "It's just . . . well, it's just that I miss you."

Heat warmed Samantha's cheeks. While she relished the notion of Greg thinking about her, she wanted to punch him for having the nerve to say so now.

"I'm not in the mood to fight, Greg. Why would you say that right now?" Her voice rose an octave as her fury mounted.

"I'm sorry, Sam. Can you give me a break? It's Thursday night, and it's already been a shitty week, and there's no good Tex-Mex around here, and . . . I miss you."

Samantha looked at her half-drunk margarita and sighed.

"I can't listen to this, Greg. You made a choice. You made that choice with no input from me, and now we both have to live with it."

"God, Samantha, you always like to make things black and white. There is no gray with you. Can't you perceive there's some nuance to the situation?"

She had wanted to let him in, if only for a moment, like old times. She didn't need to listen to his version of the blame game. "Do you want me to hang up on you? Because I am this close."

"I'm sorry . . . I'm sorry. I guess I wanted to call and say I'm sorry."

Samantha didn't answer for a while. She remained silent, closed her eyes, and listened to him breathe. She remembered nights in her apartment, lazing on the sofa, her head resting on his chest, soothed by the rise and fall. The steadiness of it.

"You're not hanging up?"

She sighed, summoning the courage to speak. "Can I ask you a question? Why did you do this to us? Why did you end it?"

This time, Greg fell silent. "I just realized . . . I made a mistake. I didn't want to settle."

An involuntary sound rose from her throat, a half croak, half gasp.

"No—God, no. Not settle with you. That's not what I mean. It was the job. The life. I pictured it, and I thought, I could be perfectly happy with this job, this life, for the next forty years and be fine. Then I would wonder, what was I missing? Had I lived up to my potential? Had I left anything on the table? I didn't want to miss out on anything . . ."

"It never occurred to you to talk with me about it?"

"I couldn't handle it. You would try to talk me out of it, with your lists and your pros and your cons and your endless debates. I needed to go for it."

"Well, I hope you're happy with your decision." She exhaled as she ended the call. Talking to him made her chest tighten. On top of everything, the last half of the conversation had only confirmed Marisa's assessment of her psyche. She did overanalyze problems and never trusted her initial instinct out of fear that she might make the wrong choice. Further reflection revealed that more often than not, she sought the choice that led to the least change. *Surely, if Greg had confided his fears, I would have been willing to consider moving or some other alternative.* She sighed. *Or maybe not.*

Maybe they weren't compatible after all. Maybe it was better this way. The pounding in her heart and the sinking sensation in her stomach made it difficult to think logically. She wanted to lay her head, one more time, on his chest, and fall asleep to the rhythm of his breathing. Instead, she finished her margarita and jumped back into more security videos.

By the second hour of the home tour, the crowd had formed.

At around the two-hour-and-fifteen-minute mark, she finally spotted something. She rewound the video and pulled up a picture on her computer for comparison before jumping from her sofa and whooping in celebration. "I've got you now, Gabby!"

Gabby had arrived at the home tour at around seven fifteen. Now, on top of Gabby's surplus of motive for the killing, Samantha possessed video evidence showing Gabby at the event.

Though her clocks signaled midnight, Samantha couldn't sleep. She wrote notes of what she'd discovered and sent it all to David. Since Bob had given the security videos to the police, she figured they could easily spot Gabby, but they might not know the full details of her motive.

She hadn't decided completely, but she was seriously considering a countersuit. It might not be bad to play some offense, especially if this woman was as guilty as she seemed.

After she typed her thoughts, Samantha grew more confident. She pressed send on the email to David and settled down enough to fall asleep.

*   *   *

The next morning, she woke still bothered by the loose ends in the narrative she'd crafted about Gabby. If she were writing a story for the newspaper, she would have needed to ask for a comment from Gabby at the least.

This isn't a news story, Sam. Yet, in some ways, the solution seemed too perfect. When she recollected Saturday night, she didn't remember seeing Mark until much later—closer to nine. Could Gabby have remained at the house the entire time with no one noticing? What if she'd left? She still could have come back later . . .

Samantha watched the rest of the videos to have a firmer idea of the timeline in her head. This time she didn't pause and rewind or scrutinize the feed as intently as before. She sought two people—Mark and his girlfriend. Since she had seen them in person, they should be a lot easier to pick out on the security film.

After two hours, the couple appeared on-screen as they walked into the house. They looked healthy and in good spirits as they crossed the threshold. Samantha stopped the tape.

Unfortunately, the camera filmed only the front door, so it didn't show people as they left the event, which they did through the side gate. It would be impossible to know for sure when Gabby had left.

With hostilities between Gabby and her husband nearing atomic level, why had Gabby even attended the home tour? It seemed fishy. However, the two hours between their respective arrivals left a sizable gap in the timeline, and Samantha didn't like gaps. Gaps made it difficult to be definitive, and to feel better about this case, Samantha wanted a solution as definitive as possible.

She needed to hear Gabby's version of events. The idea of an in-person confrontation made her queasy. The ambush had always been her least favorite part of being a reporter, though she recognized the necessity, particularly in this situation.

While David might have cautioned against it, warning her to keep her distance from Gabby, Samantha decided she needed some answers and that Galveston was the place to find them.

Despite heavy afternoon traffic on I-45, Samantha didn't mind the drive. She spent the forty minutes thinking of questions for Gabby.

Eventually, Samantha drove back to the East End near the Strand and located the pastel Victorian again. She parked on the street out front as butterflies performed a ballet in her belly. Samantha tried to exude confidence as she walked to the door and pressed the bell. A pop of color caught her eye, and she noticed a large oleander bush on the side of the house.

Look at that! The bush blossomed with hot-pink flowers. Nearly every home on the island featured at least one oleander. Its presence at Gabby's house proved little, with the exception of verifying that Gabby had easy access to the plant.

Before long, the door opened, and a teenager looked at Samantha. The girl brushed her lanky brown hair out of her face to reveal two dark circles under her eyes. She shivered, despite the heat outside, and stood mute for a long moment as she inspected Samantha.

"Excuse me, but is your mom home?"

"Wait a minute, I recognize you now. Oh my God! You're the woman. You're the one who killed my dad! Mom! Mom! Get down here!" she shouted up the stairs.

"I had nothing to do with your father's death."

The girl seemed to realize she'd left herself vulnerable and slammed the door shut in Samantha's face.

Samantha could hardly blame her. The girl must be traumatized and grieving her father. If she believed her mother's lawsuit, why wouldn't she blame Samantha for her dad's death? She stood on the porch and waited a few minutes before the door opened and Gabby walked out.

"You've got to get out of here." Gabby's hair fell from a messy bun and there were smears of dust across her shirt and face, which gave her a less-than-intimidating appearance. "You've upset my daughter."

"I'm sorry, but you and I have to talk. You're ruining my life with this lawsuit, and as far as I can see, you're the one with the best motive to want your husband dead."

"Not here," the woman hissed as she nodded her head in her front door's direction, as if to remind Samantha about the crying girl inside. "Listen, I'll meet you at the coffee shop down the street in half an hour. You can say whatever you came to say to me then."

Samantha walked away, curious. Would Gabby meet her? She drove a few blocks down the street until she reached a small beach-themed coffee shop in a bungalow and walked in. She nursed an iced chai latte for twenty minutes before the bell on the door signaled a new customer. Gabby waved a friendly smile at the girl behind the counter and sat down on the other side of Samantha.

"What do you mean by coming to my house? You have no right to show up on my doorstep hurling accusations. I'm only here to protect my daughter, to make sure you don't upset her again. I could barely get away as it is. She's still crying."

"I'm sorry if I upset her, but a few tears are hardly equivalent to what you've done to me and my finances, not to mention my reputation. The newspaper printed my picture with a story which essentially calls me a murderer, thanks to you."

Gabby sighed and looked at the floor. "I'm sorry. My lawyer pushed me into the lawsuit. He said I needed to leave the suit as wide as possible to give it the greatest chance of success."

Samantha's fury surged and her voice rose in anger. "What a cop-out. You didn't have to go along with it. Plus, the more I investigate, it seems like you yourself have the best motive for murder—not to mention opportunity."

"What are you talking about?" Gabby's voice grew higher. "Sure, it's no secret Mark and I had marital problems, but that doesn't prove I hurt him."

"It's not only the marital problems. How about the canceled reality show?" Samantha lowered her voice to a whisper. "Or how about the stolen money? I know you're short of funds to pay for your fancy house. Maybe you decided a little life insurance would help end your worries."

"How did you . . . never mind. I won't listen to this." Gabby stood as if to go.

"I know you were there that night." Samantha glared at Gabby. "The police will know it soon."

Gabby sat back down. "All right, I was there. What does that prove? I didn't even see Mark that night. I made a special effort not to encounter him."

Gabby's response puzzled Samantha. "What do you mean?"

"I only went there at the request of a potential client. She contacted me through my website and claimed she wanted me specifically because of my work with Victorian homes. Anyway, she said she wanted to do her parlor exactly like the inside of the Reilley house. She sent me a ticket for the home tour."

Samantha didn't interrupt, despite the story's strangeness.

"Obviously, I expected Mark to be there, and I didn't want to run into him, especially with Darcy. I called him and told him I planned to visit the Reilley house during the tour and suggested he make himself scarce while I attended. We agreed I would visit a little after seven and he wouldn't come until much later, around nine."

Gabby's timeline fit with the times they had arrived. Still, something sounded off about the story.

"He agreed to this?"

"I won't kid myself. He probably wanted to protect his floozy more than me, but he agreed."

"What happened?"

"I toured the house, took lots of pictures of the parlor, and left before Mark even arrived. By then, I'd driven to a different part of the city."

"You should have some proof, then, right? You have anyone who can corroborate your account?"

Gabby tugged on her necklace as her neck flushed red. "Well, that's the strange part. I had an appointment to meet this client, the one who sent the ticket. We must have gotten our wires crossed, because when I got to the meeting spot, nobody was home."

"So you've got no way to prove your story."

"It's true. I've got emails to prove it. I know it sounds ridiculous, but I knocked and knocked, and nobody ever answered the door."

"You haven't gotten back to her since?"

"Well, no . . . the next day, Mark had died, and . . ." Gabby stared at her lap. "Even if he wasn't my favorite person, he was still my husband and the father of my child. I didn't want him dead."

Gabby's story sounded strange, and yet, as much as Samantha didn't want to admit it, she found herself believing it.

I can't go soft now. I can't fall for another tale of woe . . .

Samantha needed some time to process Gabby's story and decide her next step. Stirrings of sympathy for Gabby were growing, but she pushed those thoughts down and funneled her anger into a reaction. She figured it wouldn't hurt to stir some sympathy of her own.

"I didn't want him dead either. I didn't even know Mark. I only attended that stupid party because my fiancé dumped me and I needed to get rid of three hundred bottles of homemade bitters. Now my life is even more in tatters, and you're at fault!"

Samantha stood and stormed out of the coffee shop, curious how Gabby would react.

Gabby called after her, "Wait. I'm sorry!"

Samantha marched down the sidewalk, figuring she could use any reserved sympathy later.

By one PM, Samantha realized she hadn't eaten lunch yet. Stomach rumbling, she headed out to Jimmy's on the Pier for a quick sandwich. She ordered the crab cake and a cup of seafood gumbo and listened as waves crashed onto the pier and pelicans squawked as they dive-bombed the water on the hunt for fish even fresher than her lunch. While she ate, she considered Gabby's assertion about the potential client who'd provided her with a ticket to the home tour.

On the one hand, it explains why she attended the same event as her husband. On the other hand, it's awfully convenient.

Samantha couldn't decide what she believed. Back on the road to Houston, she listened to a little Bob Schneider to lighten her mood. The tone of his mellow voice slowed Samantha's pulse, and she began to breathe a little easier.

Back at home after dinner, with no other plans for her Friday night, Samantha walked into her tiny kitchen and played around. Back among her herbs and spices, as Marisa called them, Samantha decided she should devise a recipe for Beth's peppers.

The bag held an assortment of habaneros, jalapeños, and serranos in various colors from red to orange to green. She held one out to Ruby to smell and laughed as the cat scrunched up her nose and backed away. Samantha opted to make a pepper tincture, which would be great for adding a little spice to different drinks. Wearing gloves, she chopped the stems and removed the seeds from the peppers, careful not to breathe in too deeply. She placed them in a large jar and covered them with vodka. She would leave the mixture to sit for a week before she strained the solids out. The cloudy, concentrated liquid left would be strong enough to amplify the heat in any drink.

Her tinkering done, Samantha decided she'd mix a drink. Her trip to the beach left her craving something of the tiki variety. She pulled out her bottle of homemade allspice dram and mixed some with bourbon, fresh lime juice, and a dash of her tiki bitters. She shook the mixture with ice and strained it into a coupe glass, which she carried into the living room.

She held tight to the stem when she sat down to avoid any sloshing as Ruby jumped up and settled on her lap. Then she took a sip and opened up the latest Tana French novel. She could normally burn through a five-hundred-page novel in a matter of days, but the murder deep in the woods in rural Ireland only made her thoughts turn to the murder much closer to home.

Thinking back again to Gabby's story, Samantha couldn't help but find she still believed her. Though Gabby was the obvious choice, given her motive, means, and opportunity, the pieces didn't fit as neatly as Samantha would have liked.

The timeline offered the biggest problem. The two-hour gap between when Gabby had entered the house and when Mark had arrived bothered her. The Reilley house contained enough rooms that Gabby could conceivably have sneaked into one and sat in wait of her prey. The story about a secretive client who'd given her a ticket to the show and then sent her on a wild-goose chase through an unfamiliar part of the city seemed too good to be true. Yet Gabby had seemed genuinely puzzled by it. That, Samantha decided, was difficult to fake.

If Gabby's story was true, someone had gone through a lot of effort to make sure she attended the home tour. More than that, the mysterious person had also done their best to guarantee that Gabby would have no real alibi if she left. If someone knew of Gabby's desperation to find clients after her series of mishaps, they might assume she'd jump at the opportunity to work on a potentially lucrative gig, despite the unusual circumstances.

Samantha followed the thread through to its logical conclusion.

Whoever invited Gabby to the home tour could be the real murderer . . .

Chapter Eight

The next morning, Samantha woke still thinking of Gabby's mystery client. In the light of a fresh day, the story sounded even more preposterous than when Gabby had relayed it yesterday. But on the off chance Gabby had told the truth, Samantha decided it wouldn't hurt to investigate others with a motive for Mark's death.

Apart from Gabby, the only hint of conflict she'd perceived in Mark's life had been the story about the scuffle at the meeting of the Historic Commission. Beth and Bob had indicated that the confrontation had occurred at a meeting a few months earlier. It wasn't much to go on, but Samantha resolved to spend some time tracking down the lead. She figured she could find some information in the local community rag, the historical record for the community's minutiae, covering everything from the Rotary Club pancake breakfast to the elementary school's talent show.

Samantha fed Ruby her breakfast, gathered a notepad and pen, and hopped aboard her bike. She breathed in the morning air, enjoying the slight dry coolness, which would be replaced with a sticky humidity by the afternoon.

Samantha parked her bike in front of the historic Highlands Library, an Italian Renaissance Revival–style building built in 1926. She loved the ornate details carved above the arched windows and doors and appreciated that this city, which had torn down wide swaths of its history, had preserved this delicate symbol of civic life.

Inside, she headed directly to the periodicals section, where she dug out old copies of the local Highlands newspaper, *The Times*. She began her search with editions from late February and waded through reams of stories on new restaurants, business closures, and the local neighborhood watch effort before she found something relevant.

"No" Vote on Renovation Angers Local Resident

Fireworks erupted at the Highlands Historic Commission meeting Thursday as a local resident threatened members of the commission over refusal to allow him to expand his garage.

The resident, Brian Decker, had filed a petition seeking permission to tear down an existing carport and build a garage twice its size to house both his extended-cab truck and his boat. Permission is required because Decker's home falls within the Highlands Historic District, a protected zone intended to maintain the historic character of the neighborhood.

Decker argued that he would build the garage in the style of the surrounding homes, but board members said an enormous garage wasn't in keeping with the neighborhood aesthetic.

The discussion became heated, and when board members voted against the variance, Decker stood and shouted at board members, "You'll regret this. I will destroy you!"

The newest board member, Mark Brantwell, escorted Decker out of the building, and the meeting resumed.

Samantha made a copy of the article. Now that she had a name for the unhappy Highlands resident, she could hunt for more information.

Back on her bike, Samantha stopped to buy her favorite sandwich from the local deli—roast beef with Muenster cheese on a pretzel roll. She carried it home to eat so she could finish her research on Brian Decker.

With her computer open and the scent of roast beef in the air, Samantha set out to learn what she could about the mystery man. She found a Brian Decker listed with an address on Eighteenth Street. The image on Google Street View showed a two-story bungalow with a small carport to the side.

This must be what he wanted to turn into a garage.

She scrolled through the rest of the street and viewed more historic homes—some bungalows, some Victorian style.

She hadn't seen Decker's plans, but she understood why the commission would want to rule against a hulking garage on the street, which would overshadow the quaint bungalows on either side of his house. However, to be fair to Decker, Samantha noticed two enormous garages on the end of the street, one so monstrous it could have been a second home. They must have been grandfathered in when the Historic District was created four years earlier.

Samantha remembered the controversy. It had occurred during the height of the townhome craze when bungalows were being demolished wholesale throughout Houston. City leaders wanted to protect the largest pockets of historic homes in the neighborhood from a similar fate. While those in favor won the election by a clear majority, there were plenty of naysayers who argued it would limit property owners' rights to do what they wanted with their homes.

Samantha figured Decker must have been steaming to be confronted with the enormous garages on his own street yet be told he wasn't permitted to build one on his own property.

Although murder still seemed like an extreme response to a rejection from a historic commission, Samantha imagined how rage might build on itself every day a person backed down his driveway to catch a glimpse of his neighbors' fancy garages, knowing he could never build one of his own.

It seemed a stretch, but she could be convinced if there was other proof. She had the videos, but she didn't have a picture of Decker to compare with the videos. Google had recorded more than five hundred images associated with the name Brian Decker, but Samantha couldn't identify the particular one she sought.

She would have to stake out his house. The prospect filled her with a tinge of excitement laced with fear. If Brian Decker was really a killer, she wouldn't want him to catch her spying on him or his property.

She changed into her most unexceptional outfit, a pair of gray yoga pants and an old Astros T-shirt, baggy enough to render her fairly shapeless. She pulled her hair into a ponytail and pulled on an Astros cap to hide her most defining feature, her blonde waves.

She brewed a pot of coffee and dumped in enough milk and sugar to make it palatable. Normally she didn't touch coffee, relying on tea for her caffeine fix, but every late-night movie she'd seen had taught her stakeouts were coffee-fueled affairs. Given the heat outside, she poured the whole concoction over ice into a large thermos.

Ruby followed her into the kitchen and sniffed at the unfamiliar coffee scent.

Samantha gathered Ruby in her arms and rubbed her head. "Wish me luck, Ruby."

The microwave clock flashed two. With the weather close to boiling outside, Samantha hoped Decker would be at home, enjoying the air conditioning.

Armed with the camera with telephoto capabilities she'd bought years earlier for solo reporting assignments, Samantha grabbed her thermos and headed out to her car.

Her early-2000s-model blue Sentra was nondescript enough but bordered on a little too grungy to fit in on Decker's fancy street. She parked it a few houses away but still within sight of Decker's front door, deciding that if she was asked what she was doing there, she'd say she was a maid on break between assignments.

For the first hour, Samantha jumped at every passing car, but her excitement soon gave way to boredom. She yawned, despite the coffee, and played a few hands of Spider Solitaire on her phone to pass the time. Sometime around four, a jet-black extended-cab pickup truck revved its engines as it sped down the narrow road. As it pulled into Brian's driveway, she detected a rap at her window. Startled, she turned to face an elderly woman brandishing a cane.

"You all right in there, missy? You've been here an awful long time." The woman's expression suggested she wasn't overly concerned about Samantha's well-being.

"Sorry, ma'am. I pulled over to finish a phone call. Wouldn't want to talk and drive." Samantha laughed nervously. "I'm done now. I'll head out."

She started the car and pulled away, disappointed that the truck's occupant had made it inside the house before she'd gotten a peep at him. Samantha drove out of the woman's sight line, turned at the next cross street, and pulled over to the side of the road, cursing her luck.

That nosy old woman made me miss Decker!

She sat for a few moments and was plotting her next move when a black truck very similar to the one she had seen in Brian's driveway rocketed past her car. Without a second thought, she put her car into gear and followed it, trying to stay at least a car's length behind. The truck made multiple turns and drove into a neighborhood Samantha didn't know. The driver parked in front of a low-slung cinder-block building. For a moment, Samantha worried that he'd caught her tailing him and led her to an abandoned warehouse, but when the garage door opened and two bare-chested men flipped a tractor tire across the driveway, she realized the only immediate danger might come from a trainer telling her to drop and give him fifty push-ups. The squat building housed one of the dozens of new CrossFit gyms that had sprouted up throughout the city in the last couple of years.

The man she assumed was Decker climbed out of his truck, clad only in a pair of tight shorts, and walked the length of the driveway into the gym. He offered one of the tire flippers a fist bump as he passed him.

With his slightly mussed but gelled brown hair and chiseled features, Decker looked like any of the hundreds of oil-and-gas-industry frat-boy types who crowded Houston's midtown bars every night, albeit one with a very well defined set of abs. She made sure to get a few good shots of his face and drove away.

Having identified Decker, Samantha now wanted to rewatch the security videos from the party to find out if she could spot him, but watching all those hours of tape by herself again sounded like torture. She called Marisa to invite her and Beth over to join in the fun.

Marisa quickly agreed. "We were just debating what to do for dinner. How about we buy a pizza and you make some cocktails? It'll be fun."

Samantha sifted through her cocktail recipes to find the perfect drinks. With a bottle of prosecco she'd saved in her refrigerator for her return from her honeymoon, she made the first batch—the Seelbach, a fun bourbon/bubbly cocktail named after a famous Louisville hotel bar.

The drinks were chilling when the girls climbed the outside staircase, a box of Pink's Pizza in hand.

As Marisa and Samantha plated the pizza, Beth reached into her purse. "Before I forget, Samantha, I asked one of the commission's staff about the servers for the party. It turns out they were students from City University's College of Hotel and Restaurant Management. The commission often hires students from the college to give them some professional experience. Anyway, here is the contact number at the university." She handed Samantha a piece of paper.

"Thanks, Beth." Samantha tucked the slip of paper into a drawer in her desk.

The friends ate pizza and played the videos, keeping an eye out for any sign of Brian Decker at the party. Two hours in, Mark and Darcy hadn't yet arrived on the scene when Samantha paused the videos to make another drink. "Thanks again for doing this, guys. I've already watched this once. It helps to have a fresh perspective to make sure I don't miss anything."

Marisa followed her into the kitchen. "It's sort of surreal to watch ourselves—and everyone else. It's like one of those old hidden-camera shows. So, what can I do to help?"

Marisa squeezed limes while Samantha pitted fresh cherries and placed them at the bottom of three glasses. Samantha squirmed under her friend's gaze as she muddled the concoction with sugar and a dash of her cherry bitters.

"What?" She stared at her friend.

Marisa sighed. "I know I'm the one who told you to investigate in the first place, but I'm starting to get a bad feeling. What's the end game if we find this guy attended the party? Will you try to talk to him?"

Samantha broke eye contact as she finished shaking the drinks and handed one to Marisa. "I'll be fine. Don't worry."

Marisa nodded, but her lips were pressed into a tight line, as if she wasn't yet convinced safety was uppermost in Samantha's mind.

Samantha handed Beth her drink and restarted the video. After about the four-hour mark, Mark and Darcy appeared on the screen as they walked into the house.

"There they are!" Beth rose to move closer to the television.

They all began to focus more intently, watching the video for any sign of Brian Decker. After two more couples walked inside, one elderly and hunched and one middle aged, a crowd of six or seven guests walked in together.

Beth popped out of her chair. "Pause it! I think I see him."

Samantha rewound the video and, within a few seconds, spotted the man Beth had identified.

"It's really him!" Samantha jumped up from the sofa and hooted, nearly spilling her drink and startling Ruby, who had been fast asleep on a nearby throw pillow. The cat opened one eye for a moment before curling up even more tightly, wrapping her tail around her face.

They rewound four more times to make sure, but by the end they all agreed Brian had turned up in the middle of the cluster of people arriving shortly after Mark and Darcy. That proved Brian had surfaced at the home tour at roughly the same time as Mark.

Beth squinted as if in deep concentration. "It's definitely a strange coincidence for him to be there. Then again, it's one of the biggest events in the Highlands, so it's not that unusual for a Highlands resident to attend."

"True, but given his issues with the Historic Commission, isn't it at least a little suspicious for him to show up?" Samantha finished her drink, still in a celebratory mood.

Marisa shook her head. "Maybe suspicious, but not enough to make a case on. My criminal law prof would say circumstantial evidence doesn't win cases."

Samantha had trouble containing her annoyance. "Well, it shows he attended the party at the same time as Mark, whereas Gabby arrived two hours earlier."

Marisa shrugged. "We don't see anyone exit the house. For all we know—or rather, for all potential jurors know—she remained in the house. Sorry, still playing devil's advocate here."

"What else would I need to convince police he's a likely suspect?"

"Well, I guess you have a motive of sorts, but if I were a prosecutor, I would want some hard evidence to tie him to the crime." Marisa entered full lecturer mode. "We also would need to prove he had access to the poison. Then again, everyone has access to the poison, because oleander grows all over this town. Maybe someone noticed Decker follow Mark at the party? It's a long shot, I know."

"How would we find out? Maybe Darcy would know. She might've seen if Decker approached them." Beth perked up, joining in the hypothetical exercise.

Samantha pursed her lips. "I want to talk to her anyway. Maybe she's my next step."

"Well, be careful. It's like a game of Clue. Seems like anyone in the house could be the murderer. Is it Brian Decker in the garden or Darcy in the parlor or even Gabby in the closet?" Beth laughed a little, but her face quickly turned serious again. "I'm serious, Sam. It's fun to talk theoretically, but you have to be careful."

"I'm not a fragile flower," Samantha sniped. The sight of Beth shrinking from her made her soften her approach. "I'm sorry. I didn't mean to snap at you. I'm a little on edge, and this could be a good lead. I promise I'll be careful."

Not wanting to end the conversation on a sour note, she changed the subject. "We've been talking all about me and my problems for the past few hours. How are you two doing?"

Marisa waxed poetic about an interesting case she'd debated in her constitutional law class before she interrupted herself. "Actually, Beth is the one with the news."

Samantha turned to look at Beth, who had pinpricks of red blossoming on her cheeks. "It's nothing, really."

Marisa put her hand on Beth's knee. "It's not nothing, baby. It's exciting! Beth is considering a new business venture."

Samantha raised her eyebrows, giving Beth a puzzled look. "Really? I thought you loved your job."

Beth sighed. "I love gardening, and I love building and designing gardens that reflect their habitat, but that's not what I'm doing, at least not most of the time. Everyone wants the same three trees, two shrubs, and a handful of flowers, practically none of which are even native to this region. Anyway, I'm mulling over some ideas at the moment, but nothing concrete."

Samantha nodded encouragingly. "I'd love to hear about your ideas when you're ready to share."

Beth's face flushed even redder. "Of course. In the meantime, it's getting late. We'd better get going." She stood up to leave, motioning for Marisa to do the same.

As they headed to the door, Marisa reminded Samantha of their monthly date on Sunday with Marisa's *abuela* for their cooking lesson, a tradition they'd maintained since they'd met five years earlier. "We can cancel if you aren't up for it."

"No, no. We can't cancel. I enjoy our visits. It'll be fun."

Samantha waved good-bye to her two friends and went back into the living room to tidy up. As she carried the empty pizza box and glasses into the kitchen, she wondered briefly about Beth's news. She got the sense that Beth wasn't thrilled that Marisa had mentioned it. *I guess she'll fill me in when there's something to tell.*

Before long, Samantha's mind turned to Brian again. When she'd seen him at the gym, with his ripped abs and his larger-than-necessary truck, he'd seemed more like a typical meathead than the kind of guy who would attend a Historic Commission fund raiser. There was something suspicious about him, and she intended to get to the bottom of it.

Chapter Nine

In the morning, Samantha's phone rang and David's name appeared on her caller ID.

"David. Hi."

"Samantha? Turn on the television. It's on all the local channels. They've arrested Gabby."

Samantha's mouth dropped open. "Excuse me? What?"

She ran into the living room and turned on the television, tuning it to the local ABC affiliate. She stood in silence and stared at the screen as police led Gabby from her home in handcuffs while her teenage daughter cried in the background. Samantha sympathized with the girl but took a grim satisfaction in Gabby's arrest.

"Wow! So what does this mean?"

David chuckled. "I think it means your problems are about to be over. The police must have some evidence to tie Gabby to the crime. That means her lawsuit against you isn't likely to stand. This might even be grounds to file a countersuit, particularly if a jury finds her guilty."

Samantha cried out in delight, feeling lighter than she had in days. "I could kiss you, David." She swallowed quickly. She couldn't deny her attraction to David, but this wasn't the time. "I'm sorry. I'm just excited. What's next?"

David coughed in the background, and Samantha's face burned. Fortunately, nobody but Ruby witnessed it, and she was color-blind.

"Next, I'll procure a copy of the arrest report and file it along with a brief requesting that you be dropped from her lawsuit. With police naming her as their main suspect, we might get some quick action."

Samantha could hardly contain her excitement. "That would be wonderful, David. Thank you! Then I can get back to my actual life—or better yet, figure out what I want my real life to be!"

David laughed. "I'm glad to brighten your morning. I'll let you know when I get a copy of the arrest report, and we can discuss further options from there."

"Thank you!" Samantha clicked off the phone and the television, feeling light enough to float away.

Her sense of elation soon ebbed as she pictured Gabby's daughter crying as police put her mom into the squad car. She wondered what evidence police had on Gabby and hoped it justified the anguish they were putting her daughter through.

Don't go soft on me now. You know where that's led you in the past. Still, parts of Gabby's story seemed at least somewhat believable. Not to mention there were still unanswered questions about why Brian Decker, practically Mark's sworn enemy, had bothered to attend the home tour.

Torn between wanting Gabby to be punished and not wanting an innocent person to go to prison, especially one with a young daughter at home, Samantha tried to push away any lingering doubts about Gabby's guilt.

Later that morning, when Marisa arrived to pick her up for their outing to Marisa's grandmother's house in the city's historically Hispanic Second Ward, Samantha filled Marisa in on Gabby's arrest and her own misgivings about it.

Marisa looked incredulous. "Sam, this is great news! If the police have arrested Gabby, they've got some evidence. It means you're off the hook."

Samantha's eyes widened. "You're the one who told me to investigate this like a story. If this were a story, I wouldn't be satisfied until I'd pursued every lead."

Marisa blew out her breath. "I was wrong, okay? This isn't a story. This is your life. I told you yesterday I'm nervous about you pursuing this. Can you drop the Nancy Drew routine?"

Samantha held her tongue. She didn't want to fight, so she changed the subject. "They'll never stop it with these luxury apartments." She pointed to a large complex under construction. "How many does one city need?"

Marisa nodded as she made the last turn into her grandmother's neighborhood, still predominantly Hispanic but growing more gentrified every day.

Camila had lived in her little yellow house for over fifty years. She welcomed the pair at the front door with a hug. "*Mijas*! It's good to see you! No Beth today?"

"No, she's volunteering at the community garden this afternoon." Marisa returned her grandmother's hug.

With shoulder-length white hair tucked behind her ears and a few crow's-feet that stretched upward from the corners of her eyes, Camila shared Marisa's wide smile and exuded the same warmth Samantha remembered from her own grandmother, who had passed away a decade earlier. "How about pozole today?"

When Samantha and Marisa nodded their approval, Camila grabbed her bag and followed them out to the car.

They stopped first at the open-air market on Airline Drive, where the smell of freshly cut fruit and stall after stall of mostly Spanish-speaking farmers selling everything from horchatas to barrels of dried hibiscus flowers gave Samantha the sensation of being transported to another country.

Samantha led the others to a nearby spice market to find some of the more off-the-wall ingredients for her bitters, including barberry root, white cherry bark, and cardamom pods. A heady mixture of cinnamon, cloves, and chili powder greeted visitors who walked through the door.

The trio made stops at both markets. They purchased fresh peppers and guajillo chilies at the market stalls along with a few cans of hominy and some spices at the spice market. Last, they stopped at Mi Tienda Bakery for one of the pastel conchas lining the shelves.

Brushing crumbs and sugar from her lips, Camila put her hand on Samantha's. "You look good, *mija*, despite your troubles. I'm sorry about your young man, and now this . . . lawsuit."

Camila's words, like Camila herself, were comforting. The woman's very presence soothed her like a warm embrace.

"You read the article?"

Camila nodded. "It will blow over. The headlines only last for a day or two."

"I hope you're right." Samantha smiled at Camila.

Camila smiled back. "If it helps, I'll say a rosary for you."

"It couldn't hurt."

Back at the house, the three women prepared the soup, a heavenly concoction of pork shoulder, spices, peppers, tomatoes, and hominy, which filled the house with a fragrant aroma.

While they worked, they chatted about the latest gossip in the neighborhood, including the latest controversy about a new high-end apartment complex planned on the edge of the more traditional neighborhood. "You'll see, people will be forced out of their homes when their property values increase." Camila clucked. "We've seen it happen here over and over."

Camila launched into a story about the old days in the neighborhood, where residents picketed construction sites and one friend even tried to chain himself to a tree to stop construction of a highway frontage road. "To the developers, the buildings meant nothing—little more than slums, infested with rats and other vermin. To us, it represented our history."

"Were you able to stop them?" Marisa asked her grandmother.

"Oh, *mija*, no. It's a shame, but nothing can stop the bulldozer in Houston."

Marisa often rushed her grandmother through stories she'd heard more times than she could remember. Samantha, on the other hand, could listen for hours to the history of her adopted city.

As the rich smell of pork broth and spices began to fill the warm kitchen, talk turned again to Mark's death and Samantha's involvement in the case.

Camila *tsk*ed at the news of the young girl forced to watch her mother's arrest. "Poor child."

Sensing a sympathetic ear, Samantha expressed her doubts about Gabby's guilt. "I'm sure the police know what they're doing, but a part of me thinks Gabby could be innocent."

Marisa groaned. "Ugh. Not this again. Can't you drop this?"

Camila shook her finger at Marisa with a stern expression. "*Mija*, is that how I taught you? To turn away from others' troubles?"

Marisa, appearing chastened, softened her tone. "I'm not saying she should turn away exactly. Just focus on her own life right now."

Camila shook her head. "I'm disappointed, *mija*. Samantha has a good heart." The elderly woman covered Samantha's hand with her own wrinkled palm, the paper-thin skin soft but warm. "She needs to follow it."

Samantha drew strength from Camila's words, but she didn't want to be the source of friction between Marisa and her grandmother. "I think the soup's ready." She pointed to the steaming stockpot.

They ladled the soup into bowls and topped them with chopped radishes, lime juice, and tortilla chips.

"This is heaven." Samantha savored the flavors of her first bite.

She relaxed and listened as Marisa and her grandmother joked with one another, any earlier tension gone. With a pang, Samantha thought of her own grandmother, but she appreciated the acceptance she found in Camila's warm kitchen.

Before long, Samantha and Marisa were on their way, each with a care package—Marisa's larger with "a little extra for Beth."

Samantha leaned back in the passenger's seat, full and relaxed. "I love spending time with your grandma."

"She loves it too. It keeps her young and gives her an excuse to pull out her old recipes."

They rode in silence for a few moments before Marisa turned to Samantha. "Look, I'm sorry about earlier. Abuela is right. You need to follow your own mind. But I'm going to keep worrying about you."

Samantha smiled. "I know, and I love you for it. I just want to see this through."

Marisa sighed. "Okay, but you have to promise to keep me in the loop. I want to know your plans in case something should happen."

Samantha promised.

Marisa chimed in again. "If you don't believe Gabby is the killer, who else could it have been? Do you still think it could be Brian? Or what about the waitress and her boyfriend? Beth found out where they work. You can investigate them. It's still a little sketchy that the girl came to your house."

"There could be others we don't even know about yet. At this point, I can't rule anyone out. Oh, but speaking of Beth, I hope she wasn't too upset about our discussion the other day."

"That was my fault." Marisa shrugged her shoulders. "I was a little too eager to share her idea before she's sure she can make it work. But I'm proud of her. I think it's going to be great."

Samantha raised her eyebrows. "Now I'm really intrigued. But let her tell me when she's ready."

Marisa nodded as she pulled in front of Samantha's apartment. "Now you be careful, okay?"

"I will." Samantha climbed out of the car. "Thanks again for a fun afternoon."

She climbed the stairs to her apartment with a bag of extra spices and her leftovers in tow.

*   *   *

That night, Samantha mashed a quart of blackberries with some lemon peel, allspice berries, and peppercorns and covered the whole mixture with grain alcohol for blackberry bitters. Then she began to plan her next move, a thorough online vetting of Brian Decker. With proof that he'd been at the party, she'd decided she needed to learn more about him.

Finished with the blackberries, Samantha began by stalking Decker's social media networks—Facebook, LinkedIn, Twitter, and Instagram—and found many of her assumptions about him to be accurate. Around forty, Decker held a mechanical engineering degree from Texas A&M from the early 2000s and had worked for one of the region's dozens of oil-field-services companies ever since. He seemed hard-core into fitness, with at least every other post on Facebook and Instagram being about how many pounds he'd bench pressed or how many tires he'd flipped. Six months earlier his dating status had changed from "in a relationship" to "single." Around the same time, photos of a skinny redheaded girl with a cheesy grin were replaced with selfies of more tire flips.

As Samantha pored through his posts following his fight with Mark at the Historic Commission meeting, her pulse quickened when she came across a tweet thread Decker had created about Mark. The first tweet included a photo of a particularly angry Mark shaking his fist in the air.

—*Mark Brantwell, a member of the local Houston Gestapo, aka the Highlands Historic Commission, kicked me out of a public meeting tonight, violating my right to free speech.*
—*Brantwell and his band of henchmen are trampling on the rights of homeowners like myself, telling us what we can and can't do with our own personal property.*

Tagged with a dozen hashtags, Decker's thread appeared to have drawn a fair number of nutjobs. Though it hadn't exactly gone viral, it had garnered more than 150 likes and comments. A few reasonable commenters pointed out that if Decker didn't like the commission, he shouldn't have bought a house in the

Historic District. Those rational souls were drowned out by others who seemed to agree with Decker's premise, including one particularly ominous comment from a poster named Rebel with a Cause. Rebel offered to take care of Mark and the rest of the commission and included a graphic description of how exactly he would accomplish such a task.

Samantha shivered. Those trolls weren't to be messed with. She wondered if Decker realized what kind of fire he was playing with.

Is it possible Decker's little grudge against Mark got away from him? Or worse yet, is it possible he did exactly what he intended and put Mark in the cross hairs of some gun-loving, antigovernment nutjob?

Chapter Ten

The next day, Samantha made her way to the university, hoping any talk of the lawsuit had blown over. She kept her head low as she walked toward the cubicle she used during her editing stints. *So far, so good.* Nobody made a move to talk to her beyond a few nods hello.

Before Samantha could get comfortable in her chair, her supervisor Linda stopped by the cubicle and called her into the office. Worried, Samantha made her way to the only enclosed office space in the room.

"I apologize for the call last week." Linda avoided direct eye contact as Samantha took a seat across from her desk. "The communications director read the story and panicked. You know, we finally moved past the adverse publicity from the admissions scandal. He doesn't want any hint of more controversy to hit the school."

"I understand." Though she spoke the words, Samantha really didn't understand. The admissions scandal had involved members of the board of regents using their clout to pave the way to admit donors' kids to the university. It had blown up after a lengthy investigation by the *Gazette*. A lawsuit against a lowly freelancer hardly seemed equivalent.

"Anyway, that's why I was happy to see the news over the weekend." Linda smiled. "It's always the wife or the husband in situations like these. Will they drop the lawsuit against you?"

"I'm not sure. I hope so. My lawyer is looking into it."

"They kept showing the clip of that woman's arrest again this morning, showing her being dragged from her home. Fancy home, too. What a crazy story, huh?"

"Yeah . . ." Samantha wondered what Linda's point was.

"Well, I wanted to say again, none of us ever believed you were involved with that whole situation."

"No, of course not."

"The thing is, though." Linda tugged on her sleeves, as if to straighten them. "Until you resolve the lawsuit issue, the director thinks it will be best if you have minimal contact here."

"Um . . ." Samantha's heart pounded, and her ears thrummed. "What does that mean?"

"Understand this is all temporary until you settle the lawsuit or the publicity dies down, but we can't have you interview anyone or write stories, and we can't have you edit the magazine."

Samantha stared ahead in disbelief at the words coming from Linda's mouth. "What exactly am I supposed to do in the meantime?"

Linda continued to avoid eye contact and pretended to brush some lint off her skirt. "We'll have to handle this edition of the magazine in-house. You've done excellent work, and I'm sure this will all blow over by next quarter, but you understand how it is, right?"

Samantha stumbled out of the office, stunned. She clutched her purse to her chest and walked, only half aware of her destination. She collapsed onto a concrete bench outside and cradled her head in her hands. With an almost reptilian urge, she absorbed the warmth from the concrete as blood rushed, icy, through her veins.

How can this be happening?

It wasn't as if she loved the job. She'd taken it only at Greg's urging, to provide some steady income and buy herself some time to figure out her next steps in life. Still, the sting of today's humiliation surprised her.

This is outrageous. I can't believe Linda didn't even stand up for me. What am I supposed to do now? Not only has this stupid lawsuit threatened my reputation, it's also threatening my livelihood.

She stood, wavering for a moment, before she began to walk away. An intense urge to put as much distance between herself and the campus propelled her forward.

When she reached her car, Samantha remembered Linda mentioning the footage of Gabby's arrest on the news again this morning. That could only mean a fresh development in the case.

I hope they've got enough evidence to lock Gabby up for good.

In the wake of her conversation with Linda, Samantha felt less concerned about justice and more concerned about seeing Gabby pay for what she'd put Samantha through.

On her way home, Samantha called David to ask for an update on what he'd learned from his detective friend.

"Gabby's got a bail hearing this afternoon. My buddy will send me a copy of the charging document afterward. I'll let you know what it says."

Samantha replied with a terse, "Thanks."

"Is something wrong, Samantha?"

"It's work. The university basically put my freelance job on hold while this lawsuit is hanging over my head."

"Oh, Samantha, I'm sorry. Loss of income is definite grounds for a countersuit."

"It sounds appealing, trust me. But I can't even begin to contemplate another lawsuit right now."

"No, of course not. I'm sorry. We can talk about it later. In fact, I'll draw up the paperwork for you to review. You don't have to decide anything right away, but if Gabby *is* the guilty party, you deserve to be compensated for the false claims against you."

Considering the income she'd lost, Samantha found herself more and more inclined toward the countersuit.

"Thanks, David. I appreciate it."

At home, Samantha logged in to her laptop to scrounge for a few billable hours to help tide her over in the meantime. A few clients paid her to write website content—mostly ambulance chasers who asked her to compile the latest research on topics like mesothelioma or black lung. It didn't pay a ton, but it was easy work. During breaks in her work, she hunted for alerts from news stations about the bail hearing. Samantha figured Gabby would easily make bail. In most of the cases she'd covered for the paper, defendants who were white and middle class were likely to be granted bail if they weren't viewed as a flight risk.

Late in the afternoon, a tweet from a news station indicated a one-day delay for the hearing. Samantha offered a wry smile, pleased that Gabby would spend at least one more night in jail. *It's the least she deserves.*

As she shut down her laptop, Samantha sank back into her green sofa, the weight of the day on her shoulders. She replayed the scene with Linda in her head for the hundredth time. It still smarted like a slap in the face.

These are people who supposedly know me. What will other potential clients think?

Half the city had seen her photo spread across two newspaper columns in connection with the lawsuit story. She wondered if she could ever restore her reputation. Even if Gabby dropped the lawsuit and Samantha filed a countersuit, it wouldn't be front-page news. Unfortunately, the news business didn't work that way. The paper would bury any update in the B section, if they covered it at all. Every time someone Googled her name, the initial story would likely be the first link to appear.

Samantha almost called her mom for a commiseration session but decided against it out of fear she might cave and accept her mom's offer to move back home.

She poured herself a Revolver with bourbon, coffee liquor, and a few dashes of her homemade orange bitters and downed it in a few minutes. Restless, she decided to go for a walk.

The alcohol hadn't improved her mind-set, and the walk didn't help much either. She wanted to talk to somebody familiar, someone who would be on her side. She briefly considered calling David again, tempted by the ever-present warmth in his tone when they spoke, but she didn't want to be a nuisance.

She recognized her mistake even as she dialed the numbers, but she couldn't help but turn to the one place where she'd found comfort in the past. Her fingers tingled as the phone rang, and her breath caught in her throat at the sound of the familiar voice on the voice mail. "This is Greg. I'm not available at the moment, but leave me a message, and I'll call you back." She quickly ended the call, ashamed of her desire to contact him.

What am I doing? He's not the answer to any of my problems.

She walked two more blocks and noted that the physical exertion was finally beginning to lift her mood.

On her way home, Samantha grabbed a flyer from the two-story Victorian on the corner. She liked to play her own version of *The Price Is Right*—guess the price without going over and she won the home. When she looked at the price, she'd been off by over forty thousand dollars. About to crumple the sheet and find the nearest recycling bin, she noticed a familiar face on the back page. A woman with long blonde hair as straight and flat as a horse's mane and eyes as green as a cat's stared out at her: Darcy Meadows, Mark's girlfriend.

While it shouldn't have been a surprise—Darcy had worked as a real estate agent in Galveston, after all—Samantha did a double take. She guessed it only made sense for Darcy to have joined a new firm in Houston.

She held on to the flyer as she walked the rest of the way home.

I wonder what else there is to know about Darcy.

Chapter Eleven

Still feeling low but hungry, Samantha turned her attention to dinner. She reheated the leftover pozole from Camila's and ate it while she read a book. The restlessness continued after dinner, and Samantha was unable to concentrate on her book or the television. She went into the kitchen and checked on her tincture. After uncorking the bottle, she took a whiff of the spicy mixture and determined it would be ready soon.

She wanted to get her hands dirty and whipped together a spicy ginger syrup with fresh ginger, allspice berries, and star anise. Her apartment filled with the aroma of fall spices, reminding her of apple pies and hot toddies. She mixed the syrup with bourbon, lime juice, and ginger beer for a kicked-up version of a Kentucky Mule—refreshing and spicy, just the way she liked it.

She settled onto the sofa with her drink, a notebook, and a pen, and began to write in her journal. Journaling wasn't a regular habit, but Samantha did it every once in a while to help her process her feelings. And now she felt in desperate need of some clarity. She began:

After so many low points over the last few weeks—Greg leaving me, canceling our wedding, losing our dream home—I've hit an all-time new low. My client basically told me I'm a liability.

I've been laid off before. "Laid off" is something out of your control. It's more about the business than anything personal. But this is one rung lower. It's my client saying they no longer trust me to do the work I was hired to do.

They're essentially saying, "You might have murdered Mark Brantwell. Even if you didn't, there are enough people around who think you did that we can't have you around here anymore."

Where does that leave me?

She paused for a moment, flipping through earlier pages, remembering other times she'd turned to her journal. She'd written when she'd been laid off from her newspaper job, and when Greg had left, and she'd written page after page upon learning of the elderly woman murdered by Laurie Cavendish, the girl Samantha had helped to free from prison. While writing hadn't blunted the pain from any of those experiences, it had helped her to understand her feelings better. She hoped it would do the same for her now.

With Ruby pressed against her leg on the sofa, Samantha wrote about her disappointment in Linda for not advocating for her with the university administration. She wrote about her ruined reputation and about her uncertainty regarding what she should do with her life. Last, she wrote about her competing anger and sympathy for Gabby.

Though it resolved nothing, the act of recording her thoughts did help Samantha understand some of her anger and disappointment. It made her realize her situation could always be worse. She could be in Gabby's shoes, facing a murder charge for a murder she said she didn't commit.

Her thoughts continued to pour out of her until she realized her journal entry had morphed into an itemized list about the case against Gabby. She ended with several bullet points of all she'd learned thus far:

1. *Gabby and Mark had financial difficulties, and Gabby was overextended on her Galveston home.*
2. *Mark had an affair with Gabby's best friend Darcy. Gabby retaliated by defacing Darcy's signs. Police arrested her for harassment.*
3. *Gabby attended the home tour where Mark died but arrived more than two hours before him.*
4. *She claims a mysterious client asked her to attend the party and then sent her on a wild-goose chase in the city, which left her without an alibi for the time of Mark's death.*

Reading the list, Samantha understood why police would focus on Gabby, but the evidence was all circumstantial. It also ignored other potential suspects, including Brian Decker, who had threatened Mark and who'd also attended the party. And, as Marisa had pointed out, Mila and her boyfriend, Eric, had not yet been cleared.

She wondered again whether the police had anything more substantial on Gabby to tie her to the murder.

*　　*　　*

The next day, Samantha continued to scan her Twitter feed for news about Gabby's bail hearing. By noon, when she'd refreshed Twitter for at least the fiftieth time, she found the tweet she'd been expecting. Bail had been set at $500,000.

The story, published twenty minutes later, said Gabby would remain in the custody of the Harris County Jail until she could make bond. A video clip showed Gabby gasping as though she'd been punched in the gut as the judge announced the bail amount. Despite the lack of sound, Samantha could guess by Gabby's deflated expression that she would have trouble raising the $50,000 necessary to get a bail bondsman.

Samantha gave an involuntary shudder. Having visited the county jail to interview inmates for stories, she felt sorry for anyone held there. She tried again to remind herself she shouldn't care what happened to Gabby, but the sentiment seemed spiteful.

Later in the afternoon, David sent over a summary of Gabby's charging document, which he'd obtained from his friend in the prosecutor's office, and a copy of his draft of the countersuit against Gabby.

Samantha read through the charging document summary first. It noted Gabby's previous harassment charges against Darcy, her appearance at the home tour (though Samantha noticed no reference to the gap between when Gabby and Mark arrived), and her access to oleander. The only fresh information included an eyewitness report in which someone claimed to have heard Gabby threaten Mark with death if he ever cheated with Darcy again.

The evidence hardly seemed conclusive, and the last tidbit seemed to be more of a cheap shot than real evidence. Samantha could imagine almost any woman yelling something similar upon finding her husband having an affair with her best friend. The report didn't identify the witness, but Samantha wondered if it might have been Darcy.

Other than a mention of the obvious bad blood between Gabby and Mark over his affair, the charging document contained no new evidence to suggest the charges would stick. If police turned Gabby loose, Samantha might find herself back in the suspect pool.

There's no right answer here. What do I do?

As she read the copy of the countersuit, Samantha cringed. She couldn't shake the feeling that Gabby was being railroaded and the police weren't giving proper consideration to all potential suspects. As someone recently dumped by her fiancé, something far less serious than betrayal by a husband, Samantha felt a prick of conscience at the thought of heaping insult on injury. She sent David a note thanking him for the information and telling him to hold off on the countersuit for now. She wanted to hear what Gabby had to say for herself.

Samantha worked for a few more hours summarizing medical reports and drove to the jail, hoping to get a few moments to talk to Gabby. At the downtown women's unit, she filled out some paperwork, showed her identification, and waited to learn if Gabby would approve her visit.

Samantha had conducted a few jailhouse interviews in her day, and most inmates had been more than happy to meet with her, even if they had no intention of granting her an interview, if only to break up the monotony of the day. She guessed Gabby wouldn't want her daughter to witness her in such conditions and wasn't sure who else might visit, other than Gabby's lawyer, whose privileges were valid any time day or night.

After about thirty minutes in the lobby, Samantha heard her name broadcast from the loudspeaker. She placed her purse in a storage locker and submitted to a thorough pat-down by a deputy before he led her to the visitation room, a crowded room with seats facing each other separated by Plexiglas. A small circular speaker had been installed between each pair of chairs. Catcalls, shrieks, and even casual conversation

116

echoed off the walls as dozens of visitors fought for air space in the deafening room.

Samantha easily picked out Gabby from where she stood at the back window, her arms folded tightly across her chest in a defensive posture. She seemed to shrink at every loud utterance and looked almost grateful to find Samantha on the other side of the window.

"I wasn't sure if I should meet with you or not, but I'm curious." Gabby's eyes narrowed as she searched Samantha's face. "What do you want? Did you come here to gloat?"

Samantha flinched, almost as if she'd been slapped. "What? No. Of course not."

Gabby tilted her head to the side as if to get a better angle on Samantha. "Then I don't get it. Why are you here? I told you I'm sorry about the lawsuit. Once I get all of this sorted, I promise I'll have my attorney drop you from the suit. I should never have let him involve you in the first place. I only wanted to provide for my daughter. I've got to protect her interest in all of this."

The reference to Gabby's daughter deflated some of Samantha's anger. At only thirteen, the girl must be scared to death right now.

"Do you think you'll be able to make bail and get home to her?"

Gabby looked at her lap. "I hope so. She's with a friend right now. It's all such a nightmare for her. First her father is killed, and now her mother is in jail . . ."

Samantha lowered her gaze. She perceived the worry etched on Gabby's face. It served no purpose to confront Gabby with more anger about the lawsuit.

"I just wanted to talk to you. The more I consider your story, the more I believe you. I mean, your story sounds crazy, but maybe it's meant to sound crazy. I think someone set you up."

Gabby nodded her head eagerly. "I agree, but who would want to do that?"

"I don't know, but we've got to figure it out, for both our sakes."

Gabby eyes seemed to spark with hope for a moment before narrowing again as she met Samantha's gaze. "Why would you help me?"

Samantha shrugged. "It's self-preservation. If you didn't kill Mark, I want to find out who did so I can avoid any further suggestion of my involvement. This whole situation has already lost me my biggest client. I can't afford to lose more."

Gabby lowered her eyes to her lap before refocusing on Samantha. "So, what do we do?"

"We work together. We've got to figure out who sent you those emails."

"My daughter's got a friend who's good with computer stuff."

"Good. In the meantime, make a list of anyone who might have had a grudge against your husband, no matter how small."

"Okay. I'll mull it over." Gabby smiled at Samantha. "It's gratifying to have someone believe in me."

Despite the shakiness of their alliance, Samantha offered a slight smile in return. "I'll send you an email address with my contact information through your business website for when you get out of here. Call me whenever you think of something that might be useful."

A jailer signaled the end of their time, and Samantha gave an awkward wave before she turned to leave the room. The risks of joining forces with Gabby would be worth it if Samantha's hunch proved true. Gabby could be the key to solving the mystery. Samantha only hoped they could do it in time to restore both their reputations.

*   *   *

Back in her apartment, Samantha tried to ride the burst of adrenaline for a while longer. She grabbed a quick sandwich and her notepad and tried to brainstorm ideas on other potential suspects. Brian Decker stood out as an obvious candidate, but she needed to identify others.

She spent a fruitless hour searching through Yelp and Google reviews for Mark's contracting business, trying to track down any angry customers or anyone who had made even a vague threat. Samantha could find only one contender in a man who'd complained about a shoddy home repair job and said he'd see Mark dead before he would ever work on another of his properties. A quick Google search showed the complainer to be an elderly man confined to a wheelchair. After two complete viewings of the security footage, Samantha could guarantee nobody fitting that description had been at the party.

Glancing over at her desk, she pulled out the slip of paper Beth had given her with the name and phone number of the administrator at the College of Hotel and Restaurant Management. At some point, she should try to reach Mila. Samantha still didn't consider the waitress or her boyfriend to be high on the suspect list, but if nothing else, maybe they'd noticed something during the party. She resolved to try to reach them in the morning.

With little else to go on, Samantha stood and stretched her back, practicing a few of the yoga moves Beth had suggested for easing her occasional office worker's slouch. She spotted the real estate flyer on her dining room table where she'd left it the night before and decided it would be good to learn a little more about Darcy.

While Darcy had been a real estate agent in Galveston before she moved to Houston, it seemed she'd advanced in a short time from some lesser Inner Loop properties to the Highlands area. Judging by her company's website and the number of beautiful homes on her personal listing, Darcy seemed to be doing pretty well for herself.

A Google search revealed that Darcy and Mark lived in a townhome on the cheaper side of the Highlands, near the railroad tracks, which, along with the interstate, split the neighborhood into haves and have-nots.

Samantha found herself more curious about Darcy and her actions since Mark's death. She resolved to call Bob in the morning, hoping he might be able to put her in touch with Darcy.

* * *

Without the university job, Samantha had plenty of time on her hands in the morning.

No point in putting this off. I'll call Bob.

She'd expected his voice mail at eight thirty in the morning and lost her concentration for an instant when he answered right away.

"Yes?"

"Hi. This is Samantha Warren. You know, from the party?"

"Oh yes. What can I do for you, Ms. Warren?"

"Well, I hoped I could ask you for some information. I'm still investigating Mark's death on account of the lawsuit . . ."

"I thought the police arrested Mark's wife for the crime. Our lawyers seem to think that should put an end to the suit."

"Well, hopefully. But, I'm worried she might be innocent. There are some odd parts to her story."

"I find it's best to trust the police in these situations."

"I do trust them. Well, anyway, I hoped you could give me Darcy's cell phone number. I want to ask her a few questions."

"Darcy? Oh, I'd really hate to bother her right now. She's been through so much, and she's really unwell."

"Of course. I don't want to bother her. I only have a few questions."

Bob paused as if considering what to do. "Hmm. Well, let me call her and ask if she wants to speak with you. I don't want to hand her number out to just anybody."

"Oh." Samantha tried to hide her disappointment. She supposed his explanation made some sense. "Okay. Let me give you my number. You can pass it along to her, and please, let her know I don't want to pester her."

"All right, Ms. Warren. Is there anything else?"

"No. Thank you." Samantha ended the call, frustrated. Hopefully Bob would pass her information along soon and Darcy would be willing to talk. If all else failed, she could always try her at the real estate office, or even go for a direct confrontation at her house. For now, Samantha wanted to keep things light and friendly.

She moved on to the next item on her to-do list and called the number Beth had given her for the restaurant management program at the university. When a receptionist answered, she launched into her prepared story. "Oh, hi. This may sound strange, but I met one of your workers, Mila, at a party she served at. Anyway, I wanted to hire her for another party. Can you put me in contact with her?"

"You must mean Mila Livitz. She's one of our best." The woman paused. "We don't like to give out our students' contact information. Please give me your name and number, and I'll pass it along to her if she is interested."

Darn. Samantha had hoped to get a phone number quickly and cross Mila and Eric off her suspect list for good, but life kept offering up roadblocks. She gave the woman her cell phone number and provided the name Beth Myerson because she didn't want Mila to recognize her own name.

"All righty. I'll give her the message. Thanks again for supporting our City University students."

With those errands out of the way, Samantha heated a mug of orange chai and settled in at her desk to check her emails, hoping to find a freelance opportunity or two waiting for her. Instead, she found an email from Gabby. She'd made bail and was headed back to Galveston. She'd forwarded the emails she'd received from her mystery client, which appeared to be more or less exactly as she had described them.

Dear Ms. Brantwell:

Your website says you specialize in design for historic homes. I own a Colonial Revival style home in Houston's Riverside Terrace, and I'm interested in some significant renovations. After inheriting a sizable sum, I now have the funds available for the renovation I have wanted to do for years. The work on your website impressed me, and I believe I can use your services.

I must warn you at the outset that I am confined to a wheelchair and dislike venturing from my home any longer. However, I have very specific ideas on what I would like, and I need a designer who is willing to do some legwork for me.

I'm interested in matching the style of the Reilley house in the Houston Highlands. The decor is gorgeous. I fell in love with it several years ago after touring it during one of the Highlands Historic Home Tours and want to match the Victorian style as closely as possible. I have purchased a ticket for you to attend the tour on Saturday, May 15, and attached a voucher to this email. It would be wonderful for you to view the home to find out what it would take to recreate elements in my home.

I realize you work from Galveston, so this will require some travel, which I am more than happy to pay for if you're the right person for the job. Please let me know your interest level.

Sincerely,

Ms. Vivian Caulfield

And Gabby's reply:

Dear Ms. Caulfield,

Thank you for the opportunity to work on your home. I am happy to view the Reilley house and seek ways to replicate elements in your home. Would you be available to meet at your home after the tour so I can explore your space and draft some ideas on how to carry out your vision? I look forward to working with you.

Gabby

In the next email, Ms. Caulfield confirmed her availability to meet after the tour.

Gabby, it's great to hear from you. I'm pleased you will consider working for me. We can meet after you attend the tour. As I mentioned in my earlier note, I rarely leave the house and will be available before 10 p.m. I look forward to meeting with you.

Vivian

The emails were definitely odd, but nothing in them raised alarm bells, other than the challenge of working with a client confined to her home. Samantha checked the address listed in the property tax rolls, and the home did, in fact, appear to be owned by a Vivian Caulfield.

Interesting. Maybe I should pay a visit to Vivian.

Chapter Twelve

S amantha parked in front of the house in Riverside Terrace, a neighborhood of faded mansions plopped right in the middle of one of the poorest sections of the city. The neighborhood had been built in the 1920s by wealthy Jewish businessmen who'd been denied admittance to River Oaks, Houston's most famous and luxurious neighborhood. The Riverside Terrace area lost its luster when the old families began to move away as more of the city and its suburbs opened up to them, but now, much like everywhere close to the city's core, the neighborhood had turned again due to gentrification.

Vivian Caulfield's home conveyed the grandeur of bygone days. A classic Colonial Revival, it had a rectangular brick facade adorned with an elaborate portico entrance. Though the grounds could use some upkeep, the home appeared to be in good condition. Samantha followed the footpath to the door, where she rang the doorbell.

A short, spritely woman with a tight white perm and a purple velour tracksuit answered the door. With no wheelchair, the woman didn't fit the description of Vivian Caulfield from the emails.

"Can I help you, young lady?"

Samantha stumbled with her words. She wished she had planned out what to say. "Uh . . . yes. I'm looking for Vivian Caulfield."

"That's me." The woman held her door open only a crack, but wide enough for Samantha to observe a modern foyer with sleek glass-and-metal furnishings. The decor was a far cry from the fustiness she had expected based on the email to Gabby.

"Did you attempt to hire Gabby Brantwell for some interior design work recently?"

The woman looked confused. "Interior design? No, of course not. What are you talking about? I renovated my home a few years ago. I finally got rid of all the antique clutter my mother collected and added a few modern touches."

"You didn't send an email to Gabby's website along with a ticket to the Highlands Historic Home Tour a couple of weeks ago?"

The woman shook her head. "I don't know anyone named Gabby. I don't know what this is all about, but I can assure you it wasn't me. I returned two days ago from a two-week cruise to Puerto Vallarta."

"This is going to sound like a strange question, but you haven't been in a wheelchair recently, have you?"

The woman laughed. "Hopefully not for a few years yet. Now, if you don't mind, I'm late for my kickboxing class." She grabbed a duffel bag from a table in the foyer and locked the front door behind her.

Samantha walked back to her car more confused than ever. Nothing added up. Clearly this woman hadn't emailed Gabby. Someone had, though, and Samantha planned to find out who.

By noon, when she made it back to her apartment, Samantha had decided to make another trip to Galveston.

She called on her way to alert Gabby. When she arrived at the woman's front door an hour later, Gabby welcomed her inside.

They were overpolite with one another, but an air of distrust seemed to hover over their meeting.

Samantha forged ahead anyway. "Thanks for letting me stop by. I thought it would be good to put our heads together."

"Sure. Whatever it takes to prove I'm innocent." Gabby ushered her into a front parlor decorated with tasteful period furniture, the walls painted a colorful lavender. More pops of color came from the books nestled in the built-in bookshelves.

"Oh, this room is lovely." Samantha took a seat in a wing-back chair with claw feet.

"I needed one room fully decorated to meet with current and potential clients. The rest of the house is a wreck. We've been renovating as we have money, and . . . well, we almost never have money."

"You almost had the chance at big money, right? I heard a rumor about a television show? What happened with that?"

Gabby explained that she and Mark had nearly signed a contract with the Home Renovation Network for a new pilot show on historical island renovations. Galveston was known for its sizable collection of historic homes, and the HRN folks wanted to find someone who regularly restored them. A former client recommended Mark. When they talked to him, the HRN people were thrilled to learn Gabby owned her own interior designing business.

"I think they were picturing us as the island version of Chip and Joanna, but we quickly proved them wrong. We were about to sign a contract when Mark started to get cold feet. Then I learned about his affair. Anyway, all parties decided not to proceed, given the circumstances."

"That must have been a big blow."

"Oh, I don't know. We were fighting so much by then. Pretending to play nice for a television show seemed more stressful than fun. Anyway, do you want a drink?"

"Sure. I'll take a Diet Coke if you have one."

"No problem. I'll be right back."

While Gabby went to get drinks, Samantha checked out the bookshelves. Classics were mixed with contemporary fiction and even a few well-worn mysteries. It looked like a collection built over time rather than one bought by the yard from some design warehouse. There were a few photos on the end table, including one of Gabby, Mark, and a baby posing in front of a sea lion statue at the Houston Zoo. She lifted it higher and studied the faces of Mark and Gabby, who looked as if they were in love with each other and with their little daughter.

"Congratulations. You found the one photo where we all look happy." Gabby handed Samantha a tall, frosty glass of Diet Coke.

"How long ago did you take this?"

Gabby gripped the photo and traced her finger around her daughter's face. "Oh, Chloe was around eighteen months here, so that would put this around eleven years ago."

"You lived in Houston then?"

"Yeah, Mark and I met there when I attended the university. Mark worked construction with his dad. We met, of all places, at the Art Car Parade."

The Art Car Parade was a Houston tradition Samantha looked forward to every spring. Hundreds of decorated cars paraded through downtown in a chaotic display of the inner workings of creative Houstonians' minds. Where else could you spot a giant rusty cockroach-shaped car blasting "La Cucara-cha" every time it turned a corner?

Samantha grinned at the memory. "That sounds fun."

"We dated off and on for around six years before we married and waited another three before Chloe was born. Life was great for a few years. Mark and his dad were doing really well. They were super busy, with a lot of projects, and I had just gotten started with interior design. I worked with another woman who taught me the ropes. She had even begun to hand off a few small clients to me."

"What changed?"

"Mark fought with his dad over some renovation project. We moved to Galveston, which, in retrospect, probably put the nail in our coffin."

"Why?"

"We took on too much. In Houston, Mark split the over-head with his dad. When we moved to Galveston, we paid for everything. Mark lived by the rule that you've got to spend money to make money. He spent and spent, which is what got us into this awful debt."

"How bad is it, if you don't mind me asking?"

"We've begged, borrowed, and . . . well, did everything we could to hang on to the house. He insisted we needed a house this big, while I tried to argue for a much smaller cottage. Then he moved back to Houston, and it became my problem to save the house."

"That's a lot of pressure."

"It is, and now with Mark gone, I'm not sure it's how I should spend my energy. Maybe Chloe and I should sell it and move away."

It seemed like a sore subject, so Samantha shifted gears. Taking a seat while motioning for Gabby to sit in the chair opposite hers, she asked Gabby about the emails and how the mystery person had contacted her. Gabby explained that the messages had come through her website, which automatically forwarded messages to her email.

"Wouldn't you normally talk with someone, either in person or at least on the phone, before you agreed to drive all the way into Houston or attend an event?" Samantha sipped her soda, waiting for an answer.

Gabby stayed silent, as if thinking for a moment, and then pointed out the door to a hallway with sagging walls on one side and half-restored shiplap on the other side. "It was weird. But to be honest, I've always enjoy touring historic homes, and frankly, as you can see, I need the money."

Samantha looked at the half-completed project and silently agreed. She changed topics again. "Weren't you afraid you would run into Mark?"

"That's why I called him. We arranged for me to go straight to the Reilley house while he and Darcy would go on the entire tour. They planned to arrive a few hours after I left."

"How did that conversation go?"

Gabby sighed. "About as well as every conversation with Mark those days. I got angry, he got angry, then we said what we needed to say and got off as quickly as we could."

Samantha shifted in her seat, unsure how to ask the next question.

"How about Darcy? I'm guessing you don't get along very well. Do you have any contact?"

"No way. I'm sure you read the stories about my arrest for harassment. Not my finest hour, I'll admit. But her stealing my husband pissed me off. She's vindictive. She even filed a restraining order against me. Fortunately, since they moved to Houston, it's not much of a problem."

"Is there any chance she's behind this?"

Gabby nodded her head. "I want to say no. She was my best friend once, but part of me thinks it's possible. All those stories about my arrest made her sound like such an innocent victim. Trust me, she's no angel. Darcy has a terrible temper."

Samantha kept quiet, wanting to hear more. She wondered if Gabby's suspicions were based on jealousy or whether she could come up with anything resembling a motive.

"I tried to warn Mark about her, but he never listened. Darcy wanted two things—fame and money. When she learned about our TV deal, she couldn't control her jealousy. It didn't take long before she cast Mark as her ticket to both fame and fortune."

"If that were true, why would she kill him?"

Gabby slumped her shoulders. "That's the part I haven't figured out yet."

Samantha wasn't convinced, but she wasn't ready to cross Darcy off the suspect list either. You never knew what happened behind people's closed doors. Though she couldn't conceive of a reason for Darcy to want Mark dead, that didn't mean one didn't exist. For now, she let it go.

She described her morning chat with Vivian Caulfield and explained that the woman likely hadn't sent the emails since she'd claimed to have been out of town on a cruise when they were sent. "It's strange. Whoever sent those emails knew Vivian wouldn't be there. Who could it have been? These emails may be our best chance to figure out who wanted you at the home tour. Has your daughter asked her friend about them?"

"In all the craziness, I haven't asked. Actually, they're both upstairs now."

Samantha followed Gabby from the well-decorated parlor into the hallway. They climbed stairs made of finished and unfinished pine planks and down another hall to a door in the corner.

Gabby knocked quickly and, with a mother's prerogative, walked in before anyone responded. Inside the sizable room two teens were splayed out on a queen-sized bed, flipping through anime magazines.

"Chloe, Becca, this is Samantha." Gabby bent low to pick up some clothes strewn across the redone hardwood floors. She folded a shirt and a pair of shorts and set them on a chest of drawers.

The two girls sat on the bed and stared at Samantha. "Why are you here?" the brunette, Chloe, said, sneering at her.

"Hey—cut the attitude. She's actually here to help us." Gabby shifted to her mom voice, which caught her daughter's attention.

"Sorry." Chloe sounded mildly contrite as she rolled her eyes.

"We've come to ask for your help." Samantha hoped to ingratiate herself with the teens by showing she took them seriously. "Becca, I heard you know about computers."

A pink tinge brightened the girl's pale face. "I know a bit."

"We need to figure out who sent Gabby some emails. Can you help us?"

The girl stood, and her voice grew authoritative. "It's next to impossible for anyone but a cop to pinpoint a sender's location. You can find out some things, though. Here, show me the emails."

Gabby turned on the laptop on Chloe's desk and handed it to her daughter. "Can you type in your password?"

Chloe tapped at the keyboard, and the computer came to life. Gabby pulled up her Gmail account and then the two emails. "Here they are."

Becca clicked a few buttons and shook her head. "Nope, sorry. We're out of luck. These emails came from a Google account, and they strip out the IP address. It's next to impossible to track someone from a Gmail email."

Oblivious to the mechanics of computers and networks, Samantha had assumed your average teenage hacker could help solve the puzzle. "Isn't there anything we can do?"

Becca appeared to enjoy her role as expert in the room, and she went into lecture mode. "What we need to track someone is their IP address. It's a unique number assigned to your computer or other device on whatever network you are using. You can't usually get them from an email. If, for instance, someone visited your website, you could view the IP address."

Samantha grew excited. "Wait. The first email came through a form on your website, right, Gabby?"

"Yeah. Unfortunately, I have no clue how to access it."

Becca grinned. "Leave it to me. Pull it up, and I'll get to work."

The women looked on as Becca feverishly typed. It took around fifteen minutes, but Becca located a string of letters and numbers. "This is the address linked to the user who sent the message. Now we copy and paste it into an IP address search page."

She pressed a few more buttons. The results showed who the internet service provider belonged to—in this case, AT&T—as well as latitude and longitude coordinates. Samantha could hardly believe the ease with which the computer spit out information.

"Is this where the sender lives?"

"No, not exactly. The ISP only shows the general area where the network lives. If you were police, this is the point at which you would seek a warrant, and the provider would have to reveal the name of whoever owned that unique address."

"We're not police, so what do we do?"

Becca frowned. "It's pretty limited."

"Well, I guess this is better than nothing." Samantha wasn't entirely sure how much the information could help, but she didn't want to hurt the girl's feelings after all her work. "It gives a general area and a zip code. At least we know the person who sent it lives in the Highlands. And we also know it didn't come from Riverside Terrace." She tried to point out the bright spot of an otherwise gloomy situation.

"We can always give these to the police to show them why you went to the house tour." Chloe grabbed hold of her mom's hand. "This should prove someone else wanted you there. That's some exculpatory evidence, right?"

Gabby looked surprised at her daughter. "Where did you learn that word?"

The girl grinned. "Old *Matlock* episodes."

Gabby smoothed her daughter's hair. "Well, it's an excellent idea. If Becca is right, they have the power to find out where those emails came from. But I'm not sure it's enough to draw their attention away from me. It doesn't change the fact I attended the party. There is no way to prove I was gone by the time your dad arrived."

Chloe looked at the ground. The mention of her father seemed to deflate her.

Becca, who had been quietly sitting at the desk, piped up. "When I said your options were limited, I didn't mean you couldn't do anything. There is a long shot."

Gabby's raised her head to study Becca. "What is it? We'll take a long shot over nothing."

"Well, I can build a simple IP logging link. If we can get whoever you suspect to click on the link, it will record their IP address and you could compare it. If it's the same, then you've probably got your guy, or at least the computer and network your guy used."

"Interesting." Samantha's brain worked in overdrive. "Who is the most likely person to have sent the emails? I know I've got two people in mind—Darcy and Brian Decker. First, we need their email addresses, and then we need to figure out what kind of link would attract them enough to get them to click on it."

Chloe looked at the ground again and mumbled, "I have Darcy's email."

Gabby pivoted toward her daughter. "What? Why would you have an email from her?"

"Don't get mad, Mom, please. She sent me an email about four months ago."

Gabby held her breath, appearing to wait to hear more.

"Don't even read the email, Mom. Please? Becca can send her a link or whatever, and we can find out if she's a match. Okay?"

Gabby pursed her lips for a moment, and she spoke in a controlled manner. "Chloe, I'm not mad at you, but I want to read what she wrote to you."

"I knew you'd be like this, Mom. That's why I didn't show you." Chloe grabbed the laptop. After a few minutes, she shoved the laptop at her mother and stormed out of the room.

Becca looked around awkwardly for a moment before she followed her friend. Gabby didn't seem to notice as she read the email aloud.

Dear Chloe,

I'm writing this because your father is too proud to do it. He misses you and wishes he could see you more often. Please consider our offer to have you visit our house here in Houston over a weekend sometime soon.

Best wishes,

Darcy

Gabby almost threw the laptop onto the bed. "The nerve of her, writing to my child. She had no right!"

Samantha, who had been sitting on the bed, trying to be as unobtrusive as possible, leaned over to touch Gabby on the shoulder.

Gabby flinched. "What is it?"

"I'm not the right person to advise anyone on relationships, but I think maybe you should go find Chloe and talk to her . . ."

Gabby sighed. "You're right. I'll go find her."

"Good, and when you find her, send Becca back up here to me."

Gabby nodded and walked after her daughter.

Samantha copied the email address onto a sheet of paper on the desk. After a few minutes, Becca reentered the room. "Man, that was a little awkward."

"I know. Divorce sucks. Add in all the rest of this horrible situation, and I don't know how everyone is half as calm as they are right now."

Becca sat at the computer and began to type. With a program running in the background, she turned around, locking gazes with Samantha.

"Chloe is close to her mom. She knows her mom didn't hurt her dad." The words conveyed an unspoken warning: *Don't you dare hurt this family any more than they've already been hurt.*

Samantha nodded. "Don't worry. I don't believe Gabby did it either. That's why it's important to find out who sent these emails. What kind of link do you think will work?"

Becca shook her head. "I don't know. It depends on their personality. Most people will click on a silly YouTube video, but only if they know the person who sent it. My advice is to find a topic these people would click on and send them a link they can't resist."

Samantha nodded. "I'll ponder it a bit. I can create a fake email account, but can you show me what I need to do next to create a link?"

Becca walked her through the process, from wrapping the IP logger around a typical link and then further camouflaging it using Bitly or some other link-shortening tool.

"This is fascinating." Samantha saw Becca blush. "I'm sure I'll forget all of this. Can I call you if I have any trouble? What's your number?"

"It's really easy once you get the hang of it." Becca wrote her number down and handed it to Samantha.

"Thanks for your help. You're a wonderful friend to Chloe."

Becca turned a deep crimson and closed the laptop. They headed downstairs to find Gabby and Chloe in the kitchen with an open package of Oreo cookies.

"We decided to take a snack break." Gabby held out the package to Samantha and Becca. "Want one?"

"I'll take mine for the road." Samantha plucked two from the package and grabbed her purse from the kitchen island. "Becca can fill you in on the details, but I'm heading home to Houston to think about what kind of honey to use to catch these flies."

Gabby walked her to the door. "Thanks, Samantha. I really appreciate your help . . . with everything."

"We're in this together now. I'll keep you posted if I find anything new, and you do the same."

Gabby hugged her.

It was late afternoon when Samantha left Gabby's house. On the way home, she puzzled through all she had learned.

Whoever had emailed Gabby lived near the Houston Highlands. That didn't rule out either Darcy or Brian Decker. Somehow she would have to devise a link so tempting both would click it. Since the IP address was unique to each device, she needed a link they would want to open on multiple devices.

She turned on the radio to clear her mind for a bit and watch the pelicans do their aerial dance as she listened to the Beach Boy's "Surfin' USA" on the oldies station. As Houston's skyline came into view about forty minutes later, she breathed a bit easier; she'd made it home in time to beat the traffic.

At home, she boiled spaghetti and paired it with jarred marinara. Though she usually enjoyed cooking, it wasn't much fun to cook for one person, so she did the bare minimum for sustenance. With the humidity outside thick enough to cut with a knife, Samantha shook up an Aperol Spritz to cool off. She sipped the drink, enjoying the fizz at the back of her throat, as she plotted her next move. It didn't take her long to realize she didn't have a next move. Everything she wanted to do depended on someone else.

Too revved up to read or go to sleep, Samantha walked into her kitchen to play around. Several projects were in the works, so she didn't want to start anything brand-new. Instead, she dried some citrus peels to have on hand to use in other bitters. She grabbed a lemon and an orange from her refrigerator and a vegetable peeler and began to peel long curlicues from both onto a parchment-paper-lined cookie sheet. She concentrated on filling the sheet with the zest, breathing in the clean citrus scent as she worked. After she filled the sheet, she placed it in the oven at two hundred degrees to let it dehydrate for around twenty minutes, stirring it periodically and breathing in the tang.

Her hands busy, Samantha felt her mind relax as she pushed away any thoughts unrelated to the task at hand. She was so focused she didn't even glance at the caller ID when the phone rang.

"Sam? Are you okay?"

That voice again. Her dopamine receptors hadn't yet gotten the memo that the voice on the other end of the phone wasn't worth the flush of pleasure that spread through her body when she heard it.

"Greg? I'm fine. What's going on?"

"It's just . . . you called the other night. I was still at the office, and by the time I looked at the caller ID, it was way past midnight. I didn't want to wake you. I've been swamped and only this moment had time to call you back."

She now remembered her distraught dialing on Monday night. Though she could no longer recall why she'd turned to him for comfort, she found herself annoyed that it had taken him more than a day to call her back.

"Oh yeah. Sorry. I had an awful day on Monday, and, well, some habits are harder to break than others. I know I need to stop it."

"No! I mean, I wish you wouldn't . . . stop. It brightened my day to hear your voice, but then I worried something was wrong. What happened?"

She should end the call, but a part of her wanted to hear his voice and know he wanted to hear hers too.

"Oh, ugh. Just work. The university pulled me from the magazine, at least until I sort this lawsuit out."

"No way. That's ridiculous."

"Well, it happened, and it feels crappy. You know, they talk about how they value your contributions, but then something out of your control happens and it's like you've got the plague. Whatever. It's a dumb job anyway."

"You're wasting your talents there."

"A steady paycheck is a steady paycheck. What else can I do?"

"It's a big world out there, Sam. You can go anywhere. Like New York, for instance. There are a million jobs for a smart reporter like you."

"Oh, Greg, maybe in a different lifetime."

"I mean it, Sam. There's nothing to stop you. It doesn't have to be about me. You should do it for you."

"Do it for me? I don't even know what I want anymore, other than to be free of this case."

"Please consider it. I wish I'd asked you before I left."

"Me too."

As she ended the call, she allowed herself to wonder what it would be like to escape all of this and find a new life. However, for the first time in a long while, she wanted to complete something. She wanted to solve this case.

The answer had to be in those emails.

Chapter Thirteen

Exhausted from her long day, Samantha slept in a bit and woke refreshed and ready to turn her attention to the problem of how to get the IP addresses for Brian Decker and Darcy. She focused on Brian first because he seemed the most likely suspect. But first, she had to find his email address.

Fortunately, most public records these days were online, and she knew she could likely find his email address on the application he'd filed seeking a waiver from the Historical Commission to build a new garage. The permit applications were searchable by home address, so Samantha made quick work of finding his email address.

With that in hand, she could imagine at least one topic likely to push his buttons enough to, well, get him to push a button. She drafted an email pretending to be a concerned neighbor forming an organizing committee that would lobby to end the permitting power of the Highlands Historic Commission. The email ended with the mission statement *Property rights for property owners*. Samantha also included a survey that asked residents to vote on whether they supported the dissolution of the committee and warned that organizers would track IP addresses and count only unique IP addresses. Nothing like a little reverse psychology to encourage Brian to vote using as many IP addresses as possible.

For Darcy, she tried a real estate gambit and sent her a request to review a home for potential listing, complete with a dozen photos to click. Samantha sized the photos to be huge and difficult to view on a mobile phone, hoping it would encourage Darcy to open the email on her computer as well. She sent the emails off and hoped for the best.

Four hours later, she had her first hit. Darcy emailed, requesting to set up an appointment for a walk-through of the home.

Samantha sent a note asking Becca to compare the IP address associated with Darcy's response to the one on Gabby's website.

With Darcy fresh on her mind, Samantha decided it wouldn't hurt to learn more about her. She pulled out the flyer from the Highlands home that she'd grabbed on her walk the other day. The home was listed at $890,000—not exactly the type of listing a new-to-town real estate agent could stumble into on her own. Samantha's reporter senses tingled. Darcy had a handful of reviews on Yelp between three and four stars, but hardly enough to engender the confidence one would need to entrust her with the sale of a nearly million-dollar home. Samantha decided it wouldn't hurt to ask the home's owner how she had selected Darcy.

She walked back to the house where she had picked up the flyer. On a Thursday morning, it seemed unlikely she would find the owners at home, but she decided to try anyway. On the path to the door, she noticed two giant oleander bushes in the front garden. *Geez—these things are everywhere.*

She rang the doorbell and raised her eyebrows when a middle-aged woman answered the door.

"I'm sorry. We're not doing any showings." The woman started to close the door.

"Wait. I wanted to ask you a question about your agent . . ."

"Darcy?" The woman cocked her head in curiosity.

"Yeah . . . sorry. My name's Samantha. I live a few streets over." She offered her hand to the woman, who shook it.

"I'm Sarah." The woman gave a questioning smile.

Samantha smiled back in an effort to charm the woman, who looked a little antsy, into sharing a few more minutes of her time. "I'm on the hunt for a good agent who knows the neighborhood. When I passed by your home the other day and saw the flyer, well—I wanted to ask what you think of your agent. It's hard to find a good realtor these days."

Sarah nodded. "I know what you mean. We went through a few agents before we latched on to Darcy. Honestly, she's had some personal trouble in the last few weeks. Before that she seemed okay. Our contractor, Bob Randall, recommended her."

"Oh?" Samantha hadn't expected Bob's name to come up, but this was smack in the middle of the neighborhoods where he did most of his work.

"He's one of the best in the city for historical renovation. We love this home but want a pool, and the lot here isn't big enough. We're working with Bob on another home over on Harvard. Anyway, he recommended Darcy as new but up-and-coming." Sarah's voice fell by a few decibels. "He even mentioned she might be getting a new show on HRN."

"No way!" Stunned, Samantha had no trouble conveying her surprise.

"It's supposed to be hush-hush for now, but he said she was close to finalizing a deal. The show will be about historic home renovation in a city known for demolishing historic buildings. Anyway, I love all of those home shows. I thought it would be fun to say my realtor starred in one. Since we already know Bob is one of the best, we figured anyone he recommended would have to be good."

Samantha's nerves twitched like they did when a key detail came into place for a story. She cut the conversation short. "That's awesome. Best of luck with your projects, Sarah! Thanks for the recommendation." She turned to walk back toward the sidewalk.

"Good luck to you too." Sarah closed the door.

Once out of sight of the house, Samantha practically ran to her apartment. She needed to call Gabby and get her read on this fresh information.

"Can you believe it? Darcy is about to sign a contract on a show with HRN?" Samantha paced in her living room as she spoke to Gabby.

"She wanted a chance at stardom more than anything else. I could murder her!"

Samantha understood what Gabby meant, but the words sounded ominous. She ignored the homicidal reference and forged ahead. "Wouldn't that put Darcy in the clear? If Mark promised her a television role, why would she want him dead?"

Gabby huffed. "Listen, I'm sure Mark strung her along with the promise of appearing in that show, but he had no intention of doing it. He was dead set against any show once he learned the producers wanted to play up the angle of him following in his father's footsteps."

"What do you mean?"

"I don't know what his concerns were, but he told me he didn't want any cameras digging into his father's background and sullying his reputation. I know Mark well enough to know when he's serious. He wouldn't explain his concerns, but he made it clear he would never appear on camera."

Samantha stopped pacing. "You think Darcy killed him because he kept her from her chance at fame?"

"I wouldn't put it past her." Gabby's voice was full of vinegar.

Samantha opted to continue with her questions. "Any chance you could contact the producers and ask what the deal is? I'm not sure how it all fits in, but it's a loose end and it could be important."

"I got along with one female producer pretty well. I'll try to reach her."

"Great. I'll go back to Bob to ask what he knows about it. It's interesting that he recommended Darcy to his clients. He can't have known her very well."

"Don't underestimate Darcy's ability to charm pretty much anyone into doing what she wants—especially if it's a man."

The women hung up after agreeing to check back in when either of them uncovered any additional information.

Samantha decided to grab a quick sandwich and call Bob again to ask him about Darcy and the HRN show. During their last call, she'd left it that he would give her number to Darcy and ask if she would talk to Samantha. Since Samantha hadn't heard from Darcy, she figured either Darcy didn't want to talk or Bob hadn't given her the message yet. She had just talked to Bob the day before, but she figured she could get away with calling him back on the premise of filling him in on her suspicions about Brian Decker.

She dialed the number and left a message on his voice mail. "Hi, Mr. Randall. Sorry to bother you, but this is Samantha Warren again. I've got some fresh information I wanted to run by you about the man who confronted Mark at the Historic Commission meeting. I think he might be involved in Mark's death. Please call me when you have a free minute."

She hoped it would intrigue him enough that he would call her back. Within an hour, her phone rang.

"Hello, Samantha. Bob Randall here. I'm interested to hear about this new information you have and whether it might bear on the lawsuit against the commission. I've got some time this afternoon; why don't you come by now?"

She agreed, even as her muscles twitched with nerves. She decided the nerves were a sign that she could be on the verge of a big break in the case. Maybe Bob would have more information for her.

She arrived at Bob's office at three PM. The door opened easily, but no receptionist greeted her. Still, a bell signaled her arrival, and Bob came to the front office to greet her.

"Ms. Warren, please come in." He ushered her back to the wingback chairs in his office and sat in his desk chair across from her. "Would you care for some coffee or tea?"

"No thanks, I'm good. Thank you for meeting me."

"Certainly. Since we're in the same boat, so to speak, as part of this lawsuit, it seems useful to share information."

"I agree. As I told you, I've got some new information about Brian Decker. He's the one who argued with Mark at the commission meeting. He attended the home tour that night." She told him about finding Brian on the security video, arriving at the Reilley house shortly after Mark and Darcy.

"Do you think he did it?"

"It's a possibility. Otherwise, why would he have gone to the event, given his run-in with the commission?"

Bob shrugged. "It's a good point. But lots of people enjoy our event, even if they don't support the commission. Anyway, have you mentioned your suspicions to the police?"

"I did, but I'm not sure they'll take it too seriously. That's why I wanted to meet with you. Do you remember anything more about Mark's confrontation with Decker at the Historic Commission meeting? Or did you notice anything the night of the party? Do you even remember seeing Decker there?"

Silent for a moment, Bob appeared to contemplate his answer. "It was a nasty argument. If I recall, it even made the newspapers. The man left, raging about the commission's decision, claiming he would sue us all. Apparently he hadn't read his deed when he bought the house. Either that or he thought he could convince us to give him a variance. People like him always think they can get their way if they have enough money to spread around."

Samantha knew what Bob meant. She could think of plenty of people who, once they'd reached a certain wealth threshold, had developed similarly entitled attitudes. "Why did he focus on Mark?"

"When the man started shouting, Mark escorted him out. It probably embarrassed him when Mark dragged him out of the meeting, and he took his frustrations out on Mark."

"What about at the home tour? Did you notice Decker there? Spot anything strange?"

"I'm afraid I didn't. I'm not sure I would have even recognized him if I had seen him."

So far, Bob had provided no new information.

Samantha took a different tack. "How about Darcy? Did you have any luck speaking to her? I'd love to show her Decker's picture, find out if she remembers him talking to Mark or coming close to him."

Bob's lips pressed into a thin line. "I spoke with Darcy. Unfortunately, she's not doing well. She's much too upset still to talk to anyone else about Mark. If you leave a picture, I can try to show it to her, see if she remembers anything."

Ugh. I'll never learn anything from Darcy if Bob keeps playing go-between. "Oh, that reminds me. I hadn't realized you and Darcy were such good friends."

Bob looked puzzled. "What do you mean?"

Samantha wondered if Darcy had worked her magic on Bob, as Gabby suggested. "I ran into one of my neighbors. She said you recommended Darcy to her as a real estate agent. The house didn't seem like the typical listing for a junior agent. It was nice of you to recommend her. I figured if you were willing to stake your reputation on her, you must be good friends."

Bob shook the implied question off. "Mark asked me to help her out. I did it as a favor for a fellow commission member."

"Oh. The neighbor also said you told her Darcy might have a role in an upcoming television show?"

Bob leaned back. "Mark mentioned the show, and I thought my client would find it amusing to work with a potential celebrity."

Makes sense. It hadn't taken Sarah more than three minutes to mention the show to Samantha. She could imagine the mileage she'd probably earned from sharing the gossip with her girlfriends.

"Remind me again, how did Mark end up on the commission?"

"We had a sudden vacancy, and I recommended him. We'd known each other years earlier. We worked together on a few projects when he worked with his dad. He had won some historic preservation awards in Galveston and more than met the qualifications. When I learned he had moved back to Houston, he seemed like the perfect fit."

"Nice of you to help him out. You seem to have done Mark quite a few favors. I hope he treated you half as well." Samantha laughed.

Bob chuckled. "I'm not sure the commission members would agree it's such a favor to be on the commission—it's a lot of work. As in the case of Mr. Decker, sometimes it puts you crossways with the community."

"It's also good for publicity and name recognition among a pool of potential customers, right?"

Bob frowned. "Most of the commission members serve to give back to their community and to protect these precious historic resources, which the rest of the city is so often ready to raze."

He sounded earnest, and Samantha didn't want to press him further. She decided to end the conversation on a positive note. "Well, I for one appreciate the work you and the rest of the commission do. Thanks for chatting and let me know if you hear anything from Darcy."

Bob stood and stuck his hand out to shake. "Certainly. Please, I hope you will do likewise."

Samantha walked back into the late-afternoon sunshine.

*   *   *

Back at home, Samantha continued to mull over her conversation with Bob. His answers about Darcy made some sense. She supposed it wasn't unusual to do another commission member a favor. However, the speed at which Mark had ingratiated himself enough to be worthy of so many favors seemed astounding. He'd been in Houston only eight months. Of course, Mark and Bob had known each other in a past life, which could explain the ease with which he'd pushed his way into the Highlands community.

Samantha had started to heat some soup when her cell phone vibrated from within her purse. She'd forgotten to turn on the ringer after her conversation with Bob. She had a voice mail message from David. She pressed the button to listen, wondering if there was a new development in the case against Gabby.

"Hey, Sam, it's David. Listen, this may sound strange, but I've got a gallery opening at the Blue Eye tonight in Montrose. Anyway . . . you've had a lot on your mind lately, I thought maybe you could use a little distraction. It starts at eight PM. I hope you can make it."

Samantha inhaled sharply. *Is this a date? No, he's just being nice and friendly . . . or is he?*

Her heart pounded a little at the prospect of a date with someone other than Greg. In the grand scheme of a four-year relationship, they hadn't been broken up for long, and if she was honest with herself, there were still plenty of unresolved emotions there. On the one hand, an outing with David sounded potentially awkward, but on the other hand . . .

A part of her that hadn't been engaged in quite some time enjoyed the brief tingle of possibility.

Am I overthinking this? I'm sure he wouldn't consider this a date. He feels sorry for me.

Samantha had half convinced herself not to go when she noticed the newspaper she'd left on her kitchen table this morning. Curious, she flipped to the entertainment section and found the gallery opening listed on today's calendar.

The blurb said the opening would feature some of David's earlier works and some of his latest.

I like his artwork. There's no reason I shouldn't go. I'll do it.

She ate her soup and dug around in her closet for an outfit that could fit both the date and casual-outing scenarios. She decided on a green sundress with scalloped lace and pockets and, for good measure, added a gold wrap and gold sandals. After applying makeup and brushing her hair, she decided she looked good enough. She patted Ruby, asleep on the sofa, for good luck and headed outside.

When she arrived, the gallery already teemed with people. She grabbed a glass of wine and wandered through the rooms. Though the style and technique were the same, each painting looked different from the last. She enjoyed eavesdropping on others as they told their companions what they noticed in the artwork. Where one pictured a dog with a cane, another saw a man playing an upright bass. The colors bled and shimmered across the canvases. Her favorite was a deep-purple panel with metallic golden flecks and turquoise undertones. It looked to her like sunset on a Mediterranean beach.

"Samantha!"

She heard David's voice and turned to see him.

"You came!"

Her pulse raced, and heat rose up her throat. "I . . . it sounded fun. Thanks for the invitation."

"I'm glad you made it. It's always nice to spot a friendly face in the crowd. You'd think it would get easier, but I'm always a little nervous when a show first opens."

She grinned. "Well, you have no reason to be nervous." She lowered her voice. "I've been eavesdropping, and the verdict seems to be that you're supremely talented."

He laughed a deep, mellifluous laugh. "That's nice to hear. When I eavesdrop, I usually hear people claim to see a ballerina or a seagull eating a Cheeto or something equally silly."

"To be fair, I heard a bit of that too." Samantha laughed with him, enjoying what felt like her first authentic human connection in a while.

"Listen, this will close in about twenty minutes. A small group of us plan to head to Boheme for some drinks. Will you join us?"

Samantha took a step backward. "Oh, no. Thank you, but I don't want to intrude on your night."

"Nonsense. I'd love for you to come. It's down the street, so we don't even have to drive."

Samantha had enjoyed her evening and didn't want it to end yet. "Okay, sure. I'll stop by for a little while."

"Great. We can walk over together. Now, if you'll pardon me, I have to glad-hand a few more patrons here."

"Of course." She smiled and walked into the last room, where some of his earliest works were on display. She studied those early paintings, noting how his style had evolved over the years. He had learned to refine some raw energy clear in these earlier paintings to achieve a more multitonal, multilayered effect. She continued to wander as most of the crowd filtered out, leaving only a handful of his friends.

David introduced her as a friend to a group of four others, including David's agent and a few longtime law school buddies—two men and two women. The group set off to walk the three blocks to Boheme, an eclectic bar housed in a refurbished old lighting shop from the 1920s. An immense outdoor patio, routinely rated one of the best in the city, surrounded the building.

The group grabbed a table on the patio and ordered a first round of drinks. Samantha opted for a gin drink called Flower Power and ordered the Argentinian beef empanadas for a snack.

The drink came out first. She sipped, finding it refreshing, with the right hint of lime to cut the sweetness of the floral jasmine flavor. Next, the empanadas came out, steaming and plated with a bright-green chimichurri sauce. She dug in and listened while David's friends laughed and joked about their shared histories. The friends were companionable and made every effort to include her in the conversation. She enjoyed their playful banter with David, which allowed her to perceive a different side of him.

As the stories turned to law school, Samantha excused herself and walked inside to explore the historic building. Antique chandeliers cast shadows on the original brick walls while fairy lights from the patio created a charming glow from outside the steel frame windows. Samantha grabbed a stool at the antique bar and looked at the menu.

"Can I help you?" A bartender wiped the counter in front of her.

"Sure. What do you recommend?"

He seemed to size her up. "Well, my favorite is the Spanish Gin and Tonic, but some people find it too bitter."

She could infer by his sneer what he thought of those people.

"Oh, I love bitter. I'll try it. Thanks." Samantha waited for the drink, enjoying the quieter ambience inside the bar, which offered respite from the raucous laughter outside.

The bartender served the drink over ice, garnished with cucumbers and a grapefruit peel. Samantha took a sip and let the flavors settle on her tongue for a moment.

The bartender came by and noticed her expression. "Too bitter for you?"

"No, on the contrary, it's perfect—hits all the right notes. It has me thinking of how a unique flavor combination might work with this gin."

"You a bartender too?"

"More a hobbyist. I make my own bitters. This drink has given me inspiration for a pineapple bitters . . . maybe mixed with sage."

The bartender looked intrigued. "That sounds good, actually. Do you sell the stuff?"

"Only occasionally." Samantha hoped the bartender didn't ask any more questions. She hoped to avoid any discussion of the disastrous home tour.

"Well, if you ever make those pineapple bitters, I'd be happy to try them. I'm always on the hunt for different flavor profiles for my drinks. I'm Dane, by the way." He stretched out his hand for Samantha to shake.

Samantha took his hand and gave it a warm squeeze. "I'll keep that in mind. Thanks, Dane." She paid her tab, leaving a sizable tip for the bartender as she considered his offer. It was exiting to think that someone else might be interested in her bitters. She turned to peer out the window to check on David's group but found David standing behind her.

"There you are. I wondered where you had gotten off to. My friends called it a night, but I'm still basking in the glow of a successful gallery show. Care to keep me company while I have one more drink?"

"Sure." She carried her drink and followed him.

He led her to one of the velvet sofas in the corner. "It's quieter here, so we can talk. Wait here."

He came back from the bar with a Negroni, another bitter drink.

Samantha clinked glasses with him. "Cheers to a successful gallery show."

He smiled. "Thanks again for coming out. I enjoyed seeing you there . . . and it's nice to see you here too."

Samantha couldn't identify the vibe from David. *Is he interested?*

She had enjoyed meeting his friends and seeing him in his element at the gallery opening. Still, she didn't know what she wanted and decided to keep things light and breezy. "Your friends seem nice. It seems like you guys have shared a lot of laughs over the years."

"Oh yeah. They're old law school buddies. We've kept each other sane, and they've always supported my extracurricular hobby."

"Friends are great." *Friends are great? What in the heck am I saying?* Flustered, she took another sip of her drink to soothe her nerves. Fortunately, David didn't seem to notice her inane comment.

"It surprised me to get your note the other day about not wanting to proceed with the countersuit. It seems like a slam dunk with the victim's wife under arrest."

"We don't need to talk shop right now. This is your night."

"I'm interested. Obviously, it's your decision, but I'm curious what made you change your mind. You seemed ready earlier this week."

"I don't believe Gabby is guilty."

She told him about her activity over the last few days, leaving out only the plan to get the IP addresses for Darcy and Brian Decker. While David's artistic side might applaud the creativity, she wasn't sure his lawyerly side would condone her methods.

David looked thoughtful. "Hmm . . . you have some interesting points. I admire you for trying to find out what happened. It would satisfy most people to have someone else in jail, never mind if they were guilty. However, I have to advise you to leave it to the professionals. I'm happy to pass along the information you've given me now, but please don't get mixed up any further. I don't want anything to happen to you."

Samantha's face warmed. *Is he truly concerned? Or is he flirting?*

She changed the subject, nervously chattering about her latest freelance assignment for a few more minutes before declaring she needed to call it a night.

She touched his arm lightly. "Thanks again for a pleasant time." She walked out of the bar and into the night. The slight breeze helped to cut through the oppressive heat and cool her cheeks, which warmed again as she mused about David. So far, he hadn't crossed any lines. He'd been perfectly professional, but Samantha couldn't help but sense an undercurrent of attraction. They didn't have the typical attorney-client relationship. He was more of an old friend, doing her a favor. But she had to admit, he'd gone out of his way to help her out of this lawsuit bind. *Does that mean he's attracted to me? If so, how do I feel about it?*

It was nearly midnight when she arrived back home. By the time she'd put the key in her lock, she practically floated. She'd enjoyed herself. Not to mention she had a fresh idea for some bitters on top of it all, and a professional bartender interested in tasting them. Was it possible she could actually make something of her hobby? Maybe with this mess behind her she really could start fresh, explore new opportunities and enjoy socializing solo. She allowed herself a moment to relive the spark, or whatever it was she'd experienced with David tonight. *Or maybe not solo.*

She smiled as she considered the possibilities.

Chapter Fourteen

In the morning, Samantha rode her bike to the farmers' market, where she bought a pineapple and some fresh sage. Back in her kitchen, she chopped both and left them to infuse for a few hours in a mixture of rums. After adding a handful of additional ingredients, she'd let the mixture sit for a few weeks. If it worked as she planned, it would be a nice pineapple spice bitters, and she might even take some back to Dane, the bartender at Boheme, to ask his opinion of them.

With her exercise and kitchen work done, she sat at her desk to start a few short freelance assignments. She completed an interview for a profile of a cookie delivery company for the business journal and wrote more website content, this time for a new clothing designer who had launched her own line of dresses with pockets. As Samantha waxed poetic about the dresses in her text, she shrugged her shoulders. *At least it's a product I can support.*

She was stopping to stretch when her phone alerted her to an incoming email from Becca. The IP addresses from Darcy hadn't matched, but one from Brian Decker had.

"Are you kidding me?"

Samantha jumped out of the chair with the news as excitement flooded through her. This meant that Brian Decker, at a minimum, had arranged for Gabby to be at the party. She didn't want to jump to any premature conclusions, but in one scenario, that made him a potential murderer.

What should we do now?

Becca had emailed both Samantha and Gabby, so Gabby would know the news as soon as she checked her email. Before talking to her, Samantha wanted to have a good next step in mind to discuss.

David and Marisa would no doubt tell her to turn what she'd learned over to the police. The police would be in the best position to confirm it and to question Decker. The information would help Gabby corroborate her story and could also provide her lawyer with a suitable alternative suspect. The police wouldn't be too happy with their interfering in the investigation, though. Samantha doubted the email addresses would be admissible in court either. If they weren't, she and Gabby would have to rely on the police to use the information. As convinced as the police were of Gabby's guilt, would they even pursue this lead or, if they did, give it any priority?

A second option would be for Samantha and Gabby to confront Decker themselves. If he was a killer, it would be dangerous, but with the advantage of surprise, they might get more immediate results. Of course, none of it would matter unless he told them the truth, and what would be his incentive to reveal anything? They had some proof that Decker had sent Gabby emails—or at least someone with access to his computer had. While the emails provided some leverage, Samantha still couldn't imagine Decker coughing up evidence against himself. But if he was caught off guard, he might reveal something useful.

Undecided on the best course of action, Samantha called Gabby to talk it over. They ultimately decided to turn the information over to Gabby's lawyer, who would give it to the police. At the same time, they would plan a meeting with Decker for Monday in a public place, using the same Citizens for Property Rights scheme.

A local coffee shop near Decker's home, which had a good lunch crowd but didn't get much dinner business, seemed the best choice. They figured Decker would make himself available to discuss a proposal to eliminate the Historic Commission.

Having agreed on the plan, they said good-bye. Samantha sent Decker an email invitation.

After she hit send, Samantha immediately wondered if she'd made the right choice. What if Decker really had killed Mark and he figured out they were on to him? It seemed unlikely. *Still, it won't hurt to ask what Marisa and Beth think . . .*

One quick phone call later, Samantha had wrangled herself an invitation to Friday night dinner at Marisa and Beth's house—vegetarian lasagna with veggies fresh from Beth's garden. Samantha stopped by a store to grab a bottle of Pinot Noir and drove over.

Marisa greeted her at the door with a hug, and they headed to the kitchen to help with the last preparations.

"Tell us everything." Marisa popped open the bottle of wine. "What have you learned about Brian Decker?"

Samantha poured the wine into three glasses. She lifted her glass and swirled the wine to release some of its flavors. She took a sip as she filled her friends in on the latest details of the case.

"I can't believe he sent those emails to Gabby. The plot has certainly thickened." Beth took a sip of wine.

Marisa tilted her head as she looked at Samantha and paused for a moment. "Great work tracking down the information. I assume you turned it over to the police. There's no reason for you to get any further involved, right?"

Samantha kept her face neutral. She'd wanted input, but without hearing anything further, Marisa had already started lobbying for Samantha to stay out of it. Samantha didn't mention her arranged meeting with Decker and instead confirmed that she'd sent the information to the police. Her chest tightened as she deliberately misled her friend, but she ignored the sensation, not wanting to be persuaded by Marisa's protective instincts.

"Do you really think he's the killer?" Marisa set the table while Samantha dished out a salad.

"I don't know. It's still hard to believe someone could be angry enough about a garage expansion to kill, but what other reason would he have for luring Gabby to the party?"

Marisa shrugged. "Hopefully the police will figure it out. Do you have any other hot leads?"

Samantha sliced a loaf of French bread fresh from the oven, unsure how much more to share. All of a sudden she wasn't interested in another lecture about staying safe. "Not really. There's this story about Darcy having a role in one of those HRN shows, but so far, I'm not sure how a television show could be connected to murder."

Beth pulled the perfectly browned lasagna from the oven, and the three women sat at the table.

Samantha inhaled deeply. "This all smells wonderful. I promise, one of these days, I'll have you guys over and serve something more substantial than delivery pizza."

"The cocktails are always a treat at your place." Beth dug into the food in front of her.

The lasagna, filled with zucchini, bell peppers, tomatoes, and herbs, highlighted the bounty from Beth's garden. Samantha savored every bite. "This is delicious, Beth."

As they chatted, Samantha told them about her outing to David's gallery opening and the night at Boheme's. The friends discussed Samantha's attraction to David and debated whether or not the evening should be considered a date.

Marisa left no doubt as to her vote. "He called you and asked you to go to his show. That's the very definition of a date."

"We weren't really alone. A bunch of his friends were there too."

"Yeah, until he pulled you into a dark, cozy corner." Marisa's voice took on a teasing lilt.

"We only really talked about his art show and my case."

Beth agreed with Marisa but pressed Samantha on her reaction to David's interest. "How do you feel about it? Are you ready?"

"I don't know. It felt good to be socializing again, but it's hard to picture myself dating." Samantha rubbed her neck. The conversation hadn't given her any further insight into her emotional state, but it had been sort of fun to talk about it.

They all agreed she shouldn't rush into something with David.

The discussion reminded Samantha about her chat with Dane. "Oh, yeah. I got to talking to this bartender, and I might actually take some of my bitters over there for him to taste."

Marisa grabbed Samantha's arm. "Fantastic, Sam. Maybe he'll want to buy some. I've told you a thousand times, you should set up an Etsy shop."

Samantha grinned at the fantasy. "It's a fun idea, but I have a hard enough time trying to find new freelance work, much less start a side hustle."

Grabbing the last of the wine bottle and bowls of Tin Roof Sundae ice cream, the three women moved to the living room to get more comfortable.

Beth, sitting on the edge of the sofa next to Marisa, cleared her throat. "Speaking of side hustles, I took a few more steps toward that business venture we were talking about the other day."

Samantha perked up in her chair. "That's great! I've been dying to hear about it. What is it?"

Beth wrung her hands in her lap. "It starts with that lasagna. Did you really like it?" She looked up, briefly meeting Samantha's gaze.

Samantha eased back in her chair. "Of course! Everything you make is delicious, Beth. I've always thought so."

Beth exhaled. "Well, my idea is to combine my two loves, gardening and cooking. I want to start a catering company! I've rented some space at the kitchen incubator downtown, and I've already talked to some of the folks from the community garden I work with about growing extra vegetables for me in addition to what I grow here. I think there is a niche for farm-to-table catering in Houston, with dishes based off of what's in season. I've already gotten some positive responses when I've floated the idea around to different people."

Samantha grinned broadly. "That's amazing, Beth! I'm so excited for you. If anyone can make that idea work, you can."

They spent the rest of the night discussing the logistics of the business and Beth's plans for testing out recipes at a small luncheon party for her gardening club. By ten, Samantha was rising to go. She hated to leave the cozy room, but she could barely stay awake.

* * *

In the morning, hungry despite the previous night's feast, Samantha went to check out a new bagel shop in the Highlands. She'd been assigned to write a review for a local food blog and wanted to observe it during peak bagel time: Saturday morning. The line stretched around the corner, but the hot blueberry bagel and smear of almond cream cheese more than compensated for it as Samantha's taste buds tingled with the explosion of blueberry in every bite.

As she ate her bagel on the patio outside, Samantha noticed one of Bob's renovation signs on the lawn of the cute bungalow across the street. The sign reminded her that she wanted to follow up on Bob's comments about knowing Mark before he moved to Galveston.

When she got back to her apartment, Samantha gave Gabby a call to check in. She wanted to ask her more about Mark's previous work with his father. "Gabby, I have a question. You mentioned Mark's reluctance to have the HRN cameras dig into his past. Why? What concerned him?"

"I don't really know. It was strange, to be honest."

"Could it have related to the fight with his dad? What drove the wedge between the two of them?"

"You know, he never told me the details. It involved some hush-hush development deal. Mark refused to go along with his dad's plan, and eventually we moved to Galveston."

"Do you remember anything else about it?"

"Not really. I only remember Mark saying his dad hadn't learned anything from history. He worried his dad's new project would fail, like a similar development he'd worked on twenty or thirty years earlier, before Mark's time. It had some silly name like Lisa or Melissa or—I don't know, some name popular in the eighties. One of Mark's father's partners wanted to name it after his daughter. I don't honestly know what went wrong with that project either, only that it lost a ton of money."

"Hmm. Okay. What about Bob Randall? Did you guys know him when you lived in Houston?"

Gabby answered instantly. "Before the home tour, I'd never heard of him in my life."

Strange, but maybe not so strange, since it didn't seem like Gabby had paid much attention to Mark's business.

"Did Mark and his dad ever reconcile?"

"They did about five years ago. Fred learned he had cancer and wanted to reconnect. They spent a few good years together before he passed away."

"That's good, at least."

"Yeah. Chloe appreciated having some time with her grandfather. Oh, I meant to tell you earlier. I heard from the producer I mentioned. She's supposed to call me this afternoon to give me the story on the HRN show."

"Great! There are so many little details to all of this that don't fit together yet. Maybe she'll help fill in some blanks."

They ended the call with Gabby promising to keep Samantha informed of any developments.

Samantha sat outside for a while and read a book, then came back into the apartment to work through some recipes. The lunch hour passed without her noticing, as she was still full from her morning bagel, but by midafternoon she was experiencing a few hunger pangs. It had grown hot and sticky, and her window units were not up to the task of cooling her off. The heat and humidity lay over the city like a wet blanket. In the old days, Samantha would have walked with Greg to the neighborhood stand for raspas.

She considered for a few moments before grabbing her purse. *I'll go anyway.*

Samantha walked outside and down the block to the little stand. She stood in line behind a group of kids and ordered a mangonada—basically a souped-up mango snow cone topped with chamoy, a sour-sweet syrup made from fruit and chilies. The combination was spicy, sour, and sweet, all at the same time. She sat at a small outdoor table and watched the kids play at the park across the street.

She finished half the drink, which left her slightly cooler but now too full to contemplate dinner. The trip had made her nostalgic, but she had successfully reclaimed as a solitary joy something she'd previously associated only with Greg.

Is this what it feels like to move on, to make room for someone else? Maybe someone like David?

She'd thought about David a lot since the night at the gallery—not only his attractiveness but his thoughtfulness. He didn't have to help her. But Greg was still ingrained in her everyday random thoughts. How could she close the door on four years of her life?

She wondered if there was a way she might not have to—maybe she and Greg could be friends. Maybe if she could get to the point where she could talk to him without all the old emotions rushing back, she could truly move on.

Curious to test her theory, she dialed Greg's number before she could talk herself out of it.

Can I have a normal conversation with him? Even a friendly one?

After a few rings, she got Greg's voice mail and left a message. "Hey, Greg, it's Sam. It's nothing important. It's just . . . I picked up a mangonada today. I swear, we must have eaten a million of them last summer. Anyway, it reminded me of you, and I wanted to say I hope you're doing well."

Could have been a little smoother with the delivery, but overall, it was nice and casual.

She congratulated herself on her progress in moving on from Greg and began to walk home.

On the way, Gabby called to fill her in on her conversation with her producer friend. "Apparently, once Mark refused the island show, the producers came back with another proposal for him. Someone at the network wanted to do a show about Houston."

"The show my neighbor mentioned!" Samantha's pulse raced. Pieces of the puzzle were beginning to fit into place, but there weren't enough of them.

"Yeah. Texas is always a hot spot for renovation shows, but they usually focus on smaller towns. Someone at the network pitched a show about historic preservation in Houston, juxtaposed with its reputation for demolishing anything in the name of progress."

Samantha nodded her head in agreement. "Sadly, it's true."

"Anyway, they wanted to cast Mark as the hero who would restore the city's history one historic home at a time . . . with a cute partner by his side."

"I'd bet dollars to doughnuts I know who the cute partner is." Samantha pressed her lips into a tight line, furious on Gabby's behalf.

"Exactly. Darcy, the small-town beauty queen turned big-city realtor, would help couples pick their perfect historic home, and then, once they'd decided, Mark would swoop in and 'make history feel like home.'"

Samantha chuckled.

"No, seriously. That's what they planned to call it—*Making History Feel Like Home.*"

"Wow. It's a little cheeseball, but I could see people watching it. Heck, I'd watch it." Samantha had reached her apartment again and nearly finished her mangonada. "So, were they moving forward with it?"

"Apparently Mark would never commit. All the producers flew to Houston to convince him, promising the show would be a ratings bonanza and would give him leads on more work than he would know what to do with. They met with him, and Darcy added more pressure, telling Mark the show could be her one big chance and he owed it to her. He became enraged and told the whole room he wouldn't do it." Gabby's voice demonstrated a hint of pride, despite her strained history with her dead husband. "My producer friend said Darcy threw a fit. She cursed Mark for ruining her life."

"Sounds a little awkward." Samantha collapsed on her sofa, her ceiling fan spinning at top speed. She fanned herself with a piece of junk mail from her side table.

"Yeah, the producers couldn't leave the room fast enough. They were on their way out, having decided the happy couple didn't have the right chemistry for a show, when Darcy chased after them and promised she would get Mark to change his mind. If she couldn't, she told them she would find a suitable replacement, someone as knowledgeable about historic renovation as Mark."

"Bold move by Darcy."

"Yeah, but it didn't work. The producers later decided it would be Mark or nobody. He was apparently the right mix of scruffy, sexy, and competent to endear himself to their mostly female audience," Gabby scoffed.

Samantha wasn't sure if Gabby's reaction was related to the producer's description of her husband or some mild glee that Darcy had gotten her comeuppance from Mark.

"What happened?"

"I don't know. It all happened two months ago. The network pulled my producer friend off the project a week later and sent her to work on a show about renovating cabins in the woods. She's been on location near the Great Lakes ever since and hasn't heard another word about it."

Samantha sat straight on her sofa and considered the news. "How mad would Darcy have been? How badly did she want to be on the show?"

"She would be spitting mad. Fame is all she ever wanted, and if Mark stood in her way, well, watch out, Mark! The only thing I can't figure is, how does Decker fit in?"

"Speaking of Decker, have you heard any news from your lawyer?"

"Not yet."

"All right, let me know if you hear something."

Samantha put down her phone and began to pace again as she questioned her earlier assumptions about Darcy. Samantha had seen people do plenty of crazy things in the name of ambition.

Now she wanted to talk to Darcy even more than before.

Chapter Fifteen

Samantha contemplated her next move. She wanted to ask Darcy about the television show and hear her side of the story.

Is it possible Darcy got angry about missing out on her big break and killed Mark?

In Samantha's experience, it didn't pay to ignore possibilities. Even if Darcy was innocent, she might have seen something. She had, naturally, stood closest to Mark at the home tour and would have been in the best position to see if someone acted suspicious or if anyone had access to his drink.

The question was how to reach her. Bob hadn't been a lot of help. She needed Darcy's cell phone number, but if Bob wouldn't give it to her, she didn't know how to find it short of running an expensive background check on Darcy.

Since phoning didn't appear to be an option, Samantha decided she'd have to try the last tool in her reporter's arsenal and appear on Darcy's doorstep. It would have to wait until tomorrow. She'd made it a rule to knock on doors only in broad daylight, given Texans' propensity to support the Second Amendment.

Her decision reached, she made a grilled cheese sandwich and settled down to write her review of the bagel shop. After a few hours of work, she emailed the piece to her editor and settled in to watch a little HRN before getting ready for bed.

Just as she finished brushing her teeth, her phone rang. *Greg.* She'd almost forgotten she'd called him earlier. "Hey, Greg, how are you?"

"Long day . . . but your message made me smile. We couldn't get enough of those mangonadas last summer, could we?" She detected a little flirtation in his voice and tried to keep the mood light.

"It tasted delicious, as always."

"I could go for a raspa right now. I'd make it raspberry lemon, a little sweet, a little tart, like most of my favorite things. Of course, I'd want a little taste of yours too. The best of both worlds! Maybe I should come back down some weekend. We can hit up our old hot spots."

Come back here? Samantha regretted her impulse to call Greg this afternoon. She recalled their last conversation, where he'd suggested she consider moving to New York. *Why did I call him?* She tried to end the conversation as quickly as possible.

"Ha! I'm sure you can find raspas in New York as good as the ones here. Anyway, it sounds like you're busy. I don't want to keep you. I just wanted to, you know, say I hope you're doing well."

His voice grew serious. "Have you thought any more about what we talked about before? I'm serious. I'd like to come down sometime soon. We could talk about New York."

"Oh, um . . . haven't really thought much about it. Still crazy around here with this lawsuit situation. It's hard to wrap my head around much right now. How are you? Sounds like they're keeping you busy." If she got him to talk about himself for a few minutes, it might diffuse the awkwardness.

"Yeah, it's about what I expected—twelve-hour days doing research at the firm and then, when I'm not sleeping, studying for the bar."

"Sounds rough. I'm sure you'll power through. You always do. Listen, it's late here, which means it's even later there. I should get to bed. Take care."

After an awkward pause, Greg responded. "Oh, sure. Good night."

"Night." She ended the call. It wasn't the most graceful conversational exit, but she gave herself credit for getting off the phone in record time.

She headed to bed in decent spirits. Despite the awkward conversation, the experiment had proved she was starting to get over Greg. The familiar pang of sadness after hanging up lessened with each encounter, and soon, she guessed, she wouldn't notice it at all. The trouble was, all of the sudden, he was sounding interested all over again. *But he'll be too busy to come down here anytime soon. I don't have to worry about it for now.*

*   *   *

The next morning, after finishing a phone interview for a business profile, Samantha checked her voice mail. Someone had called earlier, but she hadn't recognized the number.

"Hi, uh, this is . . . wait, wrong number."

The voice sounded familiar, but Samantha couldn't place it and deleted the message. She wrote her story and turned it in before planning out her trip to visit Darcy in the afternoon.

She'd always hated this part of a reporter's job—showing up unexpected at someone's doorstep, ready to ask them a series of personal questions. In this case, in addition to the awkwardness, it could be dangerous, given the possibility that Darcy was a murderer.

Darcy's town house stood in a long row of similar homes on the edge of what would acceptably be called the Highlands. Situated right on the border of the still-gentrifying community, the town house stood across the street from used car lots and a few other small businesses. Probably, if you climbed to the third-floor balcony of all of those townhomes and looked in the right direction, you could spot the Highlands proper, with its bungalows and beautiful oaks. The view from the garage-level stoops was nowhere near as inspiring.

Samantha walked to the door and pressed on the bell but heard nothing. She waited a few minutes and pressed again, still without response. Since she wasn't sure if the bell worked or not, she also knocked.

Samantha stood on the porch and waited a while before deciding that Darcy wasn't coming to the door, even if she was home. She walked back to her car and waited half an hour before she went through the whole process again. She tried one more time, hoping her persistence would pay off.

Finally, a neighbor out walking her dog stared at Samantha, brows furrowed, eyes squinting and trained on Samantha. "I don't think she's home."

Afraid the neighbor might call the police, Samantha wrote a note, asking Darcy to call her, and left it attached to a colorful wreath on the door. She drove home, irritated by her failed efforts and the wasted time.

Later that evening, as she strained some bitters in her kitchen, her cell phone rang with an unknown number. "Hello?"

"Is this Samantha?"

"Yeah, who's this?"

"It's Darcy. I got your message. Listen, I don't really want you coming back to my place. My neighbors said you were there for more than an hour today."

"Sorry if I caused any trouble. I wanted to reach you and didn't have your phone number. I wanted to ask you some questions about Mark and the home tour."

"I've already talked to the police."

"I know, it's just . . . for my sake. I don't know if you've heard, but Gabby sued me and the lawsuit is ruining my life right now. The more I can understand about what happened when Mark died, the more I can defend against it."

Darcy sighed. "I'm sorry. This isn't a good—"

Samantha sensed that Darcy was about to hang up. "It's okay if you don't want to talk to me now. My lawyer will subpoena you—drag you to court for a few days. To be honest, maybe that's better for me. He can be a bulldog with witnesses on the stand, and he'll be able to—"

"What do you want from me?" Darcy sounded weary.

Samantha pitied her but pressed on anyway. She needed to ask her some questions. "I want to talk. I've been investigating and discovered a few things I'm not sure the cops even know about yet. I wanted to run them by you."

"What kind of things?"

"Another potential suspect, someone who fought with Mark before he died. I only want to ask you some questions."

Darcy stayed silent for a beat. "Fine. I'll meet with you. How about right now, at your place?"

The request threw Samantha.

"Why my place? Why not a coffee shop or someplace like that?"

Darcy grunted. "Look, I'm not fit for public consumption right now. I can't be seen like this. It's your place or nowhere."

Samantha wasn't sure of the wisdom of having a potential murder suspect in her home, but she didn't want to miss the chance to talk to Darcy. She gave Darcy her address. "I'll see you soon."

After about twenty minutes, someone knocked at her door. Samantha opened it to find Darcy, less a beauty queen realtor and more a depressed widow, with deep circles under her eyes and strands of unwashed hair slipping from her ponytail. Her outfit, an old pair of yoga pants and a plain purple T-shirt, lacked the usual care of her typical couture attire. If Samantha hadn't already cast Darcy as a potential murderess, this grieving-girlfriend role might be convincing. For a moment, Samantha almost regretted dragging her out tonight.

Samantha ushered Darcy into her small apartment and offered her a seat on the sofa. "Can I get you anything? Tea or something harder?"

Darcy perked up at the suggestion. "I'd love a drink, actually. Anything, I don't care—as long as it burns going down."

Samantha walked into the kitchen to pour them each a drink. She kept it simple with an Old-Fashioned made with some of her cherry-vanilla bitters and orange bitters.

Darcy took a long sip. "This is good."

"Thanks. I appreciate you coming over. This must be a tough time for you."

Darcy took another long swallow. She looked as though she might cry, but she regained her composure. "What do you want to ask me?"

"Well, to start with, did you notice anyone at the home tour acting suspicious? Anyone strange talking with Mark or hanging around?"

Darcy shook her head. "No. I mean, he glad-handed everyone that night, you know, trying to attract future business."

"Nobody seeming to follow him?"

"I didn't notice if anybody did."

Samantha took a sip of her Old-Fashioned. "What about his drink? Who brought it to him?"

"Can I have another?" Darcy held out her glass. This time, she followed Samantha into the kitchen as Samantha made another batch.

"I got the drinks. I pulled them off a tray from one of those waiters."

"Did you notice the flowers?"

Darcy grabbed the glass from Samantha's hand and took a giant sip, shaking her head no. She sipped again before she walked back into the living room and sat down on the sofa.

Samantha offered her a coaster for the coffee table. "Did you both drink the same thing?"

"Yes. We prefer the brown stuff." Darcy raised her glass in a mock salute before taking another gulp. Suddenly, she pulled the glass away from her lips and her eyes grew wide. "Wait a minute. You're the one who made the drinks at the party, aren't you? How do I know you didn't doctor Mark's drink?"

She pushed her glass forward onto the coffee table, away from her. As she pulled back her arm, the backward momentum caused her to fall back against the sofa cushions.

"I didn't even know Mark. Why would I have wanted to hurt him?"

Darcy seemed to consider Samantha's words and nodded her head. She leaned forward and reached again for her glass.

Samantha decided she should get her questions out before Darcy got too sloshed to answer them. "Did you see Brian Decker?"

"Who's he?"

Samantha told the story of the confrontation at the Historic Commission meeting and explained how Decker had threatened Mark.

"He didn't mention anything about it. I never attend those meetings."

Samantha pulled up a photo of Decker on her phone and showed it to Darcy. "This is the guy. Did you spot him anywhere around you and Mark?"

Darcy studied the face for a few moments. "I'm sorry. It doesn't ring any bells. I told you I wouldn't be helpful."

"Can you recall anyone Mark fought with?"

Darcy finished the rest of her drink in one swallow and walked into the kitchen with her glass. Samantha watched as, without even asking, Darcy poured herself another hefty dose of bourbon and didn't even bother with the bitters. She took a large sip and walked back into the living room, flopping on the sofa and spilling a little bourbon onto her pants. She didn't seem to notice.

"There's no one," she sobbed. "He was the nicest man you would ever meet. He didn't deserve this."

Samantha moved closer, took the drink out of Darcy's hand, and placed the glass safely on the coffee table. She patted Darcy on the back and remained silent.

"The police say Gabby did this. Maybe she did. I have no idea." Darcy hoisted her glass, took another big swallow, and drained the last of the liquor. Samantha took the glass from her and offered to get her a glass of ice water. "It might be good to slow down a bit."

Darcy rested her head on the arm of the sofa, contorting her body to fit. "I'm sorry . . . I'm . . ." She closed her eyes.

Samantha carried a glass of ice water over to Darcy and pressed it into her hand, rousing her.

"Thanks." Darcy took a long gulp of the water and rested her head on the sofa's arm again. This wasn't proceeding as Samantha had planned. She decided she'd better get the rest of her questions out before Darcy fell asleep.

"I want to ask you about one other thing . . ."

"Hmm . . ." Darcy's eyes fluttered closed.

"I heard you were in the running to be on a television show . . . HRN."

Darcy shook herself awake. "How'd you hear? Anyway, not anymore." She jumped off the sofa to get another refill.

Samantha saw the bourbon splash onto her counter and walked into the kitchen to clean it up.

"I heard the producers wanted Mark to do it, but he refused, and you were furious about it."

Darcy took another swallow, this time straight bourbon with no ice. She winced as it went down. "Was my big break."

"Why didn't Mark want to do the show with you?"

"Said it would ruin things between us." Darcy could barely hold her eyes open. She shuffled back into the living room with the drink and fell back onto the sofa.

Samantha wanted to shake her awake.

"Mark was mad at you?"

"Was gonna change his mind."

"How?" Samantha wanted to throw ice water on the woman to wake her.

Darcy took a last sip and began coughing. "Only wanted him to talk to someone . . . my fault . . . so selfish . . ." She coughed again before she fell back onto the sofa.

Samantha opted for words she hoped could cut through the bourbon. "Darcy, did you have anything to do with Mark's death?"

The question had its intended effect. Darcy's eyes snapped open, and her face flashed with horror. "No! No, no, no. I loved him." She seemed lucid for a fraction of a second before she collapsed again on the sofa.

Samantha sighed and grabbed a pillow from her room, which she slipped under Darcy's head.

"Great, a slumber party with a potential murderer," Samantha muttered.

She looked over at Darcy, who had wrapped her arms around the pillow. Darcy looked exhausted, and not just from the drinks. The bags under her eyes were deep and her face thin, as if she hadn't been eating much. She hadn't taken care of herself, but due to grief or guilt? Samantha couldn't rule either out.

Wonder what she meant when she said it was her fault?

Samantha looked at her phone. Ten PM. She figured she'd let Darcy sleep it off for a few hours and then drive her home. Though Darcy seemed perfectly harmless right now, Samantha wasn't sure she could trust her. She turned off the light in the living room and went into her bedroom to think.

What a weird night.

She could hardly believe she'd been staking out Darcy's apartment only four and a half hours ago, and now Darcy was sleeping in Samantha's own apartment, snoring softly on her sofa. Besides having a ragged appearance, Darcy drank like she feared she might never drink again. She'd put away four healthy bourbon drinks in less than an hour.

Was it intentional? So she wouldn't have to answer questions?

The few questions Darcy had answered were useless. She'd noticed nothing at the party. The drinks had come from a waiter. She didn't know Decker and didn't seem familiar with the story from the Historic Commission meeting. Her responses about the television show had been unintelligible. Samantha wished she could learn more from Darcy, but her light snoring had transformed into a deeper sleep. Darcy didn't sound like she would wake anytime soon.

Frustrated to be stranded in her own room, at the mercy of a drunk stranger in her living room, Samantha pulled out her phone and checked her email. Then an idea popped into her head. She tiptoed into the living room before she could change her mind and fished Darcy's phone out of her purse.

On the assumption that Darcy used touch ID on her iPhone rather than a pass code, Samantha held Darcy's right index finger to the phone's home button. The phone blinked open and revealed a selfie of Darcy and Mark on a beach as her background wallpaper.

Samantha took the phone into the bedroom, not wanting the light to wake Darcy. She searched the call log first, copying all the recent dates, times, and phone numbers.

Next she checked text messages, but other than dozens of sympathy texts from friends, colleagues, and clients, there didn't seem to be much. Either she wasn't much of a texter or she regularly cleaned out her messages. Darcy had, after all, cheated with her best friend's husband. Clearing out texts could simply be a force of habit.

Samantha could still hear snores from the other room and went for emails next. She tapped on the Gmail account icon, and Darcy's email opened. There were hardly any emails—not even the usual spam messages. Samantha picked through a few client emails and some notes of sympathy but found nothing of note from the past few weeks.

She dug a little deeper to the few months before Mark's death. There wasn't much there either—only a few emails about events at area parks, a few back-and-forth emails with a friend about a trip to Dallas, some exchanges with her boss about a potential home listing, and several emails Darcy had sent to herself with the subject line *Notes*.

Hmm . . . this could be interesting. Samantha opened several of the emails but found only a few recipes, a grocery list, and several photos of homes with for-sale signs in front. Every time Darcy wanted to save something, she apparently sent herself an email. But she'd saved only a bunch of random tidbits. Samantha opened a few more—a *Gazette* article about which Houston neighborhoods had appreciated the most since last year and a story about the best yoga moves for improving your love life.

Samantha opened one last email Darcy had sent to herself three weeks before the home tour. She gasped when she read the subject line: *Solution to the Mark problem.* A chill ran up her spine as she forwarded the email to herself and deleted it from the sent folder. Suddenly, the phone felt like a hot potato. She went back into the living room and buried it deep in Darcy's purse.

Is the email evidence of premeditation?

Chapter Sixteen

Samantha stared at Darcy, still asleep on the sofa. She'd been passed out for about forty-five minutes, which wasn't enough time for her to have metabolized the booze she'd drunk. Samantha didn't care. She wanted her out of her apartment now.

She walked into the kitchen and began banging around some pots and pans as loudly as she could. When the ensuing cacophony yielded no results, she wetted a washcloth and rubbed Darcy's face. Darcy began to stir a little, so Samantha continued rubbing.

Darcy sat up. "Stop it!"

Samantha handed her a glass of water. "Here, drink this."

Darcy obeyed and drank the water. "What time is it?"

Samantha grabbed Darcy's purse and handed it to her. "It's late. I'll take you home now. I've got a busy day tomorrow, and I can't have you here in the morning."

"I'll drive." She stumbled as she stood.

"No, you won't. I'll take you. You can get an Uber tomorrow to get your car." Samantha grabbed Darcy's arm to help lead her down the long flight of stairs. She buckled her into the passenger seat as Darcy leaned her head back and fell asleep again.

The roads were quiet as Samantha drove back to Darcy's townhome. When they arrived, she tried to shake Darcy awake but couldn't get her to keep her eyes open for more than a few moments. Samantha walked over to Darcy's side and practically dragged her out of the car to the front porch. She fumbled in Darcy's purse for a set of keys and opened the front door. An alarm system beeped, and Samantha fumbled to press the button on the key fob to turn it off. She led Darcy over to the sofa in the living room and looked around to make sure there wasn't anything she could immediately harm herself with if she were to awaken half-asleep.

Darcy snored on the sofa, and part of Samantha wanted to search the house, but the other part of her realized she'd already been here long enough for a nosy neighbor to notice her car. She left the house, unable to lock the door, hoping the neighbors would continue their nosy watch on Darcy's town house. She got back in her car and returned to her apartment by midnight.

Samantha locked her own door and bolted the dead bolt, slightly creeped out after her midnight adventure. She'd never been a big fan of horror movies, and this weird dread lurking around every corner reminded her why. She went into the living room, turned several lights on, and pulled out her computer, logging in to her email. Ruby hopped into her lap as she opened the email from Darcy. Samantha stroked the cat's fur as she scrolled down, her pulse pounding, wondering what she might find. At first, she thought the body of the email was blank, but then she found an attachment at the bottom, below Darcy's signature. Samantha double-clicked to open it, revealing a photo of a newspaper spread from another local weekly from a neighboring county. She read from left to right, perusing a caption and photo regarding a pinewood derby competition, a story on a local school board election, and a write-up about a flower show, unsure what could be relevant on the page. Frustrated to have hit another dead end, Samantha enlarged the photo further and poured over every inch. The hair lifted on the nape of her neck when she read a column written by a local veterinarian outlining several common dangers for animals found in backyards. Much of the column was dedicated to Lyme disease from ticks, but a small section at the end mentioned poisonous plants, including the sago palm and the oleander bush. It warned readers to keep pets away from the plants.

To Samantha, the article seemed like a smoking gun. *Why would she have saved that particular newspaper, unless . . . ?*

But the longer she ruminated, the more she realized how quickly a defense attorney could explain the story away as a strange coincidence. It wasn't hard-and-fast proof, anyway. She regretted not sticking around Darcy's place and completing a more thorough inspection.

Now she needed to decide what to do with the information. Maybe she should send it to Gabby and let her lawyer handle it. Though, to her knowledge, Gabby's lawyer hadn't made a lot of headway on the Decker connection.

The mental note about Decker reminded her of her meeting with him tomorrow. Although, given the new information about Darcy, the meeting didn't seem as urgent. On the other hand, Brian had sent the emails to Gabby, which did suggest some involvement. They needed to figure out how Decker fit into the overall picture.

Samantha wanted to run the new information by Gabby but decided it was too late to call her.

*   *   *

Samantha phoned Gabby bright and early the next morning. "You won't believe what happened yesterday."

She relayed the story of Darcy's visit to Samantha's apartment, ending with her discovery of Darcy's emails.

"I didn't want to believe it," Gabby gasped, her breathing uneven. "Why would she do that? Steal him away from me, just to—"

"It's not definitive. She could have saved the article for some other reason, but, combined with the subject line 'Solution to the Mark problem,' it's very suspicious. The question is, what do we want to do about it?"

Gabby responded with a series of muffled sobs.

Samantha regretted not softening the blow before breaking the news. Mark had been Gabby's husband and Darcy her former best friend, after all. "I'm sorry. I know you need to process this. The bigger question is, what do we do about tonight and our meeting with Mr. Decker?"

Gabby spoke softly. "If Darcy did this, we don't need to meet him."

"He sent you those emails, though. He could still be involved somehow. Maybe we can learn more from him. Have you heard from your lawyer? Do the police consider him a suspect?"

"My lawyer passed the information on to the police, but he told me not to hold out much hope for them to do anything."

"What do you want to do?" Samantha asked.

Gabby's voice sounded stronger now. "Do you want to go ahead with our meeting?"

Samantha deliberated. She wanted to know more about Decker and his connection to the murder. None of it really made any sense. Maybe talking to him could fill in some blanks. "Yeah. I think we should. It's in a public place. We'll be safe enough."

The two agreed to meet at Samantha's apartment later and head to the café together.

Samantha billed a few more hours writing web content for the lawyers and pitched a gardening story to a local home-and-garden magazine. By five thirty, Gabby was knocking on her apartment door.

Upon entering, she took an appreciative gander around the living room. "This is small, but cute. You've got good style."

Samantha laughed. "It's my mother who's got style. Almost everything here is a hand-me-down from her."

Gabby shook her head. "Well, you've made it your own. I can see your personality reflected here."

Samantha regarded her walls with new appreciation for her framed travel prints and photos and shelves full of books. Over the years, she'd added her own touches to make the little apartment feel like home, and it pleased her to have someone notice her efforts. "Thanks. Anyway, are you sure about going forward with this meeting?"

"Yeah. We should be safe enough. We're meeting at a café. What can happen there? Besides, I really want to find out what this guy knows."

The two planned out their approach, deciding not to go into the café until Decker arrived in case he recognized one of them and left. They'd wait in Samantha's car outside.

At six fifteen, they parked outside the café and kept their gazes on the door. Twenty minutes later, they spotted Decker climbing the front steps and heading into the building. Samantha and Gabby waited a moment until a couple walked in behind Decker before they followed him inside the café. They watched as he looked around a minute and walked toward the counter. Though they couldn't hear him yet, Samantha guessed he had asked about the meeting, because the barista behind the counter shrugged his shoulders in the universal *I just work here* response.

Decker ordered a cup of coffee and looked around the empty room. He grabbed a seat against a wall at an empty table and pulled out his phone.

Samantha motioned to Gabby to order them some coffee while she walked to his table. "You here for the meeting?"

When he nodded, she sat in the seat next to him and slid her chair out a bit to make it harder for him to leave without squeezing past her. "My friend's getting some coffee. We'll start when she comes over."

He nodded again, appraising her. "I'm glad you guys are exploring this. The Historic Commission is a joke. It shouldn't be legal for them to determine what I can and can't do with my property."

Samantha nodded her head as Gabby walked over and grabbed the seat on his other side, pinning him in. As she placed the coffees on the table, Decker looked at her face.

He seemed to register some recognition, but it wasn't total. "Do I know you from somewhere? You look familiar."

"I should. You set me up for my husband's murder."

His jaw dropped. He stood, but Samantha and Gabby moved their chairs closer to him, trying to pin him in. Instead of sitting back down, Decker flipped the table over like an over-sized tire, vaulting across it and outside.

Samantha mouthed an apology to the barista and bolted after Decker, Gabby close behind. Samantha raced to catch him, her lungs burning with the effort, but she arrived too late. By the time she reached the corner where he'd turned, his black pickup truck had sped away.

Moments later, Gabby reached Samantha. "We lost him."

Winded, Samantha turned to face Gabby. "Want to try to find him again?"

In Samantha's car, on the way to Decker's house, Gabby bounced her knee up and down. "Are you sure this is a good idea?"

Samantha shook her head. "No, I'm not. He's hiding something, though, and if we're ever going to figure out who killed Mark, we need to find out what."

The resolve in her voice surprised her. For the first time in a long time, Samantha didn't feel like polling her nearest and dearest before she made a decision. Now she was running purely on instinct.

They drove in silence the rest of the way. Samantha cut her lights as she neared Decker's house, not wanting to draw attention to herself. There was no need. Decker's truck wasn't out front.

Gabby let out a rush of pent-up air. "Now what? Do we wait?"

Samantha shook her head. "I know another place he might have gone. You game to try and find him?"

Gabby held her breath for a moment, then nodded.

Samantha tried to remember the route she had taken when she followed Decker the first time. After a few lucky guesses, she found the right path and drove toward the cinder-block building. Decker had parked out front, as luck would have it, between a green dumpster and a light pole in an illegal parking spot. Samantha pulled behind him, angling her Sentra in such a way as to make it impossible for Decker to back his truck out. Unless he completely rammed her car, she figured, she could force a conversation.

After forty-five minutes spent discussing their strategy, Samantha spotted a sweaty Decker racing toward them, his fist outstretched as he began shouting. "Get away from my truck!"

Gabby jumped out of the car, shaking the tire iron they'd grabbed from Samantha's trunk.

His face turned ashen, but he easily snatched the tool from Gabby's hands and held it as if he was going to strike her. "I thought I'd made it clear I didn't want to talk to you."

Samantha kicked him hard in the shin, and he screamed in pain, dropping the tire iron as he fell backward. Gabby raced to pick it up before he could reach for it again.

Still on the ground, he crossed his arms in front of his face as if bracing for impact. "What do you want?"

Samantha motioned for Gabby to step away. "Did you kill Mark?"

Decker jerked backward as if shocked by an electrical current. "God, no! I didn't kill him. Look, I'm sorry for getting you involved." He aimed his remarks at Gabby. "I didn't hurt your husband."

"You sent the emails, though, right?" Samantha continued to stare at him, locking onto his face.

"I did, and I'm sorry. Your husband pissed me off with the way he treated me at the board meeting, and I wanted to embarrass him in a public setting the way he embarrassed me."

Gabby narrowed her eyes at him. "How was inviting me supposed to accomplish that exactly?"

Decker had enough sense to look sheepish. "I read about your arrest for harassment of his new girlfriend. Hey, I admired your style. I figured if all three of you were in the same space, there'd be fireworks."

He ping-ponged his gaze back and forth between Gabby and Samantha, as if to gauge how his words had landed.

"Who is Vivian Caulfield?" Samantha tried to fill in the holes in his story.

Decker shrugged again. "She's my aunt. I needed a real house and a real name on the property tax records. You wouldn't come all the way to Houston without either of those." He pulled his arms behind his back in a stretch. "I watered her plants while she was out of town. I never thought you'd go there—and if you did, the worst that would happen was you would find an empty house."

Gabby's face changed from white-hot rage to icy fury. "That's not the worst thing that happened, is it? The worst thing is you sent me off without an alibi while someone killed my husband. I don't believe you. I think you killed him."

She lunged at him with the tire iron, but he held his forearm in front of his face, and Samantha reached Gabby in time to pull her back.

Decker, his muscles tensed, composed his face into some expression of sympathy. "I'm really sorry. I didn't mean for any of this to happen, but I didn't kill your husband."

Samantha scrutinized his face, trying to decide whether to believe him or not. "Why did you run earlier—at the coffee shop?"

He tugged at his gym shorts. "It's a sensitive situation. I was with a woman at the party. She's married, and if her husband found out . . ."

Samantha glared at him. "Can you prove it?"

He stared her straight in the face. "I was only at the party for like three minutes before my girlfriend sprained her ankle wearing some ridiculous stiletto heels. Staff at the minor emergency clinic down the street can vouch for me. We were in their office less than ten minutes after we first walked into the party."

Gabby still looked as though she wanted to punch him, so Samantha pulled her away. "Let's get out of here."

In the car, Gabby hid her face in her hands. "I can't believe this. All of this happened because some meathead got his feelings hurt."

Samantha patted Gabby on the back. "We can notify the police. He's admitted he sent the emails. They'll have to investigate, and maybe it will help with your case."

Gabby sat straight and looked Samantha in the face. "All it proves is someone else wanted me at the party. It doesn't prove I'm innocent." She rested her head in her hands.

Gabby's shoulders slumped, and Samantha tried to raise her spirits. "All the more reason we need to pursue the Darcy angle."

Gabby kept her head lowered, but after a few moments, she sat straight again. "How? You said yourself the email you found wouldn't be admissible in any court. What does it prove, anyway? That Darcy knew oleander was poisonous? It's not exactly a huge secret. And the 'Mark problem'? That could be anything."

Samantha conceded that they'd uncovered no solid evidence to tie Darcy to the crime, but she wasn't ready to abandon hope of finding something.

"She knows more than she's saying. She practically blamed herself when we talked. She literally said, 'It's my fault.' "

"What do we do about it?" Gabby's expression turned hopeful.

Samantha formed her fingers into a steeple, locking gazes with Gabby. "We need to confront her again."

Chapter Seventeen

For the second time that evening, Gabby trudged up the stairs to Samantha's apartment and sat on the small green sofa.

"What do you have in mind?" Gabby lay back against the cushion.

"You probably have to get back to Galveston, so maybe this isn't the day . . ."

"Nope. Chloe is spending the night with a friend tonight. I've got another few hours in me. How do we get this proof?"

Samantha turned on her phone and opened the voice memo function. "We record Darcy. We go over there, confront her, and get her on the record."

Gabby stared at Samantha as if she'd lost her mind. "You think Darcy is a killer and you want to go over there and talk to her like there's nothing wrong? Not to mention she hates me!"

"Listen, Darcy isn't at her best right now. I don't know if it's guilt or remorse, but she put away more than six ounces of bourbon last night in less than an hour. I think between the two of us, we can overpower her if it comes down to it."

"I don't know, Samantha. If she's in such bad shape, she could be desperate, which would only make her more dangerous."

Samantha considered Gabby's words. If Darcy was the killer, she might become frantic and lash out at them if she believed they were onto her. *Hmm . . .*

Samantha riffled around in her purse until her fingers found the small, slender can of mace. "Okay, as a backup, we've got this. With two of us and this mace, at the very least, we'll be able to get away."

Gabby looked at the can and nodded.

Samantha pressed on. "The trick will be to get to Darcy before she is three sheets to the wind. She stopped making much sense after her third drink, and the fourth one put her to sleep."

"Darcy could never hold her liquor. How do we pull off the recording?"

"I'll leave it running in my purse before we walk to the door."

"Okay, but how will we get inside? Have you forgotten the woman hates me?"

Samantha pulled out her phone and found the email she'd forwarded from Darcy's phone. She sent it to Gabby's email. "We've got proof, remember? I doubt she'll consider whether it's admissible in court when we arrive at her door with proof from her own email."

Gabby stared at her lap for a few moments before raising her gaze to Samantha and nodding. "Okay, let's do it. You've got to do the talking, though. I can't trust myself to speak around that woman."

They headed out before either had the chance to change her mind.

As they climbed the steps to Darcy's townhome, Samantha pressed record on her phone and left it running in her purse, the zipper open and the can of mace within easy reach. Gabby shifted her body so her face wouldn't be visible to the doorbell camera. Samantha rang the bell and knocked. This time she didn't care if the neighbors noticed. She wanted to attract attention, hoping it would lead Darcy to invite them inside.

After the second round of ringing and knocking, Samantha heard footsteps. The door opened a crack, and Gabby stepped forward into view.

"I told you not to come back here. What do you . . ." Darcy's gaze locked on Gabby's. "What are you doing here?" She began to close the door, but Samantha stepped forward to block her.

"We want to come in and talk. We can do it out here with all of your neighbors listening, or we can come inside."

"I'm not going anywhere with her." Darcy continued to stare at Gabby. "She murdered Mark!"

Darcy elbowed Samantha in the stomach to keep her from blocking the door, but Gabby pushed Darcy into the house.

Samantha scrambled in after the two and slammed the door shut behind her.

The color drained out of Darcy's face as she looked at the two women and backed away. Almost as if someone had flipped a switch, her tone seemed to change from fright to more of a sneer. "What in the hell are you doing here? Why would you think I'd want to talk to you?"

Gabby didn't speak and merely stared at Darcy, fury practically emanating from her pores. Darcy looked a little better than she had the night before. At least it looked as if she'd showered and changed into a clean pair of yoga pants.

With the tension mounting between Gabby and Darcy, Samantha decided she needed to step in and defuse the situation. "I wanted to circle back to some of what you said last night. You sort of stopped making sense after a while."

Darcy's cheeks flushed. "I'm sorry about last night. It's been a rough few weeks, as you can imagine."

Gabby couldn't seem to stop herself from responding. "Yeah, it's been a rough year for me, Darcy. You know, the part where you stole my husband and then killed him." She practically spat out the last few words.

Darcy's mouth dropped open. "Killed him? Are you out of your mind? You're the one charged with murder!"

Samantha decided she'd better take over questioning before the situation evolved into a catfight. She turned to Darcy. "You admitted as much last night. You distinctly said it was all your fault."

Darcy covered her now-gaping mouth with her palm as she gawked at Samantha and Gabby. "I meant it was my fault he went to the home tour. He didn't want to go, but I made him. I wanted him to meet with somebody . . . anyway, I can't believe you would accuse me of having anything to do with his death. I loved him!" Darcy flounced onto her sofa.

Gabby stared at Darcy with an expression that suggested she wanted to use a pillow to smother her former friend. "Liar!" She ran toward Darcy and slapped her hard across her face. "You are such a liar! You killed him!"

Samantha jumped between the two and motioned for Gabby to take a step back, raising her eyebrows to signify to Gabby that she wanted to take the lead in the conversation.

"Darcy, listen, we've got proof." Samantha sought Darcy's gaze, wondering what the woman would say to defend herself.

Darcy spun around and turned her attention back to Samantha. "Proof? What kind of proof? You're crazy. I didn't kill

Mark." She turned to face Gabby. "I know you don't believe it, Gabby, but I loved him. You weren't happy with him anymore. You told me yourself a thousand times. It was our turn to be happy."

Gabby scoffed. "Oh, please. If you were that concerned about this great love of yours, why were you so concerned about that stupid television show?"

Darcy stomped her foot. "You can want more than one thing, you know. Yes, I wanted the television show. It would have been wonderful for both of us, and I never understood why he wouldn't go forward with it."

"So you killed him for it?" Gabby settled onto a chair near where Darcy sat on the sofa.

Darcy scooted away, as if Gabby were contagious. "How many times do I have to say it? I didn't kill him."

Gabby pulled out her phone and opened the email Samantha had forwarded to her with the photo of the newspaper spread. "What about this?"

Darcy stared at the phone, appearing puzzled as she looked at the photo. "What is this? Where did you get it? I . . . I don't understand . . ."

"You sent this to yourself, Darcy. I emailed a copy from your phone to mine last night." Samantha enlarged the photo and scrolled to the end of the veterinarian's column, pointing out the words about oleander poisoning to Darcy. "You emailed this to yourself three weeks before the murder." Samantha watched Darcy for a reaction.

Darcy looked confused and then horrified. "That's . . . I've never seen that story before. I saved that newspaper for the photo. It has nothing to do . . ." She stood and looked back and forth between the two women and briefly looked up toward her stairs. "I need you to leave now." She walked toward the front door and held it open. "Get out before I call the police and inform them that a murder suspect and her accomplice are harassing me in my home."

Samantha and Gabby looked at each other, confused, and back at Darcy.

"I mean it. Get out." Darcy shooed them with her hand.

Samantha and Gabby walked outside, not sure whether Darcy would follow through on her threat to call the police. At this point, neither of them wanted that to happen.

The two women were silent as they walked toward Samantha's car.

Once inside, with the door closed, Gabby turned to Samantha. "What just happened?"

"I don't know. It was weird, right?"

They drove back to Samantha's apartment and sat on the sofa. Both women were exhausted.

"What do you make of her story? She saved the newspaper for the photo? She never saw the story about the oleander? I don't buy it." Samantha smoothed the fringe on one of her throw pillows, running her fingers through it to work out the tangles.

She grabbed her phone and pulled up the photo from Darcy's email again to determine what photograph in the newspaper could have captured Darcy's interest. Other than a snapshot of flower arrangements at a flower show, the only photo was a standalone picture of a man named Peter Garfield and his son, Travis, a Boy Scout, holding a small wooden race car, which, according to the caption, had won the local pinewood derby. "Why on earth would Darcy care about that?"

"I don't know. It makes no sense. But I have to admit, her reaction—it seemed more confused than anything."

"I thought so too." Samantha hesitated a moment, unsure how her next statement would land. "I'll be honest, she didn't act like a murderer concerned about being caught."

"If she's not, then who is?"

"I don't know. It still seems like Darcy knows something she's not telling us." Samantha sighed and leaned back against the sofa cushions, lost in her own thoughts.

After a few moments, Gabby stood. "I guess I'd better head out now. It's not getting any earlier."

Samantha looked out the window at pure darkness. She didn't want to send Gabby out on the road for another forty-five minutes after such a draining night. "Do you want to stay here? If Chloe is sleeping over at a friend's house, there's no need for you to go back tonight, right?"

Gabby looked out the window and frowned. "It's dark, and I am super tired. Do you mind?"

"Not at all. All I've got is this sofa, but I've fallen asleep there a time or two myself. It's comfy."

"Thanks. It might not be a bad idea."

Samantha went into her room to find an extra pair of pajamas, pillows, sheets, and a blanket. She set the supplies on the arm of the sofa. "Do you want some hot tea?"

Gabby put her phone down. "You know what I would really love? One of those special drinks you made at the home tour. I left so quickly, I didn't have time to try one."

Samantha laughed. "I'd be happy to make you a cocktail. What's your pleasure, rye or gin?"

Gabby opted for rye and followed Samantha into the kitchen to watch her make the cocktails. While Samantha shook the ingredients, Gabby looked around the kitchen. She grabbed the two jars with infusions of pineapple and peppers. "How did you learn to make all of this stuff?"

Samantha poured each drink over a large ice cube in a low-ball glass and garnished them with a cherry. "I sort of taught myself. It's all about mixing different but complementary flavors. For instance, the jar you're holding will be pineapple-sage bitters. It should pair well with a gin-and-citrus combination."

Gabby set the jars back on the table and raised her drink to smell it. She took a small sip and smiled. "Mmm . . . this is good."

Samantha took a sip of her own drink and silently agreed. She sat at her kitchen table and motioned for Gabby to join her. "What's our next step?"

Gabby sat across from Samantha with her cocktail. "Oh, let's not talk about it anymore tonight. Let's pretend for the next little while we're girlfriends catching up. Tell me, Samantha, what's new with you?"

Ruby sashayed into the kitchen. Gabby grabbed the cat and placed her on her lap, where she stroked her fur.

Samantha groaned. There wasn't much new with her apart from this case, but she played along anyway. "Well, my ex-fiancé, who dumped me right before our wedding, keeps calling me late at night from New York City. Part of me likes it, and part of me realizes I need to cut it off if I want to move on."

Gabby raised her eyebrows. "Wow. How will you handle it?"

"I don't know, and now my lawyer, Greg's old boss, might be interested in me. I might be interested too, but it all feels a little strange."

Gabby took another sip of her drink. "I'm the wrong person to ask about relationships. My best advice is to trust your instincts. If it feels right with this lawyer, then give it a shot." She took a breath. "Did it feel right with your fiancé?"

As Samantha considered the question, she fiddled with a broken strip of metal trim surrounding her vintage Formica table and accidentally pricked her finger. Making a mental note to fix the trim soon, she grabbed a paper towel to wipe away the blood. "You're a perceptive interviewer. You sure you weren't a reporter in a past life? Did it feel right with Greg? I don't know. I think it felt . . . comfortable."

"Comfortable's not terrible." Gabby finished her drink.

"No, but it's not the best situation either." Samantha took one last sip and collected the glasses to take them to the sink.

She tidied the rest of the kitchen and cleaned her glassware by hand.

Gabby grabbed a dish towel to dry. "You'll figure out what right feels like. It was right for a long while with Mark and me, but then it wasn't, even before Darcy happened."

Samantha held her tongue, wanting to hear the rest of the story.

"It was everything. There wasn't enough money, and we were stressed about jobs and the business. We didn't click anymore. But I didn't hate him. Even after Darcy. He deserved better than this."

Samantha nodded her head. There didn't seem to be much left to say, so she squeezed Gabby on the shoulder. "We should call it a night. Good night, Gabby."

"Night, Samantha. Thanks for everything."

Samantha brushed her teeth and crawled into bed. She had seen the worry etched on Gabby's face and hoped they could find a way to clear her name. She tossed and turned a bit, reviewing her earlier encounters with Darcy and Decker. She wanted to check on Decker's alibi at the minor emergency clinic, but if it checked out, they'd hit another dead end. Darcy, she was certain, still hadn't revealed everything she knew. Eventually Samantha fell asleep, hoping her subconscious would make some headway in uncovering a solution.

Samantha's alarm went off around six. She walked out of her bedroom and called out, "Gabby, do you want to grab the shower first?" She walked into the living room and found her sheets, pillow, and pajamas all folded neatly on the sofa.

Gabby was gone.

Chapter Eighteen

S amantha felt a twinge of disappointment that Gabby hadn't said good-bye. *Oh well, maybe she needed to get an early start back to Galveston.*

As she sipped a cup of hot chai tea, Samantha wondered what she and Gabby could pursue next. Last night's interviews had provided no new leads, though Samantha felt certain there was more to learn from Darcy.

Staring out her window, Samantha noticed the vibrant colors of her neighbor's crepe myrtle trees, with blooms of deep magenta and light pink. *So pretty—and safe, too. Other than the million tiny flower petals that rain down with every breeze, crepe myrtles offer no danger.* Her musings made her remember the reference to oleanders in the story Darcy had claimed not to have seen in the newspaper she had saved. *What did Darcy say? She was only interested in the photo?* Samantha decided she would take another look at the photo after work to see if she could find some connection to Darcy or Mark.

Samantha spent a slow day revising an article for the business journal and hunting for other story ideas to pitch. She didn't make much headway, as her thoughts continued to turn to Gabby and Darcy. She wondered what she could be missing.

Around five thirty, she abandoned work and planned to pull up the photo again, but after looking out the window, she decided she'd been inside and at her computer for too long and needed to walk in the sunshine to clear her head.

Lost in her thoughts, she barely registered the police car parked on the street in front of her apartment.

"Samantha Warren?" a booming voice called out to her as she walked down the outside stairs to the driveway.

A police officer called to her from the street in front of her landlord's house. Her body flushed cold with fear. Had something happened to one of her friends? Her mother? "Yes?"

"I need you to come to the station with me."

Her internal temperature shifted from cold to hot and her face grew warm. "What is this about?"

"We need to take you downtown for questioning."

"What's happened? Why do you need to question me?" Samantha's pulse began to race again as she wondered what the police wanted with her.

The officer, mopping sweat from his forehead with a white handkerchief, spoke with labored breath. "There's been an . . . incident, and we believe you might have some information."

The heavyset man pointed toward the squad car and motioned for Samantha to climb into the back seat. His younger, skinnier partner stared hard at Samantha, his hands on his belt, as if itching to grab for his handcuffs or a weapon should Samantha try something funny.

Her heart raced like a jackhammer as she considered what she'd learned about criminal law. Did she have to go with him?

Could she drive herself? She needed to call David and ask if he could join her. It wouldn't be smart to face this without a lawyer present. She decided it didn't hurt to ask. "Can I drive myself?"

"We'd like you to come with us." The skinnier officer broke his silence, and his voice sounded as cold as his expression.

The officer hadn't refused outright, but his response conveyed the seriousness of the situation.

"I want to call my lawyer first."

The policeman shrugged. Samantha's hands shook as she selected David's name from her contact list. He answered after the second ring.

"David? I need your help."

"Samantha? What is it? Are you okay?"

"The police are here. They're taking me downtown for questioning. They won't tell me what it's about."

"I'll meet you there in fifteen minutes. Don't say anything without me." His voice reassured her slightly. At least she wouldn't be alone.

The drive to the police station took no time. The officer and his partner in the front seat didn't offer any comment, and Samantha didn't feel much like chatting either, though she was desperate to figure out why they wanted to talk to her.

Once they reached the station, the officer escorted her into an interview room and offered a cup of coffee. She shook her head and asked for a cup of water instead.

After a few moments, Jason Sanders, the detective she'd seen the day after the home tour, came into the room. He greeted her warmly. "Ms. Warren. It's nice to see you again. Thank you for coming down."

Samantha assumed Sanders wanted to put her at ease with his tone, but she refused to give in to it. "They gave me the impression I didn't have much of a choice."

He took a seat across the table from her. Though his tone was still pleasant, his demeanor had shifted a bit. "We need to ask you some questions about last night."

Last night? She ran through last night in her head. *Is this about Brian Decker or Darcy?* She tried to remain cool, though her mind raced with endless possibilities. "My lawyer has instructed me not to answer questions until he gets here."

Sanders closed his notebook and stood. "If that's the way you want to do it, I'll be back when he arrives."

They left her alone in the room, which was furnished with a table and two chairs and had bare walls. She tried to tamp down her panic as she wondered what would come next.

She didn't wait too long.

David must have broken several laws to get downtown from River Oaks as fast as he had. "I got here as quickly as I could." He rushed into the room. "Do you know what this is about?"

Samantha shook her head. "All I know is they want to ask me about last night."

His demeanor suggested he wasn't sure he wanted to know, but he asked anyway. "What happened last night?"

"Nothing. I mean, nothing criminal anyway."

She told him about her and Gabby's chat with Decker and their subsequent visit to Darcy. "Nothing happened. We only talked, and then Darcy sort of kicked us out."

He raised an eyebrow, and Samantha could sense he wanted to admonish her for trying to investigate alone, but he held his tongue. "All right. Let's find out what they have to say. You can answer his questions, but if I say stop, I don't want you to say anything more." He walked out to alert the detective that they were ready to begin.

Jason Sanders walked back into the room and reclaimed his seat at the table. "I need you to tell me about last night. I know you and Ms. Brantwell visited Darcy last night around eight thirty. We have you on the doorbell camera entering the house and leaving less than fifteen minutes later."

"We went to talk to Darcy about Mark's death, and, well, she didn't like some of our questions, so she kicked us out. We were back at my place by nine."

Sanders consulted his notepad. "I'll get back to why you were questioning Darcy in a few minutes, but we also have you on the doorbell camera the night before, making multiple trips to the home. Much later that night, you appear on camera escorting what looked like an inebriated Darcy in around midnight. What were you doing?"

Samantha looked at the table and then at Sanders. "Exactly what it looked like. I wanted to talk to Darcy, but she didn't answer. She later came to my apartment. I made some drinks. She consumed more than her fair share, and I brought her home."

"And what were these discussions and attempted discussions about?"

Samantha looked at David, and he nodded. "To be honest, we suspected Darcy might have been involved with Mark's death. We wanted to ask her a few questions."

"When did you last see Gabby?"

"She spent the night at my apartment last night. Why? Is she okay?"

Sanders ignored her question. "When did you last see her? Was she there this morning?"

Samantha rubbed her forehead. "I went to bed around midnight last night, and no, she wasn't there when I woke up. I figured she left early to go home."

Sanders stared hard at Samantha as if trying to gauge her truthfulness. "In your repeated conversations with Darcy, did you learn anything you deemed important to your so-called investigation?"

Samantha ground her teeth, furious at the condescension in his tone. "Listen, we wouldn't have done any of this if you people hadn't focused on Gabby to the exclusion of any other viable suspect."

David cut her off before she could speak again. "Listen, my client has cooperated with you. I think it's time you told us what this is all about."

Sanders looked back and forth between David and Samantha before speaking. "Darcy is dead, and your client and her . . . friend were among the last people to see her alive."

Samantha's jaw dropped. "Oh my God! I can't believe it. What happened?"

She looked at David, who raised his eyebrows but nodded as if to signify that she could ask the question.

"That's what we want to hear from you. We believe you're in the best position to explain exactly what happened." Sanders's tone had quickly turned from polite to icy. His chin jutted out as his gaze locked onto Samantha's.

"I've told you everything I know. How did she die? Was it oleander poisoning too?" Samantha's elbows pressed into her sides as if she were bracing for impact.

"We're not releasing any information on cause of death at this time." Sanders sat back and continued to stare at Samantha.

David stood. "All right. This interview is over for now. My client won't have anything further to say. I assume she's free to go?"

The detective stood. "She can go for now. Don't plan any extended trips, though."

David touched Samantha on the shoulder, signifying that she should follow him out. As they walked to his car, Samantha shivered despite the heat. In his car, they buckled their seat belts, and David turned to face her. "We need to talk more. I need to hear everything you said or did in the last few days, particularly with regards to Darcy."

By the time they arrived at her apartment, Samantha's shivers were mostly under control. She led the way up the stairs and showed him to the kitchen table, where he sat with a yellow legal pad and pen, ready to take notes. She put a kettle on to boil to make some tea and sat opposite him. She filled him in on all of her activity, from the IP address scheme to the meetings with Decker and Bob and finally to her interactions with Darcy.

"It was weird. Last night, when I confronted her about the article on oleanders I'd found in her email, she looked really confused and basically kicked us out. I swear, she was standing fully upright and walking when I last saw her."

David offered a wan smile. "I know you didn't harm Darcy, Samantha. What I'm worried about now is how to prove it. I'll skip the lecture about how you should have left the investigation to the professionals. What's done is done. I just want to warn you. This could be bad."

The teakettle screamed, and Samantha jumped to her feet to turn off the stove. She poured two cups of tea and took them back to the table. "What now?"

David fingered the tag on the jasmine-and-rose green tea bag. "Have you heard anything from Gabby since yesterday? It would be good to exchange notes with her on what the cops have said to her."

Samantha shook her head no. "I can try to call her."

"Do that, and then we wait for the cops' next move."

The words were of minimal comfort to Samantha, knowing as she did that the cops' next move could be to arrest her for Darcy's murder.

David seemed to sense her concern. "Try not to worry too much. If they had any evidence beyond the doorbell videos, they would have arrested you already."

A knot in Samantha's stomach grew hard, like a cherry pit.

David's expression turned more forceful. "For heaven's sake, Samantha, please promise you won't do any further investigations. Leave this to the professionals."

"Trust me. I've learned my lesson." She curled her fingers around her mug, stealing its warmth to abate the shivers.

David walked behind her, resting his hand on her shoulder, where he let it linger a beat longer than necessary to offer comfort to a client. "I have to go, but please, call me if you need anything."

She didn't trust herself to stand, so she remained in her chair, cradling her teacup. "Thanks, David."

When the door clicked shut, Samantha grabbed her phone and called Gabby.

The call went straight to voice mail.

I can't believe this is happening. Darcy was alive last night!

She tried to recall her conversation with Darcy the night before and realized she didn't have to recall it; she could listen. In all the excitement at the police station, she'd forgotten she had recorded the whole encounter. Samantha grabbed her phone and played the audio recording. Once again, she found Darcy's reaction to the email strange. Darcy hadn't acted worried, but the email had seemed to trigger something for her. If Samantha could find out what Darcy had been thinking, she might figure out what had happened to her.

Did Darcy go to see someone else? Could that someone else have murdered her?

Samantha pressed her fingers to her temples, trying to massage away her stress. She wished she could talk to Gabby. She tried to call Gabby again on her cell phone, but it went to voice mail. *Why isn't she answering?*

Frustrated, she paced like a caged animal. She needed help to figure out what to do. She sent David a copy of the recording, figuring he could turn it over to the police. She called Marisa and then Beth, but neither answered her phone. Her watch showed eight at night. Her stomach growled, reminding her she'd eaten nothing since lunch. She opened a can of soup and heated it on her stove. She ate but tasted nothing, consuming only enough to stop her stomach from rumbling. She tried Gabby again. Still no answer. She was becoming frantic. She needed information but didn't know where to find it.

Barring that, she needed to talk to someone calm and analytical. Her mom didn't fit the bill, and neither did Marisa or Beth. Even as the thought came to her, Samantha knew she shouldn't call Greg. *Why do I keep doing this?*

He answered on the second ring. "Sam?"

"Greg? I'm sorry to bother you. I know it's late and you're busy."

"No, I'm fine. Just on a brief dinner break. What's going on? You sound upset."

"I am. It's awful. I don't know where to start. It's been a horrible day."

"Baby, what happened?"

The endearment stopped her for a moment, but she didn't have time to analyze her thoughts about it. She brushed past her uncertainty and told him about the last few days, running through everything from her two visits with Darcy to her visit with Gabby to her trip to the police. "Don't worry. David was with me the whole time. He says he's got everything under control, but this waiting with no answers is driving me nuts."

"Jesus, Sam. How did this escalate so quickly from a civil lawsuit to a murder investigation? Why are you even involved? Don't you know enough to let the police handle the investigations?"

Samantha huffed, determined to end the lecture before he really got started. "Don't you know enough from having covered courts for the *Gazette* that sometimes the police don't get it right? Sometimes it takes a little outside interference for justice to be done."

He sighed. "I know, but as good of a reporter as you are, you're not equipped to handle a murder investigation. I'm sorry, but you're not."

Samantha wanted to cry. She wasn't sure what she had expected from Greg, but this wasn't it. "It's too late now. I'm right in the middle of one, and I don't know what to do. I'm scared."

"You need to listen to David. He's one of the best. If he tells you to stay put, stay put. The cops will have to show their hand eventually, and when they do, he'll know what to do."

This wasn't the rousing "never give up, be like a dog on a bone" pep talk he used to give to her when they were both reporters. Either he'd lost his edge or he'd finally completed the metamorphosis from reporter to lawyer. "Greg, I am listening to him. I'm just . . . freaked out a little."

"Listen, maybe I'll come down there this weekend. I can talk strategy with David. We'll figure this all out."

Greg in the same town? She'd finally begun to accept their breakup after being separated by more than a thousand miles. He'd been hinting about it in his last few calls, but she hadn't taken him seriously. She wasn't sure how she would feel with him in the same town.

"No, Greg. It's okay. Don't come. I'll be fine. You're right. I'll listen to David."

He spoke as if he hadn't heard her. "I'll stay at a hotel downtown. You can come stay with me. We can talk ab—"

Samantha's phone beeped. She interrupted. "It's David. I've got to go." She switched over without saying good-bye.

"Samantha, I've got some news. The police are searching for Gabby. They've got a warrant out for her arrest for Darcy's murder."

Chapter Nineteen

S uddenly woozy, Samantha swayed slightly and grabbed her counter to try to maintain her balance. "What did you say?"

"Her fingerprints were at the crime scene, and the doorbell video shows her as the last person to enter or leave Darcy's home."

"You mean the two of us, right? We were both on the doorbell video because we were together." Samantha frowned, not understanding David's point.

"No, Gabby apparently went back several hours later. The police want to question her, but they believe she's jumped bail and gone on the run. She took her daughter with her."

A familiar panic rose inside Samantha. "What do you mean? Slow down . . . how was Darcy killed, exactly?"

"The police aren't releasing all the details, but it sounded like blunt-force trauma to the head."

Samantha's stomach churned. "It could have been someone else. I'm sure someone else killed Mark, and that person also could have killed Darcy."

"Samantha, I know you like Gabby, but how do you explain why she went back a second time? You're in enough trouble right now as it is. I've convinced them for now not to charge you as an accessory . . ."

"What? How would I be an accessory?" She stooped to pet Ruby, wanting the comfort of her soft fur to blunt the blow of this fresh danger.

"You were with Gabby at Darcy's house earlier in the night. It doesn't look good . . . but I've convinced them you will cooperate. They want you back downtown in the morning for another interview. This time, we've got to explain everything you know. Not only about your meeting with Darcy. You have to tell them everything you've learned about Gabby."

Samantha's voice rose to a wail. "I swear I didn't hurt anybody."

"Of course not. We'll make sure the police are convinced. You simply have to cooperate with them."

"I'll do whatever I can."

David arranged to pick her up the following morning at seven thirty for a second interview with the detectives.

Could Gabby really have left my apartment to go murder Darcy? It's unbelievable.

Her stomach twisted as she walked into the kitchen. The tea from earlier in the evening seemed a million years ago and nowhere near potent enough for the recent chain of events. She tested out her new pineapple-sage bitters with some cold gin. The act of making the drink steadied her mind a little, while the act of drinking it wore off some of the rough edges of the day. She couldn't believe Darcy was dead and Gabby was on the run. *Did I read this whole situation wrong? Could Gabby really have done it?*

Samantha's phone beeped at her, alerting her to a new text message from Greg. **Hey! Call me when you're done. I want to hear what David said.**

Ugh. She wasn't sure if she wanted to call him back but knew he would keep calling until he reached her. She dialed his number, and he immediately answered.

"Sam! I've been worried. What did David say?"

She explained about Gabby being gone and about her second interview with the police set for the next morning. "David told me to cooperate and everything will be fine."

"Good, Sam. Give them whatever they ask for. You need to show them you aren't hiding anything."

The same advice from David had sounded smart. From Greg, it sounded condescending.

"I know. David will be with me. It should be fine. I'm mostly worried about Gabby. She wouldn't run without an excellent reason."

"Are you out of your mind? She ran because she's a murderer," Greg practically yelled. "You don't need to get any more involved than you already are. Promise me you'll keep out of it."

Samantha sighed. "I will. Now I've got to go. I need to get some sleep for tomorrow. Good night."

"Good night, Sam. I miss—"

She ended the call before he could finish the phrase. She couldn't handle hearing about his newfound concern for her, not when she hadn't come to terms with her own feelings. Mixed emotions buzzed around her head and made it difficult for her to think clearly. The last thing she needed was a muddled brain, especially tomorrow.

She finished her drink and went to bed, unsure what the next day would bring.

* * *

After a night of fitful sleep, Samantha woke early at six. She made herself some tea and went outside to grab the newspaper.

The story led the metro section: *Local Realtor With Ties to Murdered Contractor Found Dead.*

Samantha skimmed the story, noting pertinent details— *Police are searching for Gabby Brantwell, the estranged wife of murdered contractor Mark Brantwell. She's wanted for questioning in connection with the murders of both Mark Brantwell and Darcy Meadows.*

To Samantha's relief, the story didn't mention her but suggested that the police had a cut-and-dried case against Gabby. Light on details, it didn't tell Samantha much more than she had already learned from David the night before. Police had found Darcy dead in her apartment, the victim of blunt-force trauma. A neighbor out walking his dog had discovered her after noticing that Darcy's door was ajar.

Samantha folded the paper and finished her tea. David arrived promptly at seven thirty, and she ran down the stairs to meet him. Though her nerves were still doing battle in her stomach, she couldn't help but notice David, handsome as ever in a blue suit. Her heart thumped with a pang of something—attraction? hopefulness? She couldn't exactly put a name to it. But now that Samantha faced criminal charges, David's demeanor had reverted to professional. He probably thought her a total moron for involving herself in this situation.

At the police station, the detectives showed them into the same interview room they'd vacated the night earlier. Nothing had changed except for a fresh pitcher of ice water and some plastic cups sitting on the table. Samantha and David took their same seats, and David poured them each some water. Samantha observed beads of condensation roll down the side of the cup as she wrung her hands, waiting for Sanders.

The detective walked in a few minutes later and took a seat directly opposite Samantha. "Ms. Warren. Thank you for coming back. Mr. Dwyer here tells me you plan to be a little more cooperative today."

Samantha gritted her teeth. *A little more cooperative? I've been cooperative.* She nodded her head solemnly. "Yes. I want to help however I can."

"Excellent. Let's start with how you became involved in this unfortunate situation."

Samantha told her story from the beginning—her canceled wedding, her chance invitation to sell her bitters at the home tour, the lawsuit, and all of her investigations, filling in every detail she could remember up until the last time she had seen Darcy and Gabby.

"This whole time, you believed Gabby was innocent?"

Samantha traced a line in the condensation with her fingernail. "Well, no. At the beginning, I suspected her. Then I learned of the emails Brian Decker sent, and it seemed likely he implicated her for some reason."

Spencer stared at her face. "Were you aware Ms. Brantwell had a restraining order against her which prohibited her from coming within ten feet of Darcy?"

"Yes, I was, in fact. She was upset at Darcy for ruining her marriage. She overreacted."

Sanders raised an eyebrow. "You call attempted murder an overreaction?"

"Attempted murder? What are you talking about? I heard about the vandalism of the for-sale signs and a few angry comments on review websites."

Sanders relayed a story about Gabby nearly running over Darcy in the parking lot of the Island Liquor in Galveston.

Multiple witnesses had identified Gabby and testified that she sped up her car as she neared Darcy. They said she might have succeeded in running her down had another woman not pushed Darcy out of the way.

Samantha's mouth opened in shock. "Unbelievable . . ."

Sanders continued, "Were you aware Mark had filed for divorce and sought sole custody of Chloe?"

Samantha hung her head. "No. I guess maybe there were a few things I missed."

The detective chuckled. "I get it. The Hallmark Channel convinces people anybody can solve a mystery, just like the small-town baker or beauty-shop owner in their shows. But it's not as easy in real life."

Samantha's anger bubbled, like a bottle of ginger beer left to ferment too long. She raised her head. "Wait a minute. I'm a trained journalist." She looked over at David, who raised his palm as if to stop her. "All right, I admit it. I got in over my head."

The detective nodded.

"Why are you so sure Gabby killed Darcy? I watched them interact. There's certainly no love lost between them, but I swear, Gabby was fine when we left. She didn't seem enraged or anything."

Sanders raised one eyebrow as if to warn her she was treading on thin ice. "Listen, Ms. Warren, I can't divulge all the details. I can say we identified her fingerprints on what we believe to be the murder weapon."

Samantha became light-headed. It didn't sound good for Gabby.

"I'm pleased you're finally taking this seriously, Ms. Warren. Now, what can you tell us about where Gabby might have gone?"

She shook her head. "I don't know a lot about her, to be honest. I know she went to college in Houston and lives in Galveston. That's about it."

The detective stood. "Okay. Thank you for your cooperation. You will inform us if she contacts you?"

Samantha nodded. "Of course. Thank you, Detective."

They shook hands, and David led her out of the interview room and to his car. "That went better than it could have. Let's hope the worst is over now."

Samantha silently ran through the past few weeks in her head, trying to figure out how she had missed so much.

"You're quiet over there. Are you okay?"

She sighed. "I'm fine, I guess. I just feel like an idiot. How did I misjudge Gabby so much?"

"Don't beat yourself up. You operated with the facts available to you."

She shook her head and remained silent, retreating into herself the rest of the way home.

David leaned over and gave her a small hug as she opened the door to leave. "Hopefully this will all be over soon and you can put it all behind you."

"Thanks, David." She offered a wan smile as she closed his car door and walked toward her apartment.

Once in her apartment, she flopped onto her sofa, feeling drained. Before long, she fell asleep as her body tried to recover from the last several weeks.

She awoke to her cell phone ringing. It was Marisa.

"Hey, lady. Sorry I missed your call last night. I was in class. What's going on?"

Samantha groaned. "I don't even know where to begin."

She told Marisa of her two visits with the detective and about Gabby leaving with her daughter and now facing charges in Darcy's murder.

"Sam, what the hell? The last I heard you planned to turn over whatever information you had on Brian Decker to the police."

"It didn't seem like the police took the information seriously. They were focusing too hard on Gabby."

"It sounds like they had good reason. Don't tell me you still believe she's innocent."

"I don't know what to think. The police said her fingerprints were on the murder weapon and apparently Mark filed for divorce and sued Gabby for custody of their daughter. Police say she had plenty of motive to kill Mark." Samantha shook her head and hit her hand silently on the sofa arm.

"Now the police are searching for her? What a mess."

"Yeah, and I'm under strict orders not to get further involved. It's just as well. If I did anything else, I'd be liable to make a mess of everything again."

Marisa shushed her. "Don't blame yourself, Sam. You didn't know. Now, what are you doing tonight? I want you to come out with me and Beth. We'll go to a show or a movie or something fun."

"Not tonight. I need to get some rest."

"Okay, a rain check, then. I'm not taking no for an answer. We'll come get you tomorrow night."

Samantha stopped listening, her mind a million miles away. "Bye, Marisa." She hung up.

Hungry, Samantha walked into the kitchen. She made a sandwich for lunch and walked back to the living room to turn on the television while she ate. She came across the tail end of one of what her grandmother used to call her "stories," amazed to find that many of the same actors she remembered from her grandma's day were still on air.

At twelve thirty, programming switched to the local news. Following headlines about the city's pension woes and a contentious school board meeting, the well-coiffed anchor introduced another reporter in San Antonio.

"A police hunt for suspected murderer Gabby Brantwell has headed west to Alamo City, where local police have surrounded a home on the east side where Brantwell is believed to be holed up with her daughter.

"Brantwell, who has already faced charges in the murder of her estranged husband, Mark Brantwell, is now facing fresh charges in the murder of Darcy Meadows, Brantwell's girlfriend."

Samantha locked her gaze on the screen as the anchor cut to a local reporter.

"It looks like police have the home surrounded, Charlie. What have you heard from the cops on the ground?"

"Yes, Rebecca, you're correct. Police have roped off a perimeter around the house, and they believe Ms. Brantwell and her thirteen-year-old daughter are inside. Police have said it's not clear whether Brantwell is armed, but they are in contact with her. They're hoping for a quick resolution to this situation. We'll keep you posted on the latest updates."

Samantha's stomach tightened as she considered how scared Chloe must be. She hoped Gabby would turn herself in before anything disastrous happened.

The local anchors switched to more mundane topics, such as a local high school teacher who had become Instagram famous for his choreographed dances with his students; and to the weather, where a meteorologist tried to figure out how to fill a five-minute segment by repeating over and over what viewers all over Texas knew by glancing at the calendar—it would be hot.

She was about to flip back over to the game show network for a little mind-numbing *Family Feud* when the anchor cut back over to Charlie in San Antonio.

"Thanks, Rebecca. Police are now telling us Brantwell has agreed to surrender. This situation should come to an end shortly." A camera zoomed in on the front door of the house, which opened and showed Gabby and Chloe walking out with their hands raised.

After a few minutes of footage, Rebecca in Houston broke in. "Thank goodness everyone is safe. Thank you, Charlie, for bringing us the latest."

Samantha clicked off the television. She couldn't process what she'd witnessed on the television. How had Gabby gone from the woman asleep on her sofa to this desperate woman on television, running from police? A part of her still sympathized with her, though mostly for Chloe's sake. She also questioned her own instincts. Two days ago she would have said with certainty that Gabby hadn't killed her husband. Now it seemed likely that she had not only killed Mark but Darcy as well.

The whole situation reminded her of another mess she'd made when she had trusted her instincts and been miserably wrong. Seven years ago, she'd been certain Laurie Cavendish had been a helpless kid immersed in a situation she didn't understand. Samantha trusted in her heart that Laurie had been horrified by the elderly farmer's death. She'd believed the girl's friends and foster family when they'd said she wouldn't hurt a fly, all of which had turned out to be a lie. Within two years of being released from prison, in part because of the story

Samantha had written, Laurie had killed an elderly woman in her bed.

I've made a giant mess of my life and now other people's lives. When will I learn?

With little else to do, Samantha curled up on the sofa for another long nap. She tossed and turned, speculating about Laurie and Gabby and how she could have been so wrong about both of them. Sometime after nine at night she awoke to a knock on her door.

She stiffened, wondering who could be outside her apartment that late and hoping her visitor didn't have more bad news to deliver. She cautiously opened the door, almost afraid to reveal the person on the other side.

As she cracked the door, her mouth flew open and she stared in stunned silence.

Chapter Twenty

G reg stood on her doorstep, clad in a slightly rumpled gray suit, a bottle of bourbon in one hand and a fistful of flowers in the other. As soon as Samantha opened the door, he stepped inside, placed his packages on the coffee table, and pulled her into a hug. Their bodies still fit together. Her head still nestled under his chin, where she could smell his spicy cologne. He enveloped her and squeezed her hard, as if to permanently meld their bodies together. "God, I've missed you," he mumbled into her hair.

Samantha stepped out of his embrace, stunned. "Greg . . ." Tears blurred her vision as all she'd been through, from the canceled wedding to the lawsuit to the second murder, hit her all at once.

"Oh, baby, don't cry. I'm here now." He led her to the sofa and sat next to her, holding her two hands.

She couldn't get control of her emotions, so she did what her body would allow and cried harder. He pulled her to his chest, and she stayed there for a few moments, weeping.

"I've got you, baby. I've got you," he repeated over and over as he rubbed circles on her back.

She allowed him to continue for a few minutes, lost in the moment, until the word *baby* registered. She broke away from him. "What are you doing here, Greg?"

He grabbed her by the shoulders. "I had to come. I didn't want you to have to go through all of this alone."

His words were like a knife reopening the wounds in her heart. *Why couldn't you have been here? If you were here, if you hadn't canceled our wedding, none of this would have even happened. Or at least, I wouldn't have been involved.*

She looked away from him and lowered her voice. "That's the way this works now, Greg. We do things on our own. You made your decision."

He grabbed for her hands again. "I was wrong. I made a mistake. I want you to come back with me after all of this is over. We can start over, away from all of this."

A mistake? Those were the words she'd longed to hear since he'd broken their engagement. If he'd spoken them three weeks ago, it would have been as if the clouds had parted and the sun shone down on her again. Now, she didn't know what to say.

She pulled her hands away from him and stood. "It's not that easy."

He looked at her face, and his overeager smile crumpled slightly before he nodded. "We don't have to decide anything now. Let's just talk, like old times. Tell me what happened today."

Samantha looked at him and sighed, giving in. "Want a drink?" She spotted the bottle of Basil Hayden's bourbon he'd left on her kitchen counter.

He grinned. "I thought you'd never ask. I'll make it."

They walked into the kitchen. She grabbed a vase for the flowers and cut their ends off before arranging them in some water. He inspected her pineapple bitters and the bottle with the pepper tincture. "Looks like you've been busy. Where's my favorite? I've missed your cherry-vanilla bitters."

Samantha flinched at the memory of the bitters at the root of the whole mess. She didn't answer, but he continued riffling through her pantry until he came across a bottle. "Oh, here's some. Mind if I use some of this?"

She shook her head. "Go for it." She leaned against the counter to watch him work.

He mixed bourbon, sweet vermouth, and a healthy dropperful of her bitters into her silver cocktail shaker, shook it, and poured the icy concoction into two coupe glasses. He handed her one and clinked his against it. "It's a simple Manhattan, but your bitters make this drink."

They walked back into the living room. This time, while she sat on the sofa, he gave her some space and pulled in a chair from the kitchen. "Fill me in on your interview with the police."

She started with the interview and finished with the car chase and arrest in San Antonio.

"At least it sounds like David thinks the worst is over, right? You've cooperated with the cops, and as long as you continue to do so, you should be okay."

Samantha shook her head and stood to pace, placing her drink on the side table. "Don't you see? It's all my fault. If I hadn't stuck my nose in it, maybe Darcy wouldn't have died, and maybe Chloe wouldn't have had to watch her mom's arrest."

She ran into her room and threw herself onto her bed, wanting to be alone with her misery.

After a few moments, he followed her into the room. He put his hand on her shoulder and sat on the bed next to her. "You can't blame yourself. You were trying to help someone out. You were being nice. It's what you do." He turned her to face him. "You're the nicest girl I know, Samantha Warren."

She looked at him, studying his expression.

"You have the nicest eyes and the nicest hair." He brushed her blonde locks out of her face. "And the nicest lips."

He bent his head low to kiss her, softly, hesitatingly at first. She pulled away, but as the kiss went deeper, she gave in to it, closing her eyes and pulling him toward her.

*   *   *

In the morning, she awoke, stiff from what felt like a seven-hour embrace. She wriggled away from Greg and turned to study his face. *What have I done?* Yet she'd always loved this moment best. Staring at his sleeping face, she could catch a glimpse of the little boy in him and some vulnerabilities he masked when awake. Could this really be the same person who had ripped her heart out without a second thought?

She stared at him for a few more moments and then settled back into sleep again, aware that she would have to wake up and face the repercussions of her evening at some point. For now, though, she stayed in her warm bed, safe from the discussions and decisions that would come later.

An hour later, around eight in the morning, she woke again, this time to a persistent knock at her door. She bolted upright, grabbed her robe, and raced to the door. When she opened it, Marisa walked in carrying two coffees. "Hey, Sam, I know it's early, and I said we'd make plans tonight, but I didn't want you to sit around and stew by yourself the whole day. I'm blowing off my contracts class. I've got an adventure planned for us. Go on and get ready."

She looked at Samantha, and both turned at the sound of rustling coming from the bedroom. Marisa jerked her head backward as if she'd been shocked, and she looked back and forth between Samantha's robe and the door. They heard a thump and then a howl from the other side.

"Oh, uh, obviously this is a bad time." She offered Samantha a *You go, girl* wink and backed away.

Before Marisa reached the door, Greg popped out of the bedroom, rubbing his jaw and yawning. "Sorry, I tripped on your chair. You must have moved some furniture around."

He grew silent when he spotted Marisa.

"Samantha!" Marisa hissed. "What have you done? And you!" She directed her fury toward Greg. "How dare you come back here after all you put her through!" She still held the cup of hot coffee and looked as though she might hurl it at Greg.

"Marisa!" Samantha's voice stopped her friend in her tracks. "It's complicated."

Marisa held up her hand. "I don't want to hear it." She left the coffee on the counter and turned to leave.

"Marisa!" Samantha took a minute to secure her robe and jogged after her, wanting to explain herself, but she made it out the doorway too late. Marisa raced to her car and backed down the driveway without giving Samantha a second glance.

Greg stepped outside and handed Samantha one of the steaming coffees Marisa had left behind. "I guess she wasn't happy to see me, but at least she left coffee." He took a sip before wrapping his arms around Samantha's waist.

She broke away. "What are you doing?"

She ran inside, and Greg followed. "Wait! What's the problem?"

"Last night . . . we shouldn't have done that." Seeing Marisa fleeing from her apartment in horror had made her question last night's encounter.

He reached out for her hand. "Last night was amazing."

She shook his hand off and placed the coffee on the counter before darting toward her bedroom, where she closed the door. "I'm gonna take a shower."

In the bathroom, she turned the faucet to full blast. She stood under the stinging water and sobbed. She had never been more confused. For weeks she'd cast herself as a failure, in life and in love. Last night had made her feel good, at least temporarily. Then the shock and horror on Marisa's face this morning had told her she had made a mistake. But had she?

She breathed in and out, the scent of her rosemary-and-mint shampoo calming her, until her breathing was under control.

What was so bad about sleeping with Greg? Plenty of people reunited with their exes. Maybe he was exactly what she needed right now. What would be the harm in sliding back into a comfortable routine? After all, only a few short months ago she'd agreed to spend the rest of her life with him.

She slipped on her robe again and walked into the kitchen to the smell of bacon frying. Greg flipped some pancakes and looked at her, smiling sheepishly. "Sorry about Marisa. I'll bet I shocked her. Anyway, I hope you're hungry."

She smiled too. "It smells great. I'm starving."

The coffee on the counter had grown cold, so she brewed some tea instead. It was like old times, when she and Greg had mastered the choreography of working together in the compact kitchen.

With plates loaded with pancakes and bacon, they sat at the table and dug into their food. Greg finished first and carried his plate to the sink. He came back to the table and kissed her on her temple as he grabbed his keys. "Baby, sorry to leave you with the dishes, but I've got to run. I'll take a shower at the hotel."

Samantha looked confused. "The hotel? You're leaving?"

"Just to study. I'll be back tonight for . . . whatever." He grinned and raised an eyebrow but quickly turned apologetic. "I'm sorry, but I've got to stay on track with my studies for the bar exam." Within moments, he was gone.

The pancakes sank like a lead balloon in Samantha's stomach. *Did he really leave as if nothing happened? Like we don't need to talk at all about last night?*

She tried to consider it from his perspective. Even before they broke up, she'd known his studying for the bar would be a miserable experience for both of them. She had resigned herself to being a lonely newlywed for the first few months of marriage. It made sense that he would have to study, but it suddenly made their whole evening feel cheap.

Is this how it'll be if we get back together? He takes for granted that he can go off and do his own thing and expect me to wait for him?

She got dressed and came back to clean the dishes, growing more and more irritated with Greg with each dirty pan. She could have been off on an adventure with Marisa this morning. Instead she was stuck in her apartment, an entire day stretching before her and nothing in particular to do.

Filled with nervous energy, she threw herself into a cleaning binge, sweeping, vacuuming, dusting, and shining everything in her small apartment. When every surface looked spotless, she turned her attention to her desk and file drawers, deciding to sort through the mess in there.

As Ruby looked on from her perch near the window, Samantha dug through her old clips from the *Gazette* and the *Herald* until she came across her feature on Laurie Cavendish that had led her series on prosecutorial misconduct in the small town.

She stared at the girl's pockmarked face and sad eyes, which took her straight back to the central Texas town and to her interviews with the girl at the detention center.

Laurie had been frightened at first to talk to Samantha and hid behind the greasy strands of lanky blonde hair that perpetually covered at least half her face. Encouraged by the foster family she'd bonded with for nine months, she opened up to Samantha.

After multiple interviews, Samantha had believed Laurie's foster parents were right: the lonely girl would never, of her own volition, have committed such a heinous crime. Had the prosecutor not planted evidence suggesting she'd been in the room while the farmer was killed rather than waiting in the car as she'd said, Laurie would have never faced such a harsh sentence.

Nearly seven years later, even after she knew Laurie had since been accused of a second brutal murder, Samantha still couldn't reconcile the girl in the picture with the image of a cold-blooded killer.

Upon learning of the second murder, Samantha had felt shame and guilt for her part in freeing Laurie. She hadn't been able to bring herself to read any more stories about the case that would remind her of how badly she'd misjudged Laurie. Today, though, already moody and worried about following her instincts down the wrong path again, she decided she wanted details.

She Googled Laurie's name and stumbled across a blog created by one of Laurie's few high school friends and dedicated to Laurie's memory.

Front and center on the website, an article from the small paper for which Samantha had written the initial series detailed Laurie's suicide:

Laurie Cavendish, facing murder charges in the death of a Greenville woman during a botched robbery, was found hanging today in her jail cell. Jailers attempted to revive her, but they pronounced her dead at four p.m.

Cavendish, who had been released from prison three years earlier for a similar murder following hearings about prosecutorial misconduct, confessed to murdering Eva Leone, 89, in her bed. She told police she went to Leone's home to steal money to pay for her foster mother's surgery and was startled when Leone pulled out her own gun.

The elderly woman fired her gun once, grazing Cavendish's arm, before Cavendish fired back, killing her.

A short blog post written by Laurie's friend was the only other item on the website.

Laurie didn't have much of a chance in life. She made plenty of dumb choices and fell in with the wrong people, always trying to find a place to fit in. I can't justify her actions, which were unjustifiable. But I wanted to leave some reminder that Laurie Cavendish had plenty of good in her. She was a loyal friend who trusted too much and loved deeply. I, for one, will miss her.

As Samantha shut down the website, she found she could still muster some sympathy for Laurie. As the girl's friend had written, Laurie's actions couldn't be justified, but there was more nuance to the situation than Samantha had originally believed. Perhaps her instincts about Laurie hadn't been so wrong. Perhaps, deep down, she'd had a good, if misguided, heart.

Samantha closed the files and cleaned off her desk, realizing from the rumbling of her stomach that she'd been at it for hours and had missed lunch. In the kitchen, she spotted her pineapple and cherry-vanilla bitters and remembered her promise to take some over to Boheme for her new bartender friend Dane to sample. She poured a little of each into smaller bottles and stashed them in her purse. She figured she could grab a snack there for a late lunch and took the chance that Dane might be on duty.

She biked to Montrose, filling her lungs with fresh air. Outside Boheme, she locked her bike to a rack, walked into the bar area, and asked the bartender on duty if Dane was around.

"He should be in around three, if you want to wait."

With only forty-five minutes to wait, she took a seat at the bar, ordered some empanadas, and pulled out a book to read.

Engrossed in her book, Samantha didn't notice Dane's familiar face peering at her from the other side of the bar. "It's you. I wasn't sure if you were ever coming back."

She raised her gaze from her book and smiled. "Oh, hey. Yeah, life's been a little crazy, but I finished my pineapple bitters. I brought it over for you to taste."

Dane inspected the bottle. "Cool."

He poured some on a bar spoon and tasted it, nodding appreciatively. "This is great."

Samantha pulled out another bottle, her cherry-vanilla bitters.

Dane took a taste of that also. "Nice bite to it. Yeah, I could totally use both. Would twenty dollars for the pair cover it?"

She looked confused. "Wait, you want to buy them?"

"Yeah. Aren't they for sale?"

She contemplated a moment and shrugged. "Why not? Yeah, twenty dollars would be good."

He passed her the money and promised to comp her lunch as well.

"Hey, if you take requests, you know what I'd really love? Something spicy, like mouth-numbing spicy. You make something like that, bring it over."

Samantha considered the pepper tincture curing on her counter at home and wondered whether adding Sichuan peppercorns to the mix would provide the mouth-numbing sensation he wanted. "I'll think on it."

"Cool. Hey, come back sometime next week, and I'll have a new cocktail based on your bitters." He walked off to tend to other customers at the bar.

Oh my gosh! Samantha did an internal fist pump. While friends and family always praised her cocktail and bitters-making skills, Dane was a professional. Not only did he want to buy her bitters, he wanted to build cocktails around them. Maybe her situation was improving. Obviously this was only a first step, but could there actually be a way to turn her passion project into a feasible business?

She rode her bicycle home, buoyant from the encounter. A text message on her phone deflated her mood. It was from David, and it said only **Call me.** Did the police want to talk to her again? Worse yet, did they want to charge her?

With Gabby in custody, Samantha now worried about what Gabby might say to police about Samantha's involvement. She raced up her apartment steps and called David back. "I got your message. What's going on?"

She braced herself for the worst and couldn't believe his response. "I heard from Greg . . ."

Huh? Why would Greg have called him?

"He said you guys were reuniting, and he wanted to know when you might be cleared to move to New York."

Samantha exploded. "He what?"

Heat flushed through her body as her fury mounted. *How dare he tell David we're getting back together! Apparently I don't even get a say in the matter? We haven't discussed anything!*

"I told him I couldn't talk to him about your case because you're my client. Listen, I've spoken with the police, and you satisfied them with your answers for now. They said as long as you were reachable and could promise to be back if they need you to testify, you are free to move." He paused for a moment. "Are you . . . wanting to move?"

"No! I mean, I don't know what I'll do in the long run, but for now, I'm not leaving."

He paused again. "Good. Anyway, on the matter of your other case, the lawsuit? I've got excellent news. Gabby dropped the suit, so you have one less worry."

The news was anticlimactic. Though she was happy to be free of the lawsuit, there were many other concerns. "Great, David. Thanks."

David seemed as if he wanted to say something else but thought better of it. "Well, that's it for now. Please call me if you need anything else."

They ended the call, and Samantha became freshly infuriated. *How dare Greg call David!*

She selected Greg's name from the contact list on her cell phone, practically stabbing her screen and fuming while the phone rang. She didn't trust herself to leave a voice mail and called him back three times over the course of an hour with no answer.

When he walked into her apartment two hours later, he looked shocked by the onslaught of anger.

"Where have you been? Why didn't you answer me? What gave you the right to call David and say we're getting back together? Don't you think I get a say in that decision?"

He reached his hand for her shoulder. "Baby, where is this all coming from?"

She shook away from him. "That's another thing. Stop it with this whole 'baby' business. I am not your baby."

He looked crestfallen. "We've always called each other baby."

Heat infused her cheeks when she answered. "When we were a couple."

He groaned and collapsed onto the sofa. "Not this again. How many times do I need to flagellate myself? I've admitted it. I was a jerk. I made a mistake."

"It was less than two months ago. Don't you get it? You broke my heart and shattered my entire plan for my life. How do you expect me to forgive you so quickly?"

He looked at the floor. "I hoped our years together would count for something."

Samantha didn't trust herself to argue the point and focused on her other unanswered questions. "Where have you been? I called you like four times."

"I'm sorry. I turn off my phone when I get in the zone on my studying. You don't understand the pressure I'm under here. I've got to pass the New York bar."

The familiar words—excuses, really—jarred like nails on a chalkboard. Anytime she'd questioned his being unreachable in the past, he'd gone on and on about the kind of pressure he faced. She had a murder investigation weighing on her. It was becoming clear he didn't think much beyond how an event affected him. She launched into her next bone of contention. "I called to ask you why you deemed it appropriate to call David and ask about my case, not to mention telling him we're getting back together."

Greg twisted the bottom edge of his shirt with his hand. "I just wanted some information. I know how much you like having all the information on hand before you decide."

Though Greg sounded conciliatory, Samantha construed the false note in his voice as a subtle dig. "It sounds to me like you don't want me to think at all. You want to do my thinking for me."

He reached for her hand. "Of course I want you to make up your own mind. I'm sorry. I'm just eager to begin my new life, and I want you in it."

They went a few more rounds about him taking her for granted and not considering her needs or wants and her not being flexible or spontaneous. Samantha's emotions were on a roller coaster, and as much as it saddened her, she wanted the ride to stop.

"Greg, I think you need to leave."

He stood and looked pleadingly at her. "Back to my hotel, or . . ."

Suddenly, everything became clear. "You know what? No. Back to New York. Everyone tells me I need to be more decisive. Well, here it is . . ."

He moved toward her again. "No, Sam. You can't mean it. What about last night? What about starting over?"

The finality of her decision made the anger leave her body. She was tired of fighting, tired of this conversation, and tired of Greg.

"I don't think it will work out for us, Greg. I do wish you the best." She moved to the door and held it open for him as he trudged out. She sighed as he walked down her stairs one last time and offered him one last smile and wave before she walked back inside and closed the door. She lifted Ruby, who had been circling the coffee table, and nuzzled her.

Though she was a little sad, the decision lifted a weight off her shoulders. She could let go of her anger and feel grateful to Greg for forcing them into this kind of decision. He really wasn't right for her. It was obvious to her now.

Chapter
Twenty-One

At seven thirty, her stomach growled. She wanted company but didn't want to rehash the entire scene with Greg. She texted Marisa, hoping her friend wouldn't still be angry about this morning. **Sorry for the weirdness this morning. Greg's on his way back to NYC for good. You guys free for dinner?**

Marisa responded in less than five minutes. **Pick you up in fifteen.**

She smiled. This was the stable relationship she needed in her life. The friends opted for pizza at one of the half dozen new brick-oven places that had proliferated throughout the Inner Loop. They shared a bottle of wine among the three of them while Samantha offered a few details of her two days with Greg.

"You seem happy." Beth swirled the Pinot around her wineglass.

"You know what? I am. It feels good to have ended things on my terms. We can both move on now. By the way, how are things with your new venture? How was the garden club?"

Beth described the party. She'd served mini veggie calzones with fresh produce from her garden. "It went well. Everyone raved about the food, but I'll be honest, it was a lot of work.

And this was a group of friends. I'm not sure I can pull it off on my own, catering for strangers."

"So you'll hire someone." Samantha took a sip of her wine. "It sounds like you are really onto something. You don't want to give up your dream because of a lack of manpower."

Beth nodded her head. "I've thought about it, but I'm not sure I can make the numbers work to hire someone. Really, what I think I need is a partner. I'm considering a few options."

Beth's words struck a chord with Samantha. She was happy for her friend, but she couldn't help but feel a twinge of jealousy that she was moving forward with her dream. Samantha's dreams these days felt ill defined. Once upon a time, her greatest dream had been to become a reporter, to write stories that mattered. But that dream had begun to fade with her layoff from the paper, and now, after all that had happened, it just didn't feel right anymore. She had the whispers of new dreams fluttering at the back of her mind, but she hadn't yet given them room to grow. She thought back to her encounter with Dane earlier in the day, again wondering if there might be some way to transform her cocktail passion into a paying gig.

Conversation drifted to other topics, and Samantha told her friends that the wrongful-death lawsuit had been dropped.

"Are you convinced now that Gabby is guilty?" Marisa offered the last slice of pizza, but with no takers, she ate it herself.

"It seems likely. Her fingerprints are on the murder weapon, and she was the last person to appear on Darcy's doorbell camera the night she died, after the two of us left Darcy alive earlier in the night. I can't make those facts fit in any other scenario."

Beth took a sip of her wine. "Except . . . if Darcy was already dead when Gabby came back the second time."

Samantha shook her head. "How would the killer have gotten there? No one else appeared on the doorbell camera between when Gabby and I left and when Gabby came back."

Beth didn't answer right away. "What if the real killer was already in the house before you two arrived the first time?"

Samantha tilted her head questioningly. "What do you mean?"

"Well, if someone arrived before you and Gabby did, they could have come down after you and Gabby left, killed her, and been out of there before Gabby came back. There's no way to know from the doorbell camera whether Darcy was alive when Gabby came back. All we know is Gabby reentered the house."

Marisa scoffed. "Beth, you watch too much *Murder She Wrote*. In real life, the most obvious explanation is usually the right one."

Beth gave Marisa an annoyed expression, then shrugged her shoulders. "You're probably right."

But Beth's comments had piqued Samantha's interest. She reflected on the visit with Darcy. Darcy had seemed distracted and somewhat nervous. The questions they'd asked her could explain some of her nerves. Still, Beth had raised an interesting alternative.

The friends finished their wine and got the check. Marisa suggested they get a nightcap somewhere else, but Samantha begged off.

The couple dropped her off at home, and Marisa made plans to meet later in the week. Samantha waved as they drove away and walked inside to make some tea.

She tried to read her book for a bit, but her thoughts kept turning to Beth's suggestion. *Is it possible someone was hiding in Darcy's house while we were there? If so, who?* She remembered what had nagged her after she and Gabby left Darcy's house. The email, which had seemed like such a smoking gun to Samantha, had barely seemed to register as meaning anything at all to Darcy. Not only that, but she had seemed shocked when Samantha pointed out the paragraph about dogs being poisoned by oleander. *What did she say? She saved the newspaper for the photo. She seemed earnest and confused when I asked, as if she couldn't understand the newspaper's relevance.*

Samantha had promised David she wouldn't get involved, but surely it wouldn't hurt to do a little internet searching. Although still fairly convinced of Gabby's guilt, she realized she'd never actually looked into that photo to figure out why Darcy might have been interested in the man. She pulled up the photo on her phone and read the caption again: Peter Garfield. She plugged the name into Google along with *Montgomery County* and within moments found his website. Peter Garfield was a contractor, and he apparently specialized in Victorian cottage renovations.

Goose bumps rose on her arms. The subject line in Darcy's email to herself was *Solution to the Mark problem*. When Samantha had first read the subject line, she'd assumed the worst—that Darcy planned to kill Mark. But what if her problem was merely Mark's refusal to appear on the HRN show with her? Could she have invited Peter Garfield to be Mark's replacement on the show? His website suggested he worked regularly on historic renovations, so he certainly had the skills. And judging by his photo, with his muscular frame and barely scruffy beard, he certainly had the look HRN seemed to want for their television personalities.

But why did Darcy have this particular photo of Peter with his son rather than a picture from his web page? And what are the odds of that picture appearing on the same newspaper spread as the story about oleander poisoning? Is it possible it's all a coincidence?

But the more she thought about it, Samantha didn't think so. She remembered Darcy's reaction when she'd seen the blurb. Something seemed to have clicked with her, and she'd immediately kicked Samantha and Gabby out.

Was it possible she realized someone had attempted to frame her for Mark's murder three weeks before it occurred? And if so, who?

Samantha suddenly wished she could strategize with Gabby about this new bit of information—before remembering she'd already all but convicted Gabby in her head.

I need to stop this. More harm than good can come from theorizing.

Samantha pushed her laptop aside and went to bed.

* * *

The next morning, Samantha pulled out her laptop to get some work done. Her thoughts had shifted back to the case when an email from Gabby's daughter, Chloe, appeared in her in-box.

Dear Samantha,

I'm sorry to bother you, but I'm afraid you might be my mom's last hope. She made me promise not to call you because she doesn't want to get you any more involved than you've already been. The police believe she did it, and they aren't considering any other options. I swear to you she didn't do it. I'm safe for now—staying with Becca's family. I can't stand the idea of Mom stuck in prison. Please help!

Chloe

The poor girl. Samantha couldn't imagine what it must be like to have your father murdered and your mom thrown in jail for the crime. She wanted to respond to the girl, but she wasn't sure what kind of hope she could offer when all the evidence seemed to confirm Gabby's guilt. She shouldn't get involved again. Then again, it wasn't right for Chloe to have to take on the burden of proving her mother's innocence. She decided it couldn't hurt to message her back. Maybe her mom had told her something that would help prove her innocence or, at the very least, hint at someone else's involvement.

Dear Chloe,

I'm sorry about your mom. I really wish I could do something, but the police insist all the evidence points to her, including her fingerprints on the murder weapon. Did your mom say why she went back to Darcy's? Or anything that might help?

Samantha

She pressed send, somewhat anxious about her decision. She didn't want to get the girl's hopes up, but if she could help without endangering herself or others, she should try.

After half an hour, she received a reply.

Mom said she got a text from Darcy around four in the morning telling her she wanted to talk to her but to come alone. Mom thought Darcy would confess, so she went. The door was unlocked when she got there. She walked in and found Darcy on the hall floor, bleeding, with a coat rack laying on top of her. Mom lifted the coat rack off to check if she was still alive, but when she realized Darcy was dead, she ran. She came to get me, and we drove to San Antonio. I wish I knew more.

The text message explained why Gabby would have gone back to Darcy's. The explanation about her lifting the coat rack off of Darcy seemed plausible. None of it seemed enough to make police consider someone else as a suspect. *Though, if I'm not careful, they won't hesitate to add me back in the mix.*

Samantha wrote one last email telling Chloe she couldn't promise anything but she would try to find out more. *Stay strong*, she wrote the girl.

A lump formed in her throat as she pondered all Chloe had been through, from her father's death to her mother's arrest to the standoff with police. Now, with Gabby back in jail and unlikely to get bail, the girl must feel so alone. Samantha wasn't going to turn her back on her now.

Samantha tried to pinpoint what she could be missing. There must be something she'd overlooked along the way, and when she figured it out, everything would fall into place.

She decided to try to follow up on the lead she'd dropped yesterday and called the phone number listed on Peter Garfield's website. When she got his answering machine, she left a message, asking him to call her back.

With that done, Samantha determined she needed to go back to the beginning, or at least Mark and Darcy's beginning in Houston. Something still nagged her about it. Mark had moved to Houston eight or nine months ago. How had he cultivated this brand-new, successful life right away?

While she'd heard from Bob, she realized she'd never asked Beth what she remembered from when Mark joined the commission. She called her.

"Hey, Beth, I know this is coming out of the blue, and I promise, I'm not getting involved where I shouldn't, but something's been bothering me."

"You're sort of scaring me, but I'll bite. What's going on?"

"Do you remember when Mark joined the Historic Commission? I know there was a vacancy, but why did the other person leave?"

Beth seemed to expel her breath all at once. "I'm really not sure. I think maybe he retired. You could ask him yourself. He's a professor at the architecture school."

"What's his name?"

"Reingold, I think. Arthur Reingold."

"Thanks. I may pay him a visit."

It wasn't even lunch yet, so Samantha decided to try to make an appointment to visit Reingold in the afternoon. The department assistant confirmed that he would have time to talk with her during his open office period around two.

Before her appointment, she grabbed a sandwich and turned on the television to watch the news. Gabby's initial hearing was scheduled for this morning, and though Samantha would have liked to attend, she couldn't risk it because of the warnings from police to keep her nose out of the case. Given the publicity, the local television stations would likely offer gavel-to-gavel coverage.

The first station she turned to was broadcasting scenes from the courthouse.

Because the courts didn't allow video cameras during open court, the news networks could only show B-roll footage of scenes from within the courtroom right before the hearing started. The sight of Gabby in her orange jumpsuit made Samantha flinch. Gabby looked helpless sitting at the defense table, staring at its polished wood.

The reporter stood outside the courtroom to do her live shot, informing the audience of Gabby's not-guilty plea. Her face molded into one of tight-lipped seriousness, the reporter informed viewers that a judge had denied Gabby bail because prosecutors considered her a flight risk. After completing a run-down of the gruesome murders of both Mark and Darcy, the reporter offered the prosecutor's theory that Gabby had committed the crimes out of jealousy.

Samantha shut the television off and got ready to leave for her meeting with Reingold.

After checking in with the admin, who confirmed that Professor Reingold was in the lab and ready to meet her, Samantha walked in, feeling a little like Gulliver in a village of Lilliputians with all the miniature-sized buildings on display at the surrounding work desks. There were miniature airports and schools and shopping centers in various stages of design. She had always enjoyed the creativity of design—the freedom inherent in designing for design's sake or to solve a particular problem, knowing that the building wasn't likely to see the light of day.

A balding man with lively eyes strode over to Samantha and thrust his hand in her direction. "Arthur Reingold. I understand you want to speak with me."

Samantha took his hand, answering his powerful grip with one of her own. "Yes, Professor. Thank you. Samantha Warren. I'm a freelance writer working on a story on historic buildings in Houston. I understand you used to be on the Highlands Historic Commission?"

Reingold, who appeared in good humor, gave Samantha the once-over. "That's right, until eight months ago."

He led her over to a set of chairs in the corner with gold leaf poles jutting out at obscure angles and seat slings made of a coppery, gossamer-looking fabric Samantha didn't believe would hold her weight but did.

"Did your term expire?"

"No. Actually, my term ran through next fall, but the chairman asked if I would mind stepping down a little early."

This news piqued Samantha's interest. "You mean Bob Randall?"

"Yes. He wanted to recruit some new hot shot contractor to the board. I had recently won a commission that would take a lot of my time, so I didn't mind stepping down a little sooner than planned. What kind of story are you looking at?"

The discrepancy between what Bob Randall had told her about a sudden vacancy on the board and Reingold's assertion that Bob himself had asked him to step down intrigued her.

"I'm still trying to find my focus, but I want to feature some historic properties demolished in Houston and contrast those with efforts going on in the Highlands to preserve entire districts."

Reingold grabbed a pencil tucked behind his ear and twirled it. "There are so many magnificent buildings that have been destroyed over the years in this city, which is why the work the Highlands group is doing is so important. I was proud to be a part of it. If you want more current information, though, you probably want to speak to Bob."

Samantha pulled out her notepad and pen. "Thanks. I've talked to him a few times before. I'll reach out to him again. In the meantime, can you suggest any places I could do some research on historic buildings in Houston? I'd love to read the history of some of the demolished buildings and the history of what people built in their place."

Reingold directed her to some periodicals in the architecture library, which he said regularly featured historic buildings in the city at risk from the wrecking ball.

"What you really want is the Houston Architecture Forum." He described a message board started over ten years ago by two colleagues that had evolved over time into the best searchable database for Houston building histories and construction updates.

Samantha smiled. "That sounds perfect. Thanks, Professor Reingold." She stood to leave.

"Send me a copy of the article when you're done."

She waved as she left the studio. Though mildly remorseful about leading him on about her true intentions, she saw little harm in pretending she would write a story. And hey, the topic did interest her. Maybe she would get around to it someday.

As she walked across campus, Samantha passed by the College of Hotel and Restaurant Management, and her mind went back to Mila.

The wrong number on Sunday. It was her.

A kernel of an idea grew in the back of Samantha's mind, but it needed time to form. Though she didn't believe Mila or Eric was guilty of murder, she didn't like loose ends. She flipped through the call log on her phone. Though she'd deleted the voice mail, the phone number remained in her incoming-calls list. She dialed it.

After a few rings, a familiar voice answered. "I know who this is. What do you want? Listen, the police cleared Eric, and anyway, we ended things, so I don't have anything else to say to you."

"Wait, Mila. Please don't hang up. I only want to talk to you for a minute. Please? I'm outside the college right now. Are you on campus? I can buy you a cup of coffee. You owe me at least one conversation for scaring me half to death at my apartment."

"I don't owe you anything. You sent the police after me."

"I'm sorry, but what did you expect me to do? It's a murder investigation, after all. How about not only free coffee, but I buy you a whole meal? I've heard they've got pretty good sandwiches and even better cake at the café."

As much as things had changed since she'd been in school, Samantha had never met a college kid who would turn down a free meal.

The girl sighed. "All right. Fine. I'm in my dorm room now. We can meet at Cougar Café in fifteen minutes."

"Thanks. See you then." Samantha disconnected the call and wandered inside the Hotel and Restaurant Management building to find the café, a student-run enterprise designed to give students management experience. It specialized in experimental coffees and teas. She ordered an iced apple cider chai and waited for Mila.

As promised, the girl walked in fifteen minutes later. Samantha spotted her curls first and met her at the counter to pay for her coffee as well as a panini and a slice of the café's famous hot chocolate cake.

"Thanks for meeting me like this." Samantha ushered the girl toward a table in the corner.

"Thanks for the meal." The girl took a sip, giving herself a foam moustache. "Like I said, police cleared Eric, and I broke up with him, so I don't know what else I can tell you."

"The dead man's wife sued me, and it's nearly ruined my reputation. I lost my job, even. I'm trying to clear my name, and I want to ask you what happened the night of the home tour. Why did you think Eric might have done something?"

The girl sighed. "He's jealous all the time. That's why I ended it with him. At the party, I talked to the dead guy, Mark or whatever. He gave me this crazy-big tip, twenty-five dollars, and told me to forget what I had seen. The thing is, I hadn't seen anything."

Samantha raised her eyebrows but didn't say anything, waiting for Mila to continue.

"Anyway, I told Eric about it, and he didn't believe me. He assumed something must have happened between me and the guy for him to give me such a big tip. Eric stormed out of the party. That's when you found me crying in the garden."

"That happened at least twenty minutes before Mark collapsed."

"I know. The next day, I didn't really know what had happened to the guy, but I worried Eric might have come back to confront him or something. It turns out he didn't. He went to his sister's apartment and got drunk. Her roommates confirmed it. He's got an alibi."

The story confirmed that Samantha's instincts were correct. Mila and her now ex-boyfriend hadn't had anything to do with Mark's death. But maybe, without knowing it, Mila still knew something.

"Back to the money Mark gave you. Why do you think he did that? What did you witness?"

The girl shrugged. "Nothing, I swear. I walked into the room to ask if anyone needed a drink, and Mark was talking to some old man. I didn't hear what they were talking about, but everyone smiled, so I didn't really think anything of it until the guy handed me the cash."

"Do you know the other guy?"

"I don't know. Just some old guy. Other than my grandpa, they all sort of look the same to me. Anyway, I've got to get to my next class. Thanks for the meal." Mila walked out of the café.

Samantha left, considering the conversation as she walked to her car. If nothing else, it gratified her to cross two more names off the suspect list, though now she had new questions. Who was the old guy who had been talking to Mark, and what could have been so important about their conversation that Mark would pay Mila to keep quiet about it?

Back at home, Samantha couldn't decide on her next move. She walked into the kitchen, hoping her subconscious could make sense of everything while she worked on one of her bitters projects.

At the farmers' market earlier in the week, she'd purchased several pepper varieties, including the tiny chiltepin peppers that grew wild in parts of Texas. They were small but spicy, measuring over 100,000 Scoville heat units. When combined with Sichuan peppercorns, the spicy mixture should bring enough heat to clear the sinuses of her Boheme bartender friend Dane.

She threw the peppercorns and peppers into her spice grinder and ground the mixture. With her hands on autopilot, she began to recall her day, trying to find the loose thread present in all of her discussions.

As she sealed jars with her spice mixture in grain alcohol in preparation for letting them rest on her kitchen counter for several days, her phone rang.

A number with a Galveston area code popped up on the caller ID.

Chapter
Twenty-Two

"Hello?" Samantha took a deep breath before answering the phone.

"Samantha? It's Chloe."

"Oh, it's you. I saw the Galveston area code, and I wasn't sure who to expect."

"I'm sorry to bother you again, but I found something. I think it could be important." The girl sounded breathless.

"What did you find?" Samantha's pulse began to race.

"It came in the mail today. I guess Darcy boxed up a bunch of my dad's stuff and sent it to me. At first, I didn't want to go through it, but then I had to." Chloe began to sob. Her breathing turned ragged.

"Easy . . . take a deep breath. What did you find?" Samantha held her breath as she waited for Chloe to be able to speak again.

"A notebook with some drawings of furniture he planned to build for my room. I guess Darcy thought I would want to keep it." The girl sobbed again.

Samantha let go of the air she held, now more confused than anxious. *What could be so important about some furniture?* "Go on."

"In the back of the notebook on some blank pages, I found a letter or note of some sort. I don't really understand it."

Samantha caught her breath again. "Can you read it to me?" She grabbed a pen to write the message down.

" 'I'm bidding on the McCormick project. If I don't win, everybody will find out about the Jennifer situation. We both know you don't want that to happen.' " Chloe's voice wobbled as she spoke the words. "What could it mean?"

Samantha believed she understood what it meant, or at least what it might mean, but she didn't want to say the words aloud to the girl. "I don't know, Chloe. Did you find anything else? Any other papers or notes?"

"No."

"Does the name Jennifer mean anything to you?"

The girl sniffled. "There are a million Jennifers out there. I have no idea what this letter means." Her voice began to grow louder and shriller.

"It's okay. You did the right thing in calling me." Samantha tried to keep her voice even-keeled to instill some calm in the girl. "I want you to do something else. Call your mom's lawyer and give him the notebook Darcy sent you. Tell him everything you told me."

The girl sobbed again. "Do you think it will help Mom?"

"I hope so. I don't know what it means yet, but let me try to figure something out."

Still sobbing but in a more controlled manner, Chloe thanked Samantha and disconnected the phone.

Samantha read through the words again. *This sure sounds like blackmail to me, but who's the target? And who or what is 'the Jennifer situation'?*

* * *

Samantha grabbed her laptop, headed to her sofa, and began to Google the name Jennifer. She might as well have Googled the word *dog*. Chloe was right. There were a million Jennifers out there. It had been one of the most popular names in the 1980s. Mark had probably known dozens of them during his life. *How can I find the right one?*

It was clear that an aimless Google search would produce no results. Sometimes she'd gotten lucky with Google while reporting, but not with a name as generic as Jennifer. She needed a way to do a more targeted search.

She remembered the forum Reingold had mentioned and pulled up the website. It wasn't sleek, but it contained a treasure trove of information about everything going on development-wise in the city. Each individual neighborhood was represented, from the Highlands to Montrose to Pearland and even all the farther-flung suburbs. There were pages for practically every development project for which permits had been sought or variances requested. It all appeared to be citizen led, but these citizens were savvy about pulling records, and they were happy to share gossip.

Samantha poked around the site and discovered an area dedicated to different developers. First, she plugged in Mark's name, but nothing appeared other than a link to the same article she'd read earlier in the community newspaper about his fight with Decker at the Historic Commission meeting. This being an architecture forum, most of the comments were favorable toward Mark and unflattering to Decker.

Samantha sighed. *There's nothing new here.*

On the off chance it would reveal something, Samantha typed in different variants of Mark's name and the name Jennifer. Her eyelids grew heavy as she scrolled through hundreds of random comments, most having nothing to do with anything of interest. About to concede defeat, she stumbled upon a post about a failed midtown high-rise tower development from someone named "Captain Obvious," asking if anyone remembered the "colossal failure of the Jennifer project?"

Alarm bells went off in Samantha's head as she instantly perked up. *Could this be THE Jennifer?*

There were no real responses to Captain Obvious's post, dated three years ago. She looked around for other posts by him and found a few in the last year—one about a recent bar development in the Washington Corridor and one about the East End. She hoped he still visited the forum. Even if he wasn't a prolific poster, he might be a lurker.

Seeing no harm, Samantha responded to his Jennifer post. *This is so funny—I just heard about the Jennifer project today and came here to find more information about it. Would love to hear what you can share.* She signed it Nose for News, pressed post, and hoped for the best.

Samantha clicked backward through the thread, trying to find anything else that might be relevant. After a few clicks, she stumbled across the Brantwell part of the search—a post about a different failed midtown development project started by Fred Brantwell, Mark's father.

It was getting late, but Samantha realized she wouldn't be able to sleep until she'd exhausted her searching. She plugged *Fred Brantwell* into the forum search engine and began to put together a blueprint for his development history.

It appeared, going back through the forum, that Fred had started out building tract homes in farther-flung suburbs like Pearland and Clear Lake. There didn't seem to be anything remarkable about the developments mentioned in the forum.

Most of what commenters wrote was reminiscences about various strip centers or restaurants located nearby.

Later in his career, in the late 1980s and early 1990s, Fred had moved inward toward the city proper and generated some controversy, at least according to some forum posters. He'd bought cheap property and tried to redevelop it into luxury residential towers. Sometimes the plans fell through and the developments never got off the ground. In other cases, they were built but to the ire of neighbors, who opposed the density and the loss of some single-family homes near the projects.

The trip through history brought to mind her earlier unanswered questions about Mark and Fred and the project that had soured their relationship, sending Mark to start over in Galveston. Gabby had mentioned an earlier, similar project named after one of Fred's partners' daughters . . . something about a name popular in the 1980s.

She mentioned Lisa, but could it be Jennifer?

Samantha threw her laptop aside and rose, needing to pace. She walked the perimeter of her living room rug over and over as she tried to piece together everything she had learned. All the facts were jumbled in her mind, so she grabbed a notepad and pen and sat on her sofa to jot down some notes.

1. *Fred and Mark fought about a development project, causing Mark to leave Houston. Mark believed the project would fail, exactly like another earlier project named after someone's daughter. Could that be the Jennifer?*
2. *Mark quit lucrative television show after producers began to dig into his past, saying he didn't want his father's reputation sullied. Could this have related to the Jennifer project?*

3. *Chloe found a note referencing some form of blackmail and the Jennifer situation in Mark's notebook.*

Reviewing her list, Samantha tried to piece together a scenario to explain the murder. *What if someone blackmailed Mark, threatening to ruin his father's reputation over some development deal gone bad? Maybe someone involved in the HRN network show learned about Mark's dad's development projects and blackmailed him. Could that person have killed Mark—and later Darcy if she had learned about the blackmail?*

It was possible. However, Samantha thought of another possibility. *What if Mark did the blackmailing? But why would he blackmail someone over his own father's development?*

There were still too many missing pieces for Samantha to make a coherent story out of anything. She went to sleep thinking about the biggest black hole in the story.

What exactly was the Jennifer, and how could it relate to Mark's murder?

Chapter
Twenty-Three

The next morning, Samantha raced to her laptop and read a response from Captain Obvious.

Hi, Nose for News. Finally, someone who remembers something about the Jennifer! I remember walking by as a kid and seeing the signs for it. It was supposed to be a luxury high-rise over in the Second Ward, with a view of downtown and a rooftop pool. They demolished some old houses to build it. I remember some neighbors made a big fuss about it. Didn't do any good, though. They tore them down anyway. Then, after everything, they never even built it. Guess Mr. Brantwell and his partners didn't realize there was no downtown view good enough to get white folks to ignore the view from the other side.

Intrigued, Samantha wanted to learn more. Could this have been the same project at the heart of the rift between Fred and Mark? She wrote Captain Obvious back.

Thanks, Captain Obvious! Do you remember where the Jennifer was supposed to have been located? What year was it being built? It's strange more people on here haven't commented on it.

She closed the website down for now as something niggled in the recesses of her mind. *That name, Jennifer. Why does it sound so familiar?*

She'd met plenty of Jennifers over the years, but all of the sudden, her mind stuck, like a record on a scratch, on one particular Jennifer she had stumbled across recently. As hard as she tried to will it to the surface, though, she couldn't remember anything specific.

She worked on a few freelance stories and stopped for a quick bite to eat before curiosity got the best of her, and she logged back into the forum. Once again, she found a response waiting from Captain Obvious.

It was in the early 90s, though I can't be much more specific. I think it was over near Chestnut and Holcord—at least that's the route I walked every day walking to my grandma's from school. I remember staring at the sign and imagining living in such a fancy place, but over time, nothing happened, and the sign eventually fell down. As for why nobody else has commented on it, I don't think it was particularly well publicized, given the demographics of the area.

Samantha read the message and pondered the subtext left unsaid. If mostly minorities in a minority area had complained about something, it might not have been written about at the time by even the *Gazette*. There were other sources for such news. She shot off a quick response.

Thanks, Captain Obvious. You've been a tremendous help. I'll do more research on the Jennifer, and if I find anything, I'll share with you!

After posting her message to the forum, Samantha shut down her computer and decided it might be time for another trip to visit Camila.

She figured Camila hadn't eaten dinner yet, so she stopped off at Mi Tienda for some pork guisada tacos. She didn't want to show up empty-handed.

When she rang the doorbell, Camila came to the door almost immediately. "*Mija*! What are you doing here?"

Samantha held out her dinner offering. "I wanted to ask you a few questions, and I thought I would bribe you with dinner."

Camila waved her inside. "I wish you had told me you were coming. I would have cooked for you, but those tacos smell delicious!"

They gathered some bowls and plates and laid out the taco feast on the kitchen table. As they dug into their tacos, Camila asked Samantha how she could help.

Samantha didn't want to alarm her friend with reference to the murder case, so she decided on the same white lie she had told the professor. "Your story the other day about those new apartments under construction in your neighborhood got me thinking about historic properties torn down over the years in Houston. I'm doing some research on some forgotten ones and wanted to ask what you can tell me."

"I'm not real good with names or dates anymore, but I'll try."

Samantha took a big bite of taco, and the juicy pork gravy spilled out onto the plate. "Did you ever hear of a project called the Jennifer? It was supposed to be a big high-rise development but never happened. Over near Chestnut and Holcord, I think."

Camila closed her eyes, as if to help her concentrate. She reopened them again and shook her head. "Honey, I've got nothing."

Samantha rubbed the back of her neck and tried to hide her disappointment. Though she'd considered it a long shot, she had hoped Camila could provide some answers. "That's okay."

Camila snapped her fingers. "I might know somebody else who can help. Remember my old neighbor who chained himself to a tree to keep those houses from being wrecked? Let me call him. He might know something."

Samantha smiled, gently biting her lip. "That would be great! Thanks, Camila."

Camila took a bite out of her taco and daintily dipped some chips into the salsa verde. "We'll do it right after dinner."

The two enjoyed the rest of their meal, though Samantha restrained herself from racing to finish.

Finally, after crunching one last chip, Camila stood and wiped her hands. "Let's call Carlos."

She pulled out an ancient address book from the top drawer of her rolltop desk and flipped through it until she found the name she wanted. Camila owned a cell phone, but it seemed she preferred to keep phone numbers the old-fashioned way.

She dialed the number and smiled when she heard an answer. "¡Carlos! Es Camila de La Garza de la calle Coronado. ¿Cómo estás?" She paused, nodding her head and making knowing grunts at what sounded to Samantha like a lengthy list of aches and pains. Camila looked at Samantha and switched to English for her sake. "Listen, I'm here with my friend trying to get some information on some old development project. I told her you might know something about it. It was called the Jennifer?"

Samantha couldn't hear the voice on the other end of the line well enough, but Camila grinned.

"Can you tell my friend about it?"

After another slight pause, Camila grinned even more broadly and nodded her head at Samantha.

"*Gracias, Carlos. Te veremos pronto.*"

Samantha's heart pounded. She still wasn't sure what significance the Jennifer would have on this case, but it struck her as important. She hugged Camila and suggested they stop back off at Mi Tienda on the way to pick up a tres leches cake to take to Carlos as a thank-you for his help.

Carlos met them at the door of an old shotgun house, which looked as if it was in need of a paint job but was otherwise neat as a pin on the inside. Camila introduced Samantha, and he welcomed the two of them into a living room as mismatched as it was cozy, filled with a collection of thrift-store finds and family heirlooms. Samantha and Camila took a seat on a well-worn but comfortable sofa with curved claw feet and rich red velvet fabric.

"Sorry, it's a little crowded in here. My wife used to collect furniture, and I haven't had the heart to get rid of it since she died."

Camila stood. "It's lovely in here, Carlos. Let me get some plates for the cake and maybe start some coffee. You two can talk."

Carlos grabbed a shoe box full of photos and pamphlets and sat on the sofa next to Samantha. "This is what I found."

He pulled out photos showing an art deco movie theater in the middle of a shopping center and some other photos of small shotgun-style homes similar to his own. "This was the first shopping center in our part of town. The movie theater was the only place some of us felt welcome for years. It's all gone now."

Unfortunately, the news didn't surprise Samantha. She had seen similar historic buildings decimated all over Houston for years. She could understand the particular hurt caused by the destruction in this community. "How horrible. What happened?"

Carlos shook his head. "Greedy developers happened. The owner of the theater couldn't pay his lease. These developers bought all the land in a square-block radius on the cheap. At first, people didn't know what they planned to do with it, so there the community hoped the buildings might be saved."

He showed her flyers he'd collected, mostly in Spanish, calling for the neighborhood to band together to save the theater.

"What about these homes?" Samantha inspected a photo of shotgun houses.

Carlos shook his head again and tut-tutted. "Demolished too. Most of the homes were empty at the time and some were in disrepair, but they don't make homes like that anymore. They should've saved them."

Samantha set the photo on the coffee table and flipped through other items from the shoe box. "When did you learn what their plans were?"

"When they arrived with a wrecking ball and started demolishing those houses. My buddies and I immediately jumped into action. We tied ourselves to a column outside the theater, and I swear, they wouldn't have thought twice about swinging right through us if the cameras weren't there."

The mention of cameras piqued Samantha's interest. "Cameras? What happened?"

Carlos nodded. "Another buddy filmed the entire thing. We tied ourselves to the column. A crowd of people shouted at the workers to stop. They stopped for a while until one developer showed up, calling us names. He said he had a court order and he would call the cops if we didn't get out of there."

Carlos dropped his head and looked to the ground. "We didn't want trouble with the police, so we left. We should have stayed, though. One of my buddies stayed and filmed the whole thing. Within five minutes, the man crawled into the cab of the wrecker and did the job, knocking down our history in ten minutes flat. He did it with a smile on his face."

Carlos gazed at the ceiling, his face suddenly showing his age as if he were reliving the affront to his history.

Samantha hated to interrupt his memories but wanted to ask if he could tell her more. "So that was the Jennifer?"

Carlos nodded. "It was supposed to be, anyway. Those guys erected a sign showing the fanciest high-rise you've ever seen. They planned to slap it right smack in the middle of our community and market it based on stunning views of downtown." Carlos laughed a bitter laugh. "They didn't know their market very well."

"It didn't work?"

"No disrespect to yourself. I know you're a friend of Camila's. But at the time, no white woman would be caught dead living on this side of the interstate."

Now Samantha hung her head in shame for how white leaders had treated this city's Hispanic population. "Did anything ever get built?"

Carlos scowled. "Sat empty for years until someone bought it off those guys and built another strip mall, same as any other strip mall in this town. Now there's a convenience store and a liquor store and a dollar store."

He gazed at the floor and shook his head, seeming to relive the decades-old defeat. Camila came into the room with coffees and slices of tres leches cake. As they enjoyed the creamy cake, talk turned to the neighborhood and Carlos and Camila exchanged gossip. Before long, they were standing to leave.

On the way to the door, Samantha turned back and asked Carlos about the film from the cameras.

"I've still got it, but there's no way to watch it," he said. "Don't have the projector anymore."

"I'd love to see it. Would you mind if I borrowed your films? I think they might have a projector that would work at the university."

Carlos shrugged and walked to a compact room at the back of the house. He came back with another shoe box. "It's in here somewhere, but I'm not sure which one it is. I haven't watched these in years."

Samantha thanked him and offered him a hug as she left, promising to bring back the films soon. Camila smiled at Samantha as they drove back to her house. "Did Carlos help you with your project?"

Samantha smiled back. "I think so. I really appreciate you taking me to visit with him."

Samantha dropped Camila back off at her home. Camila hugged her tightly, and warmth coursed through Samantha's body.

"Come again anytime." The elderly woman waved as Samantha walked back to her car.

Samantha returned the wave as she pulled out of the driveway. She drove by the site of the planned but never built Jennifer and understood Carlos's disgust at the nondescript strip center standing in its place.

As she drove home, Samantha experienced the familiar adrenaline rush that usually came from being on the trail of a hot story. The sensation seemed sort of ridiculous, considering the story stretched nearly thirty years in the past. But the information from Carlos and the tapes in the box on her passenger seat could be the key to solving the mystery.

At her apartment, Samantha brought the box inside for safekeeping. She wished she could watch the movies tonight, but the library closed at seven. She fingered the brittle film reels wrapped in layers of tissue paper inside the box. Though tomorrow would be Sunday, the campus libraries would be open, and she could find a projector to play the films. She couldn't wait to learn what was on them.

*   *   *

In the morning, she packed the reels of film in a backpack and carried them with her to the university. Though it was Sunday, the libraries remained open for students to study or do research. While she'd been relieved of her duties at the university's magazine, she still had the pass that granted her access to the libraries for research purposes. She crossed the campus, for once quiet enough to hear the mockingbirds' shrill cries, and climbed the steps to the main library. She showed the librarian the tape reels and asked her for help in finding a projector she could use to watch them. The librarian directed her upstairs to the special collections room, where another librarian told her she couldn't check the projector out but could watch the films in one of the library's viewing rooms.

Samantha bounced from foot to foot, excited to finally watch the tapes. She struggled for a moment to load the projector as the brittle tape continued to slip off the reel. Cursing under her breath, she called to the librarian for help. Samantha could hardly stand the woman's slow and deliberate pace as she fed the film onto the reel but held her tongue as she realized the process was working.

The colors were faded and the images somewhat grainy, but Samantha could identify certain Second Ward landmarks in the first of the films she played—the open-air market and the warehouses long since turned into loft spaces and, of course, the towering Houston skyline in the background. There were a mix of home movies and clips from neighborhood parties as well as some footage offering a flavor of life in the neighborhood. She observed, interested, as a younger version of Carlos and his friends shifted in tone from serious to silly. The footage was raw, but there were a few scenes that it seemed Carlos and his friends had clearly planned out with a future documentary in mind.

She rewound and fast-forwarded through hours of videos, getting the hang of the clunky projector, not entirely certain what she hoped to find, until, miracle of all miracles, she found it. On the screen in front of her, she recognized the art deco movie theater from Carlos's pictures and subsequent scenes in front of the homes and the rest of the surrounding neighborhood. It pained her heart again to behold the beautiful buildings before what would be their imminent destruction.

She held her breath and watched as Carlos and his friend tied themselves to the ornate columns in front of the theater. A wrecking crew stopped mere inches short of toppling the concrete awning on top of them. The action in the scene seemed to stop for a moment as the camera panned around to show the crowd of protesters holding picket signs and other onlookers pausing in their daily life to witness the destruction of a fixture of their neighborhood.

She stared, transfixed, as the crowd parted and a man with a hard hat walked through it, cursing the protesters and threatening Carlos and his friend, who were still tied to the columns.

When the camera panned in for a close-up, Samantha gasped as she recognized a much younger Bob Randall threatening the crowd with arrest if they didn't disperse.

When the crowd finally moved off and Carlos and his friend relented, allowing themselves to be removed from their chains, Bob climbed into the wrecker's cab and aimed the first blow directly at the theater marquee. The whole building crumbled in a matter of a few minutes. She stared in horror as a cloud of dust rose and young children were led away by their mothers, who wanted to keep them safe from the rubble, which now flew freely through the air.

Samantha flipped the switch on the projector to stop the film, and all of the various puzzle pieces slipped into place. She remembered her first meeting in the man's office, when she'd asked about the photograph of his daughter, Jennifer. Bob, Houston's patron saint of historic preservation had once been the quintessential evil developer. He'd partnered with Fred Brantwell, and together the two had reduced a community's history to little more than rubble for a quick buck. She could imagine exactly how well footage like this would play for Bob's current clientele of liberal preservationists in the Highlands. They would be horrified by his callous display of indifference, and it would certainly tarnish his image, not to mention hurt his business.

Suddenly, all of those favors done for Mark and Darcy made a little more sense. *Mark must have been blackmailing Bob, threatening to share his sordid history with the community. If word got out, Bob would have been vilified and his livelihood and standing in the community threatened.*

Samantha wondered aloud, "Would that be enough to justify murder?"

She watched the footage again and gawked at the hateful expression on Bob's face as he ordered Carlos and his friends to leave his property.

Samantha took out a notepad and pencil and jotted down every instance she had heard Bob's name over the course of her investigation.

1. *Bob asked Reingold to resign from HC so he could appoint Mark*
2. *Bob helped Darcy get the high-commission Highlands job*
3. *Bob did several favors for Mark and Darcy*

Combining all this with the video evidence in front of her, Samantha grew more certain. Bob had served as host during the home tour and could easily have poisoned Mark's drink. She remembered her conversation with Mila about Mark talking to an old man. Could Bob have been the old man? Could they have been discussing the blackmail?

She pulled a photo of Bob off the internet and texted it to Mila.

Quick question. Any chance this is the old guy who you saw talking to Mark?

As she waited for a response, Samantha turned her thoughts to Darcy. If Bob had killed Mark, it seemed likely he had also killed Darcy. But why? Could she have somehow learned about the blackmail and confronted Bob?

Samantha played the film a few more times and recorded the grainy footage onto her phone. She saved a copy in her camera's photo album and, taking a page out of Darcy's book, emailed a copy to herself. She packed up the films, wishing now that she could lock them in a vault somewhere.

At home, Samantha stashed the tapes in the back of her towel closet, figuring nobody would look there in her apartment. Though still uneasy with the films being in her apartment, she realized that Bob had no way of knowing the tapes existed, much less that they were in her possession. With Gabby still in jail, Bob likely believed he was sitting pretty, certain to get away with at least one and maybe two murders. Samantha would do everything possible to make sure that didn't happen. She just didn't know how quite yet.

Her phone buzzed with an incoming text. Mila had responded.

Could be. Looks similar. Couldn't swear to it.

Ugh . . . She wished the girl could be a little more definitive, but she took the response as at least partial confirmation of her theory. Now she needed to figure out a way to get the police to pay attention. She couldn't imagine they would view a thirty-year-old film as evidence in two contemporary murders. She needed more recent evidence.

I need a confession.

Chapter
Twenty-Four

She spent the rest of the afternoon and evening stewing over how she could get a confession out of Bob. Without access to Mark or Darcy's townhome, she gave up on finding further proof of the blackmail scheme or concrete proof of Bob as the target. *There has to be a way.*

She needed to convince Bob to break into Mark and Darcy's townhome by hinting that there might be more evidence of the blackmail scheme there. If she could catch him in the act, it might give police enough incentive to look a little harder at him.

By the next morning, Samantha had a rough plan in place to lure Bob to Mark and Darcy's townhome. She walked into the living room to knock superstitiously on her coffee table, the only nearby wood in her apartment, and dialed Bob's cell phone number. The call went straight to voice mail.

"Hi, Bob. Sorry to bug you again. I don't want to get into too many details on the phone, but Mark's daughter called me with some crazy story about how her dad might have been blackmailing someone. It doesn't make a lot of sense. She keeps saying it has something to do with Jennifer or something. Anyway, I promised her I would check into it, but since you knew him best, I wanted to ask you a few questions."

She hoped the reference to Jennifer would be enough to get him to return her call. Samantha twisted her watch on her wrist and paced in her small living room as she waited for some response. She didn't have to wait long. Within fifteen minutes, her cell phone rang.

"Ms. Warren. I received your message. I'm not sure how you think I can help you."

"Oh, Bob, thank you for calling me back. I'm sure my message sounded crazy. The whole story sounds crazy, but I promised Chloe I'd investigate. Poor kid can't believe her mom could have killed her dad and Darcy. Anyway, I wanted to at least run the story by you to ask your take on it."

"I'm heading to a job site right now and can't really talk, but if it's really important, you can stop by my office around noon."

"Perfect. I'll see you then."

She disconnected the call, feeling good about the first part of her plan. Her palms began to sweat and her fingers tingled as she considered how best to confront Bob.

Before noon, with the inside of her mouth dry as cotton, she drove to Bob's office and found it empty when she walked inside. Her heart beat faster without the reassuring presence of the receptionist out front. She had counted on there being at least one other person in the office, certain Bob wouldn't try to hurt her within earshot of someone else. Now, forced to walk alone into the home turf of someone she believed to be a killer, she could hear her personal safety alarm bells ringing full blast.

Should I leave?

I can't. I've come this far. If I play dumb enough, he won't know how much I really know.

She walked ahead, hoping she could lay her trap quickly and get out.

"Hello? Bob?" she called out into the empty room.

A woman popped her head around the corner. It was the receptionist, and she held half a sandwich in her hand. "Oh, I'm sorry. I was just on my lunch break. Bob's in the back."

After a moment, Bob Randall appeared at the front. "Ms. Warren, hello again." He stuck out his hand to shake.

She returned the pressure with a slight squeeze and a smile, despite the wave of cold rushing through her insides. She kept her voice calm. "Bob, thank you for seeing me again. I hate to keep bothering you. Hopefully this will be the last time."

He ushered her back to his office and took his seat behind the mahogany desk. Samantha moved her gaze to the credenza behind Bob's desk and noticed he had removed the photo of his daughter.

"What can I do for you? You mentioned something about blackmail?"

Samantha nodded. "Yes, as I mentioned, Mark's daughter, Chloe, contacted me with this crazy story. To be honest, it doesn't make a lot of sense. She claims she found evidence of blackmail while going through some of the papers her dad left at his house. She could only tell me it had something to do with a real estate project called the Jennifer."

She peered up from her lap, where she had been playing with a zipper on her purse, to glance at Bob's face and observe his reaction. He sat in unmoving silence.

"Anyway, she thinks he must have gone through with the blackmail, because she remembered finding a box labeled 'Jennifer' at his townhome in Houston. She had looked through it, thinking her father had another girlfriend named Jennifer, but her dad yanked it away from her before she could read it. All she noticed were some pictures of maybe an old movie theater and what looked like some film canisters."

"This is an interesting story, Ms. Warren, but I'm still not clear how you think I can help." His expression remained neutral, but Samantha thought she could detect at least the faintest hint of perspiration forming at his brow.

"I'm sorry. Chloe refuses to believe her mother is a murderer. She wants to find an alternate suspect for the police to consider, and she thinks the person Mark blackmailed might have murdered him to stop the blackmail. Darcy too, presuming she knew about it. I know it's a long shot, but since you knew the two of them best of anyone in Houston, I wondered if you thought Mark was capable of blackmail."

Bob pursed his lips as if he were truly considering the possibility. "I didn't know him very well, Ms. Warren, but I couldn't imagine him blackmailing someone." He stood, ready to usher her out of the office.

Samantha stood too. "I told her not to get her hopes up. Anyway, maybe the police will find the box at Darcy and Mark's place and something will come of that. Thanks for your time."

As he walked her to the front of the office, she turned back and locked gazes with him. "You've lived here a long time, right? You ever hear of any project called the Jennifer? Funny name for some real estate development."

She noticed a slight twitch of his upper lip as he shook his head. As she waved good-bye, she breathed an enormous sigh of relief to have escaped the close quarters with Bob. Now she could only hope she'd planted enough seeds of interest to get him to fall into her trap.

Samantha drove home, ready to work on the rest of her plan. She believed Bob would go to Darcy's place and try to hunt for the mysterious Jennifer box. Now she simply needed to

275

watch and catch him breaking in, which meant another stakeout.

She rode her bike to a taco stand on the cross street near Darcy's house, ordered some tacos and a drink, and climbed the roof deck, which had a view into the townhomes across the street. She carried her good camera with the telephoto lens in her messenger bag. With a heat index of 101 degrees outside and only a wooden pergola for shade, the roof was empty.

While most burglars would wait until the dead of night to attempt a break-in, Samantha suspected Bob might find more cover in the middle of the afternoon, when most neighbors were at work and he could play the part of the contractor. Plenty of studies had shown that if you wore the right clothes, most people wouldn't question whether or not you belonged.

As she sipped her soda and wiped away the sweat, she finished her tacos and waited. After about an hour, she noticed what looked like a contractor's truck pull in across the street from the town house. She grabbed her camera and began shooting photos as a man, who looked to be of Bob Randall's build, got out of a truck and fiddled with a cable box.

Is that him? What is he doing? She aimed her camera, trying to get a closer view of his face. At the same moment, a couple mounted the stairs with a tray full of tacos.

The woman, spotting Samantha with her camera, called out to her. "Cool camera! What are you shooting?"

Samantha whirled around, thinking fast on her feet. "Oh, just an art project. I'm about done here."

She gathered her things and left. If it had been Bob down there, she hoped she'd gotten his photo. She didn't want to stick around to find out whether the couple would accept her explanation. The last thing she needed was a run-in with the cops.

In her car, she flipped through the photos she'd shot. The one close-up revealed a man with a red goatee, clearly not Bob Randall. A better angle of the truck showed an AT&T decal. She'd spent the better part of fifteen minutes taking hundreds of photos of an internet service technician.

Frustrated, she sat in her car and tried to decide what to do next. She wanted to bounce some ideas off someone and dialed Marisa's number. She decided the scolding she would get for involving herself in the investigation again would be worth the chance to talk to someone with a fresh perspective. The phone rang a few times and went to voice mail.

"Hey, Marisa. It's Sam. Listen, don't yell at me for getting involved in this case again, but I'm convinced Bob Randall is the actual murderer. It's a long story, but your grandma and I visited a man who had videos of Bob from thirty years ago when he demolished some historic properties in the Second Ward. I think Mark and Darcy must have known about it and were blackmailing him or something. Anyway, I could really use a fresh perspective on what to do next. Call me."

That won't freak her out or anything! Samantha threw her cell phone into the center console and began to pull away.

Just as she'd put her car into drive, her phone rang with a number she didn't recognize. *Who can this be now?* Samantha put her car in park again and picked up the phone. "Yes?"

"Is this Samantha Warren? This is Peter Garfield, the builder. I'm sorry it's taken me so long to get back to you. I just got back into town from an extended vacation."

Samantha bit her lip, wondering if the call was the result of some divine intervention. "Oh, Peter, yes. Thank you for calling me back. Listen, I'm a writer and, well, this is going to sound strange, but do you know a Darcy Meadows? She might have contacted you about a television show?"

The man paused a moment and exhaled. "I already told her I'm not interested. It's a nice idea, but I've got my hands full right now."

"So you did talk to her?"

"Sure. She called me about a month ago or so, mentioned Bob Randall had given her my number, but as I said, I'm too busy with my business right now. Plus, I don't like the idea of all of the up-front costs not covered by the network."

"Wait, did you say Bob Randall? Do you know him?"

"Of course. Everyone in the region who's active in historic renovation knows Bob. What did you say this was about again?"

A flutter started in her stomach. This man's story could help explain her theory of the murders to the police. If Bob had given the newspaper clip to Darcy, he'd almost assuredly intended to frame her for the murder he planned to commit. *Darcy must have realized that when I showed her the blurb about oleander poisoning.* "I'm sorry to belabor it, but just to be clear, Darcy told you that Bob recommended you to her for the show?"

"Yes. I've already said so. Now, can you please tell me what this is about? I've got a lot of other calls to make." The man's voice, though still polite, had taken on a frustrated edge.

"I'm so sorry to bother you. You've given me what I need for now. I really do appreciate it. Have a nice day!" Samantha ended the call, putting her phone back in the center console. Peter had been the man in the photograph of the clipping she had found in Darcy's email, and Bob had introduced him to Darcy, which suggested that Bob had sent Darcy the clipping. Samantha grinned as she put her car in drive and headed home, already planning the story she would tell the police.

She pulled up to her apartment around four. She needed a shower after her stint on the roof of the taco shop, so she raced to the top of her apartment steps and opened the door. She threw her purse on the sofa and was carefully laying her camera on the coffee table when suddenly a gloved hand covered her mouth and an arm pushed her into the kitchen and down onto a chair.

"Don't scream. I've got a knife." Bob's voice was low as he pressed the blade of a knife against her neck. He grabbed her hands roughly and, still holding the knife, wrapped duct tape around her wrists behind her back.

Samantha's chin and lips trembled as she considered that she might be about to die. She wanted to shut her eyes and escape inside her mind, but another part of her refused to give in.

"I . . . I won't scream." Her mouth dried like cotton as she struggled to swallow. "How did you find my place?"

Bob jerked the chair around so that Samantha faced him. "Oh, your little friend Beth helped me. I told her you left your notebook in my office and I wanted to take it by your apartment."

The mention of Beth offered Samantha a glimmer of hope. *If Marisa checks her voice mail and talks to Beth . . .* The odds were against her.

Samantha lifted her face to stare at Bob. "What are you going to do to me?"

Bob smiled again, this time a more sinister smile. "I'll make you a little cocktail. I know how much you like those. First, though, you're gonna tell me where the film is."

"I . . . I don't know what you're talking about. I told you, if there's a film, it's at Darcy's house."

Bob shook his head. "Don't bother lying. I was onto you the second you searched for the photo of my daughter, Jennifer, on my credenza. I know you've got something, so where is it?"

Samantha swallowed again, thinking of the backpack in her towel closet, wondering how much she should try to bluff. "I don't have it."

He *tsk*ed. "You know too many details—the old theater, the old houses. That story has been forgotten by anyone who matters for thirty years, and it won't come up again."

She opted for a different tack. "It was the nineties. People tore down buildings all over Houston. Nobody will fault you for one mistake more than thirty years ago. Not after all the outstanding work you've done restoring and protecting buildings throughout the Highlands."

Bob slumped his shoulders and looked briefly deflated. "It won't matter. All it takes is one story from the past to bring a principled person to ruin." His voice rose, sounding defiant. "I'm not going to lose my legacy."

Samantha could hardly think with her pulse thrumming in her ears. She considered every conceivable escape plan but couldn't find a scenario to help her get out alive.

Bob looked at her expectantly. "I don't have time for stall tactics. Where is the video?"

Samantha followed her gut and offered some version of the truth. "I . . . I don't have it. The film was on eight-millimeter, and nobody has those projectors anymore. I have a copy of some of it, though. I can show you . . . on my phone. It's in my purse on the sofa."

He walked into the living room and retrieved her purse. As he riffled through her purse for her phone, she remembered the shard of broken metal trim on her table. It was a few inches to her left. She took a chance and slid her chair slightly closer to the jagged edge.

Bob glanced at Samantha at the sound of the chair scraping against the floor, but his attention shifted quickly back to her purse as he pulled her phone out of it.

"What's your pass code?"

She offered the five-digit code for unlocking her phone and observed as he opened her photo app. While he grew absorbed by the film playing on the phone's screen, Samantha slowly reached her wrists to the jagged trim and began to saw the duct tape. She heard the protesters shouting in Spanish and followed his expression as he observed a younger version of himself send the wrecking ball through the lobby of the old theater building. He looked . . . if not remorseful, at least pained by his actions.

"Why'd you do it?"

He looked at her, startled, as if he'd forgotten about her. "I was young. Mark's dad convinced me to invest. The Jennifer should have been my legacy. I named it for my Jennifer, my monument to her. Something she could always see so she could be proud of her daddy."

"You destroyed other people's history." The words slipped out, destroying Bob's reverie.

"The building was a fire hazard and a public nuisance." His tone clipped, Bob no longer seemed willing to travel down memory lane, so Samantha brought him back to the present. She wanted the details, the full confession.

"Mark blackmailed you? Threatened to reveal your part in the project?" The duct tape started to split, but she held her hands firmly together to avoid his notice.

"At first, his requests were simple, like the position on the commission and a few jobs thrown his way, but then he got greedy." Bob appeared distracted as he continued to scroll through Samantha's phone.

"What about Darcy? You were there the night Gabby and I went over there, weren't you?"

He laughed. "You should feel a little guilty for your part. I never would have killed her if you hadn't put certain ideas in her head."

His smirk chilled Samantha, who held perfectly still under his gaze. "Wh . . . what do you mean?"

"I waited upstairs when you two arrived. Darcy and I had been discussing your little theories about Decker. You convinced her he had something to do with Mark's murder." He chuckled. "She felt guilty for not noticing anything because she'd been so preoccupied with her plan to have me convince Mark to do the show with her. After my friend Peter refused to consider it, she wanted me to take another shot at changing Mark's mind. She dragged him to the home tour to talk to me—unaware, of course, that Mark and I were not exactly the best of friends."

"You killed him instead." Samantha let the words slip out.

Bob looked irritated at the interruption. "Of course I killed him. Darcy was dumb as a post and wouldn't have known anything until you started connecting the dots for her. Initially, you had her convinced that Brian Decker was responsible, which was just fine. But when you showed her that article about oleander poisoning I'd sent to her, she realized I'd tried to frame her as a potential suspect. When you left, she turned on me and threatened to turn me in."

"So, you killed her." Samantha bit her tongue. Nerves were making her speak out of turn.

"You've got a knack for pointing out the obvious." Bob turned his attention back to Samantha's phone. He typed something on the touch screen.

With his attention diverted, Samantha split the final fibers in the duct tape. "There's one other thing I wondered about. Why didn't you ever appear in the doorbell video from the night Darcy died? I don't understand how we appeared and you didn't."

He smirked at her. "You gave me that idea too . . . after I heard you say you'd emailed yourself that article from Darcy's phone. I realized if I used her finger, I could have access to all kinds of things, including the app where the camera feed is sent. As long as you view the app on your phone, you can delete any video you want."

He continued typing on Samantha's phone until she heard the telltale whoosh of an email on its way into the ether. "It's amazing what you can do with access to someone else's phone, like send a suicide note off to their nearest and dearest."

As he finished with her phone, Samantha yanked her wrists free. She jumped out of the chair and leaped toward her kitchen counter. Bob threw the phone against the floor, smashing the glass as he lunged toward her with the knife.

He was too far away, and the sharp steel only grazed her arm as she grabbed for a bottle on her kitchen counter. Her hand clasped her five-pepper tincture, guaranteed to make a grown man cry, and she squirted it directly into Bob's eyes.

He screamed and clawed at them as if they were on fire. She grabbed another knife from the block on the counter, but before she could turn away from him, he threw himself against her, sinking the sharp blade into her chest, right under her armpit. Unbearable pain seared through her, forcing her to release a blood-curdling scream.

In the chaos, neither noticed the pounding on the stairs up to the apartment. Bob jumped when the door slammed open and Marisa leaped into the apartment.

"He's got a knife!" Samantha screamed as Bob stabbed at her again, this time catching her forearm and lightly grazing her.

Marisa grabbed another large bottle on the counter and, using it as a cudgel, hit Bob over the head with it, knocking him out temporarily.

Samantha hurt too much to move but motioned to Marisa to knock the knife out of Bob's hands. Marisa kicked it out of his hand and crushed his fingers under the hard heel of her boot. She whipped out her phone and dialed 911 while she searched the room. Samantha knew they needed to restrain Bob, so she pointed her chin at Marisa's belt. Recognition lit up Marisa's eyes, and she ripped the belt off and quickly wrapped it tightly around Bob's wrists.

"Are you okay?" Marisa turned to Samantha, horrified as blood continued to pool beneath her on the floor. She grabbed some kitchen towels from a drawer and pressed them hard against the wounds.

Samantha grew colder as shivers overtook her body. Within about ten minutes, sirens sounded in the distance. Before long, paramedics and police rushed in to take both Samantha and Bob to the hospital.

At the hospital, Samantha learned she had been fortunate not to have severed any major arteries or punctured any vital organs, but she would have a nasty scar. The doctor told her it might fade some over time, but likely she would carry some reminder of her experience for the rest of her life.

Resting in her bed, Samantha smiled as Marisa and Beth walked in with a bouquet from Beth's garden.

"Oh, Sam, I'm so sorry. I feel so guilty. If I hadn't given Bob your address, none of this would have happened."

Samantha shook her head. "There's no way you could have known, Beth. It all happened so fast. I didn't really have time to tell anyone of my suspicions."

Marisa reached for her friend's hand. "You could have died, Sam. Thanks goodness I listened to your message during a break in class."

Samantha shuddered. "You saved my life, Marisa. How did you know to come to my apartment?"

"Beth left a message earlier in the day and mentioned she'd given Bob your address and she hoped it was okay. When I heard your message, I raced over there as fast as I could."

Wincing as she readjusted herself in bed, Samantha asked for an update on Bob. As Marisa explained that she'd heard he had only superficial wounds, Detective Sanders walked into the hospital room.

"Miss Warren. I'd like to have a few words with you."

Marisa and Beth backed away toward the hallway, miming that they would be back later.

"Detective, I . . ."

"First off, Miss Warren, I believe I warned you to stay out of police business." He pulled his lips taut as he stared at her.

Samantha cowed under the weight of his disapproval. Then he smiled.

"Secondly, nice work. I can't say I ever pegged Bob as the killer. Though I might have figured things out if you had shared some of your discoveries rather than confronting him alone."

"So, does this mean . . ."

He nodded his head. "He's confessed. We've got him for both Mark's and Darcy's murders. We released your friend Gabby this morning to go home to her daughter."

"Thank heavens."

Sanders stood up from the chair where he'd sat next to her bed. "Well, I'm glad to hear you'll make a full recovery. We'll take your statement once you get out of here, but I'll let you get some rest now."

Samantha offered a slight wave as he walked out into the hallway. "Thanks, Detective."

Over the next few days, she had visits from Chloe, who thanked her profusely for helping to free her mom, and Gabby, who promised to help with any interior decorating needs. Camila and Carlos chided her for confronting Bob alone but celebrated her takedown of the man who had wrecked part of their history. David came bearing flowers and a recommendation for another lawyer who specialized in civil claims for pain and suffering.

"No thanks." Samantha shuddered at the idea. "I've been party to enough lawsuits this month to last me a lifetime."

David smiled. "So, what's next for you?"

Samantha grinned back. "I've gotten the message over the last several weeks that everyone thinks I don't trust my instincts enough."

"You've turned over a fresh leaf." He frowned and pointed to her bandaged chest. "Seems like maybe you followed your own instincts to the extreme with Bob Randall."

Samantha nodded. "Despite the injuries, it worked out. I've decided I'll keep it up. I've got an idea I'm working on. Stay tuned for details."

David lifted his eyebrows. "I'm sure you'll make a success of it, whatever it is. And if you need some legal help, I'll recommend someone."

Samantha grimaced. David's words almost sounded like a brush-off. *Am I wrong about him? Does he not like me?* "Are you tired of me so soon?" She tried to keep her voice light, to make a joke of it.

David looked at the floor. "These past few weeks have taught me a few things too. I don't really want you as a client anymore."

Samantha opened her mouth in shock, not sure what to say.

David smiled at her. "I know this isn't exactly the most opportune time, and maybe you're not ready yet, but sometime, when you are, I'd love to take you out on a date."

Despite the painkillers coursing through her veins, Samantha's pulse raced. She reached out for David's hand and smiled. "I'd love to."

* * *

A few days later, following her release from the hospital, Samantha stopped by Marisa and Beth's house and rang the doorbell. Beth answered in an apron smeared with flour. She dusted herself off and pulled Samantha in for a hug, being careful of her still healing wounds. "Are you okay? You're looking good, but are you sure you're ready to be walking around like this?"

Samantha hugged her back. "I'm fine. I'm good, even. I just wanted to talk to you about something."

Beth ushered her into the kitchen and pulled out a stool near the island. "Please, take a seat. I've got to finish kneading this dough before it turns into concrete. Are you here to see Marisa? She's at her contracts class now."

"No, it's you I wanted to see, Beth. I wanted to ask the latest with your business plan. You mentioned looking for a partner. Have you found one yet?"

Beth's face fell slightly as she continued to pummel the dough. "No, but it's okay. I'm just going to have to start smaller than I wanted to. I'll only take small jobs that I can handle myself until I can start earning enough to grow the business."

Samantha began to jiggle her knee as she spoke. "Listen, I don't want you to feel obligated because we're friends, but what would you think about me as a partner? I've still got a little of the money I'd saved for the down payment on the house I gave up, and I want to invest in something for my future. I'm not as good as you in the kitchen, but I like cooking, and I can follow directions. Plus, I was thinking I could provide a cocktail service to complement whatever food you make."

Beth's face brightened as she dropped the dough and raced over to Samantha to enfold her in another hug. "Are you serious? Because that would be amazing."

Samantha looked stunned. "Really?"

Beth laughed. "You're not going to believe this, but I wanted to ask you myself. Marisa thought I should wait. She didn't think it was the right time, given all you've been through. But I think we'd make a great team. Between your craft cocktails and homemade bitters and my locally sourced food, we would have a unique concept."

Samantha felt the pent-up tension leave her body. This felt right. "So, do we have a deal?"

Beth grinned. "Not just a deal, but a partnership." She reached out and shook Samantha's hand, chuckling as a wad of sticky dough momentarily plastered their hands together.

Beth washed her hands and returned to the dough, preparing it to proof on the counter, while Samantha got to work making a celebratory cocktail. She scavenged through Beth's cabinets and refrigerator to find the ingredients for a French 75, shaking some gin, lemon juice, and simple syrup together with ice before pouring it out into two flutes and topping it off with prosecco. The friends sipped their cocktails and read through Beth's existing business plan, making tweaks here and there as they discussed their options.

* * *

Over the next few weeks, Samantha's life became a whirlwind of activity. She and Beth worked up contracts with local vendors, tested out recipes, and held a few more test-run dinners. Samantha scoured the classifieds and located a food truck, which she purchased at a discount from a prior owner eager to move from her mobile cupcake shop to a brick-and-mortar storefront. She and Beth took out a small business loan to help buy the truck and customize it both for use at outdoor venues and as transportation for other catering jobs. With Gabby's design know-how, it was soon ready for business, emblazoned with the name and slogan *Cocktails and Catering: From our garden to your table.*

Chloe and Becca helped Samantha and Beth launch a new website, which had tons of traffic after Samantha was featured in dozens of stories and interviews about her part in bringing down Bob Randall.

Their catering service was booked solid for parties for the next two months, and Samantha had dozens of orders for specialized bitters, including some from local bars, after Dane, her bartender friend at Boheme, shared her bitters with some buddies in the business.

Samantha's life had done a complete 180-degree turn, and she finally felt optimistic about her path forward.

One afternoon, Samantha was working side by side with Marisa in her kitchen, which looked like a high school science lab gone wrong. Row after row of jars filled with twigs, bark, and leaves were marinating, suspending in an amber liquid.

Bits of bark and seed pods collected in a strainer, looking like wet, chewed mulch, as Samantha poured another jar of the murky liquid into a vat on her counter.

"I'm glad you didn't listen to my advice." Marisa grabbed an empty jar, appearing to reel for a moment from the angel's share of the hundred-proof bourbon still lingering in the air, before setting it down and turning to face her friend.

"What do you mean?" Samantha carefully labeled each jar with the contents and the date. Her counters were filled with concoctions, and she could barely keep track any longer of all the projects she had going on at once.

"If you'd bought the house like I suggested, you never would have ended up with all of this."

Samantha laughed, pleased at the controlled chaos in her kitchen. "Yes, it's a little overwhelming."

The bottling finished for now, Samantha pulled out her shaker and a few bottles and made a variation on an African Flower with bourbon, amaro, crème de cacao, and her lavender instead of orange bitters.

They carried their cocktails into the living room and sat together on the sofa. Marisa sniffed at her drink before taking a sip. "I can really taste the lavender. It's not the most obvious combination, but it really works."

Samantha took a sip and smiled, silently agreeing with Marisa's assessment. "I trusted my instincts."

"You seem to be doing that a lot more these days." Marisa gestured with her glass toward the kitchen, filled with bottles of bitters for Samantha's new business. "You and Beth are really making this work. I've never seen her happier."

Samantha grinned. "She's a great partner. I know it will still be hard sometimes, but if the last few weeks have taught me anything, it's that sometimes great things can happen when you aren't afraid to take risks."

Marisa clinked her glass against Samantha's. "I'll drink to that."

Recipes
Beth's Homemade Gingersnap Cookies

2 cups sifted flour
2 teaspoons baking soda
½ teaspoon salt
2 teaspoons ground ginger
1 teaspoon ground cinnamon
½ cup butter (room temperature)
¼ cup shortening
½ cup brown sugar
½ cup white sugar
1 egg
¼ cup molasses
Cinnamon sugar for rolling (3 tablespoons white sugar and 1 teaspoon cinnamon mixed together)

Preheat oven to 350 degrees.

Sift together flour, baking soda, salt, and spices.

With a mixer, blend together butter and shortening for one to two minutes or until creamy. Add sugars and continue mixing. Beat in egg and molasses until well incorporated.

Gradually add the flour mixture in three parts to the butter mixture, until a soft dough forms.

Roll dough into 1-inch-diameter balls and coat them in cinnamon sugar before placing them on an ungreased cookie sheet.

Bake 12 to 14 minutes or until tops of cookies are slightly crinkled.

Beth's Fresh-From-the-Garden Lasagna

6 tablespoons olive oil, divided
4 garlic cloves, finely chopped
1 28-ounce can crushed fire-roasted
    tomatoes
2 14.5-ounce cans diced fire-roasted
    tomatoes
2 teaspoons salt, divided
1 teaspoon pepper, divided
1 onion, chopped
1 red bell pepper, chopped
1 zucchini, finely chopped
1 eggplant, finely chopped
2 tablespoons chopped fresh basil
1 tablespoon chopped fresh oregano
¼ cup red wine
2 cups baby spinach, roughly chopped
1 pound lasagna noodles
1 pound small-curd cottage cheese
1 egg
2 teaspoons Italian seasoning
2 cups Italian-style shredded cheese, divided
1 cup shredded Parmesan cheese, divided

Preheat oven to 375 degrees.

In a medium-sized pot, sauté garlic in 4 tablespoons of olive oil for 1 to 2 minutes. Add crushed and diced tomatoes, 1 teaspoon salt, and ½ teaspoon pepper to the pot and mix. Cover and simmer for 15 minutes.

In a large pan, heat remaining 2 tablespoons olive oil until shimmering. Add onion and cook at medium heat until translucent. Add zucchini, eggplant, and bell pepper to the pan; stir. Add fresh herbs. Sauté mixture until vegetables soften. Add wine and cook until the liquid boils off. Add tomato mixture to the vegetables and continue cooking at medium heat. Add chopped spinach and stir until spinach wilts. Cover and let simmer for ½ to 1 hour or until sauce thickens.

In a large pot, boil lasagna noodles according to package directions. Drain noodles and let sit in cool water.

In medium bowl, mix cottage cheese and egg with remaining salt and pepper and Italian seasoning. Stir 1½ cups Italian shredded cheese and ½ cup Parmesan into the cottage cheese/egg mixture.

In a large lasagna pan, begin with a layer of sauce (enough to cover bottom of pan). Next, add a layer of lasagna noodles, followed by more sauce and a third of the cottage cheese mixture; spread evenly around. Add a second layer of noodles, sauce, and cheese mixture. Add a third layer of noodles, sauce, and cheese mixture. Top with remaining noodles and remaining sauce.

Cover pan with foil and bake 40 minutes. Remove foil and sprinkle remaining cheeses over the top of the sauce.

Reduce oven temperature to 350 degrees and continue baking 15 minutes. Broil top of the lasagna for 2 minutes or until nicely browned.

Let lasagna stand 5 minutes before cutting and serving.

Samantha's Take on an Attorney's Privilege

2 ounces rye whiskey
½ ounce orgeat
2 dashes cherry bitters

Add ingredients to a shaker filled with ice. Stir until well chilled and strain into a coupe glass. Garnish with a cocktail cherry.

Samantha's Cherry Gin Fizz

1½ ounces gin
½ ounce fresh-squeezed lime juice
½ ounce cherry simple syrup (see recipe below)
2 dashes cherry bitters
Champagne or other sparkling wine

Add gin, lime juice, cherry simple syrup, and cherry bitters to a cocktail shaker filled with ice. Shake until well chilled and strain into a coupe glass. Top with champagne. Garnish with a cocktail cherry.

Cherry Simple Syrup

1 cup water
1 cup sugar
1 cup fresh pitted cherries, chopped

Boil water and sugar; stir until sugar is dissolved. Add cherries and simmer 8 to 10 minutes or until cherries have softened. Remove mixture from heat and mash cherries with a potato masher or wooden spoon. Allow mixture to cool and strain through a fine-mesh strainer, removing cherry bits.

The mixture can be refrigerated for up to a month and used in cocktail recipes or to flavor lemonades or other drinks.

Acknowledgments

This book would never have been possible without the help and support of so many people.

Thank you to my editor, Melissa Rechter, who believed in my characters enough to take a chance on a new writer. Thank you also to the rest of the Crooked Lane team who helped to shepherd this book into reality.

A huge thanks to my agent, Dawn Dowdle, for pulling me out of the query trenches and helping me breathe life into my story.

I'm so appreciative of the support and guidance from the Guppy Chapter of Sisters in Crime and all the members who read query letters and multiple versions of my synopsis. Special thanks to my friend Lis Angus, beta reader extraordinaire, who helped me to identify and fix plot holes along the way.

My parents always encouraged my writing and offered unending love and support. I want to thank my mother for paving the way by publishing her own books and never failing to dream big dreams for me. My father didn't make it to see this book published, but I know he would have been proud.

Acknowledgements

To my husband, Edward, thank you so much for the love and support and everything you have done to help make my dream a reality. You are my favorite cocktail connoisseur.

To my daughter, Evaline, my assistant baker and number-one recipe tester, thank you for always inspiring my creativity.

Lastly, thank you to all the readers who have taken the time to read my story.